MW01243217

IN LOVE WITH A LAS VEGAS OUTLAW 2

By: Londyn Lenz

LONDYN LENZ CATALOG

(in order)

Finessed By A Detroit Boss (1-3Completed Series)

Seduced By A Heartbreaker: A Miami Scandal

Fallin' For A Detroit Rydah (1-3 Completed Series)

Tis The Season To Fall For A Thug

She Fell In Love With A Real One (Spin-off of Fallin' For A Detroit Rydah)

Lucas & Paige (Spin-Off of Seduced By A Heartbreaker: A Miami Scandal)

In Love With A Las Vegas Outlaw

KEEP UP WITH ME:

My Facebook Reading Group: Londyn'z Bestyz

Facebook Author Page: Author Londyn Lenz

Please SUBSCRIBE to my YouTube channel: Through Londyn Lenz Reading Group

Email: Londyn_Lenz@yahoo.com

Last Time....

NINA

Once again Angel popped in my head, those puppy does. It was making me feel something other than the nothing before. It wasn't much but I still was feeling, which was good. I guess it really was getting to me because I started thinking how I hadn't talked to Talia in about a week. She had texted me and even called me, but I didn't answer. I didn't mean to do her that way, so I decided to go see her tonight.

My best friend was a night owl, so I knew she was up. I didn't want to call her because I knew she wouldn't answer to get me back for not answering. I tapped my finger to the beat while Destiny's Child sang to me. The ride seemed quicker with the music and I had forgot what that was like. Usually, I feel like I'm in this car for hours, especially when I'm on the freeway. Everything would seem to move in slow motion and the lights would annoy my eyes.

Not tonight though. I turned down the block of Talia's house. Well, it wasn't her house, but she still lived there. As I got closer to her house, I saw Marlo's Caprice parked out front. That made me turn my music off and I sat there for a second, trying to think why his car would be outside her house after ten o' clock at night. I couldn't even take my mind off of the awful thoughts, because there was nothing I could think of that made sense.

No reason for him to be here except the obvious. Getting out my car, I wasn't even thinking about Marlo, it was Talia. My supposed to be best friend. I would never do this to her. I got to the door and knocked, making sure to not stand in front of it. Knocking twice, the porch light came on and I heard it being unlocked. When Talia opened the door, her eyes fell and grew so wide when she saw me. I looked at her and what she had on; a short robe.

That nothing feeling came back and I balled my fist up. The next thing I knew, I punched her so hard she fell back and her mouth gushed with blood. Stepping over her crying on the floor, she called my name, but I went straight to her room and pushed the door open. I didn't see anybody, but I thought this nigga was hiding because his car was for sure here. Punk ass was probably in the bathroom, so I turned around and pushed open the closed door next to her room.

"Nina, no!" Talia yelled my name as soon as the door flew open.

I was so ready to let this nigga know I caught him with her, but what I wasn't ready for was to see Marlo ass naked, fucking Talia's brother. He was sweating and they both were so into it that they didn't jump from the door, it was Talia's loud voice. Marlo looked like he saw The Grim Reaper in the flesh. My mouth was wide open and I felt so disgusted but it got worse when Marlo and her brother, Tino, rushed and separated.

Marlo's dick was hard, and I didn't see a condom on. My stomach turned and I ran out the house so fast. All I heard was my name being called, but I was in my car pulling off so fast it was insane. What the entire fuck! Once I got far enough, I pulled over, opened the door and threw up all on the curb. I wiped my mouth with the back of my hand and had to catch my breath. A man. Marlo was fucking a man, Talia's brother. She knew it and to make matters worse, Marlo wasn't using a condom. No way was I going home, so I pulled off into my new direction.

"Hey boo, what are you doing here?" Christian asked when she let me in.

Symba came from the back and asked, "What's wrong?"

I didn't even know where to begin, so I just said the first thing that popped in my mind. "If y'all are off work tomorrow, can you go with me to the clinic?" I asked and their mouths dropped.

"Not that." I hurried and laid anything they thought to rest. "I need to get a STD test."

Their faces changed and Christian snapped first. "What did that nasty son of a bitch do now?"

"Nina, hell yea, we will go with you tomorrow." Symba added. "But you need to leave Marlo's struggle ass where he's at, for real. Fuck him and that bitch he's with."

"You mean nigga he's with." I looked at her and said.

"Um, what!?" They both said.

I sat down and looked straight ahead, shaking my head slowly. "He's fucking Tino; I just saw it with my own eyes." I could hear both of them gasping in shock.

"Wait, wait. Tino, Talia's brother?" Christian asked.

I nodded my head yes. "Oh and Talia knew." I said, still looking straight ahead and shaking my head slowly.

"What the fuck!? That damn bitch! Let's go fight her ass right now." Symba said standing up.

"No need, I already busted her lip wide open." I took a deep breath. "Look, I'll give y'all full details tomorrow. I promise, right now I'm tired and just want to sleep," I said standing up.

"Understandable. You can shower, I'll get you

something to sleep in. Wanna slumber it in my room?"
Symba asked me and Christian, and we agreed.

While they laid next to me sleep, I was in deep
thought. Marlo played so much with my life and I allowed it.
From the moment I met him, I was stupid in love. Gave up so
much of myself, morals, decisions and myself piece by piece.
I needed to change. I'll die if I stay this way and it won't be
by his hand but by my own. At that moment, I knew that's not
what I wanted.

**

"How do you feel?" Christian asked me as we sat in
TGI Friday's.

We all went to the clinic and I was tested. Then we
went to T-Mobile and I bought a new phone and got a new
number. I had to call the clinic and give it to them and wait
two days for my results. I had no feelings towards it, I just
wanted to know. I didn't hope, wish or pray for anything
when it came to it. We all know I have no room to do any of
that, I just wanted to know so I can know how I needed to live

the rest of my life.

"I feel pretty good," I answered after we ordered our food. I told both of them the whole story of last night. Talia was calling both of them back to back. Symba answered and cussed her out, Christian got some words in too, and she stopped calling. I knew Marlo was looking for me, but I didn't want to see or talk to any of them.

"That's how you should feel. Nothing will come back positive for you Nina, as nasty as Marlo is, that doesn't mean anything. You'll be good and nothing will come back positive," Symba said, smiling at me.

"Thank you, auntie." I looked at her smiling back with my eyes. Our food came and we ate, talked and it was feeling better being around them.

The next two days were normal, minus me not being at home. Marlo had been to Mama's house and Grandma's. They didn't tell him anything except to get away from their house before they shoot his ass. I was still at Christian and Symba's house when my phone rang. Sitting up, I saw it was the clinic calling me. I was in the living room so when I answered, I ran in Symba and Christian's room, mouthing to them who was on the phone.

"Yes this is Ms. Curwin." As I listened to her, Symba and Christian had their fingers crossed, looking so anxious.

I closed my eyes and breathed out. "Ok, yes thank you so much." I hung up, looked at them and said. "I'm all good." I was happy, but a smile didn't come. I was more relieved now that I knew.

They both did all the smiling and screaming for me. Symba's annoying ass started twerking.

"Oh my goodness, this came at the best time," she said looking at me and Christian with a wide grin.

"So remember Dominick?" She asked Christian.

"Yea fine guitar dude, what about him?"

I didn't know who Dominick was, but I just listened.

"Well he wants me to meet up with him and he has two friends—"

"Nooo. No." I said cutting her off and so did

Christian.

"Come on y'all, please? I already told him I was bringing two friends. Talia is no longer in the equation and Nina, this is perfect for you. Nobody is asking y'all to marry these men. Just meet them and have some good conversation," Symba pleaded.

"Girl I'm not even in the mood for no white boy right now," Christian said, waving her hand.

"White? Girl you talking to white boys now?" I asked Symba. I had nothing against white guys, it just wasn't my thing.

"I swear you two are so close-minded. Christian you just said Dominick was fine."

"Fine as fuck, but that don't mean his friends are on his level. They could be some Sears catalog looking dudes who can't play a sexy ass guitar, but play the clarinet or some shit."

That was funny and I was laughing on the inside because Christian was so serious.

"I do whatever y'all ask me. I'm just asking for this one favor. I doubt his friends are lame and ugly. If they are, I swear we can leave." Symba crossed her heart and started begging.

"Pleaseeeeeee!"

I looked at Christian and shrugged my shoulders. "Fuck it, I'm in." I said.

Symba's eyes looked at Christian, all hopeful.

"Ugh! Ok, ok I'm in, but I swear if they ugly, I'm calling the police and saying I was kidnapped," she joked.

"Thank youuuu my favorite nieces." She kissed and hugged all on us.

Oh Lord, I hope I didn't just agree to something I was going to regret.

MARLO

"I'm not going to ask you again. Get the hell off my door-step. Nina isn't here and even if she was, I still wouldn't let her talk to you. But I thank you from the bottom of my heart Marlo, because whatever you did finally drove her away from you."

SLAM!

Man, this old hoe had me fucked up! Coming at me all disrespectful and then slamming the door in my face, hell naw!

BANG! BANG! BANG!

"Open this fucking door old ass lady! Open the fucking—"

The door flung open and I was looking at the front of a rifle.

"You better get your black ass off my porch before I blow all that gold out your mouth." Her calmness was pissing me off even more.

I had my heat in the car but that's a good thing, because I couldn't have killed Nina's grandma. I balled my fist up in anger and said, "You never liked me from the first moment you met me. It never occurred to you that I'm the best thing for your granddaughter?"

"Not one time. I'm old school and I smelled the stench of shit coming from you a mile away. Now, get off my porch." Standing there with the gun on me, she literally waited until I was off her porch.

I got in my ride, slamming the door hard with frustration. I took my phone out to check it and once again, no missed calls or texts. Throwing my phone on the seat I pulled off and headed home. This shit was like a nightmare for the past two-weeks. The night replayed in my head over and over. Nina walking in that room seeing me in that position wasn't supposed to happen. Her ass ran out the house before I could even explain.

For you bitches who think I'm a fag, fuck you

because I'm far from gay. Talia's brother was the realest as they come; a goon to the fullest in these streets and we have been doing business together for a while. I've sold dope for him back around the time Nina was a senior in high school. That same money that took care of her, bought her first car and kept a roof over her head. It bought clothes, shoes, diapers and toys for our child.

One misunderstanding and she takes off like a thief in the night without hearing me out. Stupid bitch got a new number and had muthafuckas keeping her from me because I could not find her ass. I had been over her mama's crib and she swore she didn't know where Nina was at, either. The older African nigga she worked for was crazy as hell; he told me he'd send some people my way if I came back to his business.

He probably was fucking Nina. What other reason would he be protecting her like that? The bitch got the nerve to think I'm dirty. The only thing that was making me not flip out and kill everybody was their reaction when they saw me. Clearly, Nina didn't tell them what happened which saved them all. I don't need nobody thinking I'm gay, in love with a man, or none of that shit. I'm all pure man; I love pussy and everything about it.

I'm not the only person who has a friend they fuck, nothing more nothing less. I didn't need my damn girl running around telling people shit she didn't know about. After today, I was about to chill out, live my life and wait for her to come back to me.

We all know Nina does this. She calls herself being done with me, but after a few weeks she always realizes how I complete her. It ain't much out here for her without me, so she comes right back. I'll let her cool off and when she does come back, I can explain to her that what she saw wasn't shit. Ain't no other way for this to go; me and Nina were forever.

"Have you spoken to her?" Talia asked when she opened the door to her brother's house.

Talia was fine, slim, fine face and always got some weave that stopped at her little round ass. You couldn't pay me to fuck her though, because that's Nina's best friend and I wouldn't do her like that. I'm not stupid though. If I would have tried to fuck Talia, I know she would spread that pussy to me in a minute. Every bitch in Nevada wanted to fuck ya' boy Marlo, but I keep this dick reserved for Nina only.

I was on some dumb shit back when we first started talking but I chilled and left the hoes alone. I mean I'd get some mouth from a hoe, but I wasn't fucking no pussy. That's why Nina needed to recognize that I don't have her out here looking stupid. I don't fuck a bunch of niggas either for you thot heads who think I do. Like I said, I ain't no damn fag.

"Naw, but I'm not worried. This is what she does; just chill and she'll come around," I told her, going to the kitchen and grabbing a beer. This hot ass, muggy weather made any indoor place without A.C. feel like the inside of an oven.

"This is different Marlo, she caught you—"

"Shut the fuck up." I clenched my jaw, staring at her hard as hell in her eyes because she was crossing a line.

Turning her nose up she said, "Nigga fuck you. Don't forget who has been keeping your secret since you and my brother been locked up together. I betrayed my best friend not for you, but for my brother. Don't get no damn attitude at me because you slipped up."

I put the beer down and walked towards her. I was over bitches disrespecting me today.

"Tino!"

I stopped when she called her brother's name. Scary ass trick.

Smiling while still looking at me, her raggedy ass said, "You've got company!"

I stepped back a little with my squinted eyes still on her as Tino walked in the kitchen.

"Well, I gotta work. I'll let y'all talk." Picking up her cheap purse she walked in the kitchen laughing.

"I'm glad you're here; we need to rap," Tino said and walked back to his room. We were the same complexion. He was taller than me, wore a platinum grill and a little lighter muscle built. Like I said, he's a straight heartless goon, will rob or kill anyone. He's put me and my boys on a lot of robbery hits whether it was a home invasion or robbing local dope boys.

"Speak your mind," I told him, leaning against his dresser.

He folded his arms and stood a few inches in front of me, looking like I was the enemy. "You fucked up, you know that right?"

"How the hell I fuck up? I did the same shit I did any other time. You think you the only one who will lose street credit if some false shit get out?!" I got a little hype because he had me fucked all the way up.

"I'm the only one who's street credit got real value, muthafucka!" He yelled with his nostrils enlarged like he was ready to charge.

That was it for me. Too much disrespect on me in one day. I didn't care about shit else except Nina coming back so we can get right and I could explain myself. Balling my fist up, I swung and hit Tino in his jaw. As soon as he realized what I did, he took a swing back at me in my stomach. I dropped to my knees, coughing and holding my mid-section.

Tino grabbed me by the back of my neck like I was the one who took dick up the ass. When I was on my feet, I elbowed him hard in his stomach. Swinging for his face, I missed and he got me good in my jaw. Then, I heard his gun cock.

"Nigga I will end you right here, right fucking now." He was breathing hard like I was and we both were looking on edge.

"Look, I don't know why Nina showed up that night. But I know she hasn't said anything—"

This punk ass tightened his lips and pressed the gun hard on the side of my throat. "You betta make sure she doesn't say shit. As a matter of fact, I don't trust no bitch in their feelings. When you get to her, you better handle that shit or I'ma handle her and you."

"Man, I can't kill my damn girl, fuck that. Trust me,

she won't say a word. If she does, you can take out my own mama." My eyes were on his, intense as hell as I spoke the truth. "Real shit homie." I assured him again.

He slowly lowered his gun but still looked at me. "This better be buried Marlo, on my life, I will hold you to what you just said."

I held my hands up. "Like I said, if I don't do what needs to be done then you can handle yo' business."

Chuckling at me he asked, "That bitch means that much to you that you'll be willing to end yo' own mama's life?"

"Without question," I told him and I was about to head out.

Tino stopped me and started unbuckling his belt and jeans. "You here now, might as well give me some dick."

I looked down at his hard on when he dropped his pants and I pulled my shirt over my head. Might as well work off some frustration from all this bullshit going on.

GUNNA

"Did you let The Law know exactly who the hell I was?" I asked Sincere when he came down the stairs of my house.

We didn't get a chance to meet in part one. I'm Gunna. Naw, that ain't my real name, but that's not of importance. Who I am is what matters. I'm the number one pimp from Philadelphia and I'm that muthafucking nigga. Everything about me was life, from my prison built body filled up with tattoos, down to the lint between my toes. I could always get women to do anything for me, and I mean any damn thing. I've had a bitch spend her whole child support check on me, max out her bridge card filling up my fridge and then I'll send her ass home to her empty shit.

You name it and I guarantee a woman has done it for me, even if I don't ask, especially if she thought I was about to walk out on her. Now, a man with that much power of the opposite sex was meant to pimp these bitches. I ain't never,

ever loved any of them except for my aunt who raised me. I respected that woman with everything in me and she had my heart. The rest of the female species were bitches, bottom hoes who were good for two things: making a dick shoot out and making me money. If they weren't doing one or the other, then they didn't need to be in my face. I started in the game in high school with two girlfriends. Kinsley High's most popular cheerleaders were most wanted by niggas. One dude pulled out twenty dollars and said he would give it to me if he could see my girl's titties. I took his money and told him where to meet her at.

When I told her, of course she bitched and cused out, but I warned her that if she didn't do it, then I was dumping her. She'd no longer be Gunna's bitch and there were so many girls wanting to be in her position. I offered her ten dollars of the twenty and she flashed old dude. Once she was done, I rewarded her with some good ass dick because like I said, she was my woman. Now, that's one rule I did have when I call you my woman: you are not allowed to cheat on me.

You do, then that's when I have to get physical and then throw yo' ass out on the streets. From there, I was in business. It started with flashing titties, then a flash of pussy and ass. Because the two were my girls, I wouldn't let them fuck or suck. But word spread and soon niggas in school wanted to see other body parts besides my two girls. That was more work for me as far as talking other girls to agree to it so, I upped my prices.

Girls were making about forty dollars a day and in high school, that was a lot. Time went on and I stayed in the pimp business; wasn't nothing fancy about the way I did business. I had eight hoes who lived with me. They all are bad as hell and very good at what they do. I made money off this, enough to never go hungry and buy whatever I wanted. I left Philly because money was declining and every time I visited Las Vegas with my hoes, I cleaned up.

So, I purchased a four-bedroom home, let the hoes have the bedrooms upstairs and I decked the entire massive basement out for myself. I had my hoes on some ride or die shit for me, shooting guns and will pop any threat that comes near me. They were fine as hell but would turn gangsta at the drop of a hat. Money and Sincere been my homies since high school. Name one 'bad guy' who doesn't have a posse behind him? That's what they are.

"Yea I did and it still was disrespect. What's your next move? You want me to talk to Angel alone?" He asked me, sitting down on the edge of the small stage I had with two poles in the middle of it.

"Naw, I wanna get at him myself. As long as you went to see them first to introduce me, then it's all good." I told him while moving a chess piece. I dug the shit out of the game chess. One of my hoes bought me a gold and silver Egyptian chess set for my birthday.

"Let me kill that nigga Quest. He threw a knife at Money's arm and fucked him up."

Still deciding what next chess piece I was going to move, I said, "I get he's your brother, but Money is also a grown man. You or him won't do shit, they're the fucking Law. We heard about them before we even got here. Don't yo' stupid ass know they expect you to make a move because of what they did? You don't handle men like them with their capabilities sloppy." I spit some facts at him.

"Why do you want to put our girls in that complex anyway? We had a nice thing in Philly and could have even better here. We don't need The Law or anybody else, we got some good custos here. Fuck them law niggas."

I sat back in my chair and looked at my homie while he went on his rant. Picking up two chess pieces, I put them in my hand and walked over to him, placing the pieces on the side where he was sitting.

"This is the most important piece on a chess board, the king." I put it in his face then picked up the other one. "This is what you and everybody else in my life is: a pawn. *We* didn't build shit, *we* didn't have shit in Philly. *I* am the king, the best damn piece on the board. No other one is above me. If I say don't make a move, then that's what I mean." I looked him in his eyes with a snare.

"Not a move, got it," he said, nodding his head and holding his hands up.

"Good, glad we have an understanding. The Law owns this state and I want in with the business they do and the business I do. Me and them could own more than Nevada, make more than a few thousands a month. Them niggas so solid on they shit that they took over an entire complex up under Las Vegas nose. This is about money and nothing else for me. Not beef, blood or a takeover. Money is what I want and collaborating with them will make me millions."

"What if they don't cooperate? I get where you're coming from Gunna, but they might not see shit your way."

I chuckled and picked the king piece up again, looking at it. "Then The Law quickly becomes The Past. But that's if things get that bad. Once I meet with Angel we should come to an arrangement." I walked back over to my seat where I was playing and looked down at the board.

"They don't wanna be pawns on my board, then this king will knock they ass off." I tipped three of the pawn pieces over.

After Sincere dipped out, I grabbed two of my girls that had dates at Caesars Palace Casino. I didn't buy these hoes cars because they weren't my woman. As long as they paid me my money each date they had, then what they did with their money was on them. Clothes, jewelry, shoes, spas, weave and designer bags was all these bitches cared about anyway.

"Do y'all thang and don't rush. The more his old ass feels special, the more money he pushes out," I told them while I parked my car. I didn't mind waiting for money; hell I'd wait all day.

"Yes sir, I promise we'll be good." Cherry answered me and she and Kat got out my Navigator truck.

I didn't like them calling me that 'daddy' bullshit like most pimps. Call me 'sir' because to me, it sounds like a man who requires respect and no one would challenge me. Cherry was white and been with me since we were twenty-one and we both were thirty-four now. She was the only hoe I had that I invested money in. Fake ass, titties and lips; men loved her, especially old ass men who was into that life-size Barbie look.

Kat was white too; a sexy Kylie Kardashian look-a-like. Oh yea, did I forget to mention all my hoes were white? I haven't fucked with black women in my circle since high school. I'll date and fuck a black girl all day, but ain't enough money in the world to have me dealing with them as my hoes. They talk too damn much, quick to kick a custo in the balls for being rude and quick to slap other hoes in the mouth. Basically, they were just too much drama.

Anyway, while the girls handled their pussies, I decided to go get something to eat at my spot, *In-N-Out Burger*. I needed a double cheeseburger fresh from the hot grease, a big ass milkshake and a large fry. I had more than enough time to eat, burp, smoke and probably get a quickie from the big titty manager who worked there that I fucked on from time to time.

"Excuse me, I asked for no onions on my order." I heard a woman speak.

I looked at Ms. Thick-Thick, who was so damn fine. I almost choked on my food.

"I'm sorry, let me fix that for you." The manager, who I fuck on, said to Ms. Thick-Thick.

Her whole mood changed from hot and ready when I walked in here and ordered my food. Renee was her name and it wasn't shit to us. Just some good nuts and anytime I came to *In-N-Out*, my food was free, whether she was here or not. With Ms. Thick-Thick here, I was feeling like fuck Renee with a virus dick. I wiped my fingers with the napkin and got up to head in her direction.

"Who eats a cheeseburger without onions? Shit don't even sound right," I said to her, leaning on the counter trying not to look at her beefy thighs in this dress she had on that hugged her bottom.

Turning her body around facing me, she looked at me

up and down then said, "It sounds good to me and like my breath will be fresh still." The little giggle she did was cute. I peeped her teeth were white as hell and straight. Turn on number three. I like how she had on some cute high-top gym-shoes with a fitted dress.

"That's why it's good to keep a mint or gum on you. Gunna, what's your name?" I asked her.

"That's something deserving and I'm not sure you're there yet. But, it's nice to meet you, Gunna."

I laughed and made sure to flash my award-winning smile. I had straight white teeth on top and my bottom row was dripped in a 24-karat gold grill; bitches loved that. "Trust me Ms. Thick-Thick, I deserve everything you got and you will give it all to me in due time. Until then, can I at least know how you doing on this beautiful day?"

Her open smile and squinted eyes she gave me made her look like she was appalled at what I said. But I spoke facts. Every woman I meet always gives me their all and then some.

"I'm doing good, just leaving school. How are you?"

"Why you wasting your time getting that expensive piece of paper? You know there's money out here that doesn't require that, all you gotta do is get a hustle." I told her truthfully. College is a waste of time. A way to get people in debt for something that ain't useful.

"My mama always told me a black woman should never have any holes people can poke through. She already blessed me with the physical; education and making something of myself is my hustle," she said, putting her right hand on the back of her wide hips.

"Let me ask you this, what do you do to make money? Slaving in school doesn't pay any bills."

Laughing she put some of her big, shoulder length hair behind her. "Gunna, are you offering to cover my bills, rent, car note or anything? No, of course you're not, so cut the shit and just ask me for my phone number." She ended at the same time the cashier came back with her new order. Ms. Thick-Thick looked back in my direction like 'what'chu gon' do nigga?'

Now she had me thrown back a little by how blunt she was. I took my iPhone out while still looking at her fine ass and said, "Give it to me, then."

Walking towards the door with her back to me she shot off her number. "702-686-4932."

"Aye, slow down. I didn't get it all." I said as she walked out the door, not looking back and heading to her 2020 Nissan Sentra.

"702-686-4932." *Four* guys repeated her number in unison.

I looked at them niggas and they were punching her number in quickly as if she was talking to them. I just shook my head at their thirsty asses. I wasn't trippin' though. Ms. Thick-Thick would definitely remember me when I call.

DOMINICK

"Hello."

"How big did you smile when you saw my name pop up on your screen?" I said into my phone after Symba's sexy voice spoke into my ear.

I was seeing her tomorrow since I last saw her at the club and I couldn't wait. We'd been talking on the phone and texting a lot which was a new vibe for me. I did it with other women but not as much. Symba had me on point with every text and phone call. If I did miss it, I was making up for it. I liked talking to her aside from her voice and those low moans she would do and never knew I heard.

I dug how cool she was; her response to the questions I'd ask her, and her comments about anything we talked about was different. One thing I learned without her telling me was Symba lived her life to the fullest unapologetically. I admired that because that's how I was.

She wasn't searching for a relationship, nor trying to be a social media goal. There was no filter for what came out her mouth, same as me.

Another thing I learned was she ran over boys. Treated them like shit in her own sexy way. They didn't stand a chance of locking her down. Notice I said boys, because that's what they were; a man would never let her run them down and over. I'm a firm believer of having a weakness for your woman and being soft for her, but getting disrespected, played or handled by her like your dick is a giant clit, no fucking way. If or when I decide to make Symba mine, all of that would die. I'd rise her up on my shoulders like a true Queen, but best believe she'd rise me like the King I was, too.

"You live to annoy me. I didn't even crack a smirk, Dominick."

I chuckled quietly. "Liar, you feel the same way you do as when you say my name." She smacked her lips and I followed up with, "It's all good, he wakes up as soon as you speak anyway." (He as in my dick) "I'm not ashamed to admit my shit, though." I smirked and paused so I could catch that low moan she does when I turn her on, which was a lot.

"You're a bad boy," she squeezed out.

"That I am. So how are you today, Symba? How was class?" An education was an absolute turn on and she was filled with knowledge, even at the age of twenty-four. I was thirty and had to get my G.E.D. because I was stupid and didn't finish high school.

I knocked that out at twenty, went to community college, transferred my credits and got my master's in business. Now my goal was my guitar/ motorcycle shop. I wanted a garage attached to it for bike repairs. I had it all in my head and written out in a business plan. Now, I just had to make it become a reality. Symba told me about her dance school she wanted. We had yet another thing to add to the list that we bonded on.

"I'm ok, school was—

"You know what, can you hold that thought for me gorgeous? I got to take this call coming in. Give me one minute." I said to her.

"Oh, that's fine." She responded sweetly.

"Sixty-seconds." I told her and I hit my mute button, sitting my phone on top of my 2020 Escalade EXT.

"Come on Dominick man, please!" This punk ass joke pleaded and yelled.

It fell on deaf ears because I turned my nose up at him and slammed his head in my back door twice. The third time, I leaned my weight on my left arm that was on the door, crushing his head while picking up my phone. I could hear his cranium cracking as I unmuted Symba.

"See, less than sixty-seconds." I smirked when she giggled. "Now, continue telling me about your day baby." I said, waiting for this fool's head to crack all the way open. I'd have to take my truck for a deep cleaning, but whatever.

"Class was pretty good. After I was done, I went to get something to eat and then harassed my nieces."

"That sounds like a smooth day; you'll be harassing me tomorrow, right?" I asked in reference to me seeing her.

"Of course, my nieces are down too. The other girl with the straight hair you saw me with won't be with me. My other niece is coming instead, but trust me, she is breathtaking."

Pressing the door harder on his head I responded, "Oh I believe you. I don't think you run around with ugly duckling lookin' chicks."

"You know me so well." Symba was making me laugh too with her wittiness. "What did you do today? How was work?" She asked me.

I looked down at the muthafucka whose head I was smashing and said, "I crushed work pretty good today, I'm actually still at it."

"Really? Do you need to call me back?" It was cute how she really thought she was inconveniencing me like I wasn't the one who called her. But, I did have to wrap shit up with this clown I just killed. I could see blood pouring down from his head. "You know what, I do need to finish up, but I wanna do our usual and hit you up tonight."

"Actually, I'll be busy tonight, but I'll just see you tomorrow." Her voice was soft when she said that.

Little did she know I didn't give a damn; we talked every night and that wasn't about to change. Don't think I'm the only one on some clingy shit already. I was busy last night, and she cut it short with her attitude that she tried to hide. I was working on my bike with my boys but Symba wasn't trying to hear it. The way she played it off like it was no big deal was fake. Her tone was laced with annoyance. So, I cut it short and talked to her all night; wasn't no thang to me.

"Aight gorgeous, we'll talk." I said and we both hung up.

I put my phone in my pocket and went back to punk ass. Opening the door, he slid down all the way, brains and shit all on the inside of my door and on the ground. Angel and Quest walked out of the dark alley looking at what I did.

"What?" I asked, stepping over him. "Ain't like we needed his brain."

We were seven hours outside of Las Vegas in Reno. We got a call from this popular car dealer ship Arab dude. He owned two casinos in Las Vegas and a few properties as well. Anyway, he had some enemies in Reno who were coming at him hard, so he called the best to come handle it. Of course, besides our expensive fee, we require to keep the body after our doctors tested the corpse and made sure the organs were useable.

What wasn't would go to Burt's funeral home and get burned. This was six bodies right here. We caught them off guard when we met them in an alley to do what they believed was a drug deal. Before they knew it was a set up, I broke two of their arms. Quest stabbed the other two in the neck and Angel rammed the other two headfirst into each other over and over. Easy money and some organs to sell on the Black Market.

"You love making a mess, crazy ass white boy."

Quest joked.

"Says the muthafucka holding two heads in his hand." I pointed out. No matter what, his ass had to cut some shit up.

He grinned and said, "I had to let my babies have a moment," referring to his knives.

"Both of y'all some twisted fucks, making more work for ya'selves." Angel cut in as we zipped the bodies up in the morgue bags and loaded them in the back of his van.

"Oh shit I forgot to tell y'all, this chick I met at the club is coming through the complex tomorrow. She's bringing her two nieces for y'all."

"What? Hell naw, D, last time you hooked me up a dick appointment almost turned into a WIC appointment." Quest's loud ass objected. I was talking to this girl a while back and she put her sister on Quest. Yea he was with Kamila, but he was a grown man and could handle his own when it came to his dick, so I didn't stop it. Chick ended up getting pregnant and causing a lot of drama.

"Nobody told your crazy ass to knock that girl up." I

laughed because he was shaking his head 'hell no'. "One of her nieces is chocolate as hell, bad." I told him, nodding my head.

"Oh word?" He rubbed his hands together. He had an obsession with chocolate girls. "That's all you had to say, I'm in. I'm giving Kamila her walking papers anyway."

"Shut'cho same ol' song ass up. You and her will do some awful shit to each other and both of y'all will still stay stuck on stupid," Angel said making me fall out laughing.

Quest indeed repeats the same stuff about leaving Kamila alone, but he never will.

"Fuck you fool. I'm for real this—"

"Blah, blah, blah, nigga." Angel cut him off, laughing along with me because Quest hated getting cut off.

He looked at Angel like he wanted to fight. I finished laughing and had to get his attention. Angel was still laughing hysterically, pissing him off even more.

"Quest." I said, trying to cover my laugh.

"I'm cool, I ain't even about to argue wit' no nigga

who got a nose ring. Fuckin' hoochie mama."

When he said that, on God, I felt my gut trying to bust out. I was cracking up hard as hell and so was Angel. That's why they were my boys; we would snap on each other and it still was love.

"What her other niece looks like?" Angel asked me after recovering from the strong laugh.

"Not sure." I wasn't about to lie.

"Aw fuck naw, D, you'on even know what your chick bringing me?"

"She ain't ugly, I don't see my chick having ugly family members. On God, she that fucking bad and so is her first niece. You got a better chance of hitting the lottery," I told him honestly.

"Dats yo' ass nigga if she looks like a fucking horse," Angel threatened with all seriousness.

"Fuck you." I laughed and gave him the middle finger. "When she fine as hell, I want twenty-thousand Franks." I held my hand out to him, offering a bet. We always betted on petty and big shit.

"You on bro." He laughed, shaking my hand.

"Have y'all gotten any more of them funny notes?" Angel asked me and Quest.

An envelope was mailed to my parent's house, no return address, and inside was a picture of the doctor I killed who treated Denise. It wasn't his corpse, just a profile picture of him in his white doctor coat. I killed him in front of his house out of rage of my sister dying. That was my favorite person and I was hurt. He didn't have any sympathy for us because we didn't have the right dollars in the bank to pay for a new heart at the time.

So, I snapped and killed him with my bare hands the same night she died. An eye for an eye meant blood for blood in my book. Anyway, only two people who knew about the kill were the two people in front of me, or so I thought. Quest's mother was in a psych treatment center. Someone sent her some flowers and the card said, 'From an old friend of Quest'. We knew off rip it was the same person who sent me the picture.

"I haven't," I responded.

"Me neither." Quest added. "But something is funny as fuck in the game; I'm killing on sight when I find out who fucking with me."

"Hell yea, I never told a soul aside from y'all about doc," I said.

"Somebody either wants something from us or it's from the both of y'all. Either way, they fuck with one they get all three, so they fucked regardless. Don't nobody fuck with The Law and live to brag about it. Naw, whoever the fuck it is either got a death wish or they stupid as hell." Angel spoke truth.

"Big facts." I nodded my head. "They know us on some personal shit; my parents' address and Quest's mama's location. Once we get they ass, they gotta die and everyone they know." I felt the rage and anger building up in me. I didn't like being threatened, blackmailed or any of that shit. A whole different side of me comes out when I feel myself or my brothers being fucked with.

"Yo' you ever look at yourself in the mirror when you get pissed?" Quest asked me.

I looked at him confused and Angel snickered. "Bro you look creepy as hell. I been telling you since we were kids you could play Michael Myers." They both started laughing.

I squinted my eyes at both of them. "Ain't shit funny; y'all some damn geeks." I turned my nose up at them as I threw the last body in the van, closing the doors. We had a seven-hour drive back. Angel was driving the van and Quest rode with me in my truck.

"Swear, Kamila stay blowing me up." Quest said as he answered his phone.

I just chuckled and kept driving while listening to music. We've been on the road for about an hour now. It was almost seven o'clock in the evening, so I decided to call Symba. Putting my phone to my ear with my left hand still on the wheel, she answered after the third ring.

"Dominick, I can't talk right now." Her pretty voice

said.

My eyebrow arched up. "Why?"

She did a light giggle. "I don't get questioned, boo." Her voice was laced with sarcasm and comedy like I told a joke. "I'll hit you up later."

"Don't hang up this phone." I said calm with no anger at all; my voice was naturally deep but I really wasn't mad. "I don't care what you're doing, I wanna talk to you."

"And the story will remain the same, I'm busy."

"And the ending ain't about to change, I said don't hang up this phone. Either talk to me now or I'll come where you are and talk." Now, I was almost five-hours from her, but she doesn't know that. If I was in Las Vegas right now, I would hold up to what I said for real.

Scoffing, she said, "You don't even know where I'm at, good-bye Dominick." When the phone hung up, I laughed and shook my head.

This is why I loved black women. They were such a challenge and it made my dick rock hard. I quickly looked at

Quest who was caking with Kamila as I dialed the number I needed.

"D, what can I do for you?"

"Sup Cyrus, I need eyes on someone real quick." He was our guy who could get us the location of anyone in Nevada. When we said eyes, he knew we needed him or one of his guys to physically get sight on the person. Otherwise, he'd just text us the location.

"You're in luck, I'm actually out now so as long as they're in Las Vegas, then I can do it."

"Cool, Symba Greene phone number 702-686-4932." I gave him her name and phone number.

"Ok, let's see what we got." I heard him typing in his laptop mount that he always had in his car. "Located her driving in the direction now, do you want pictures?" He asked me.

"Nope, I got a better idea," I told him while I cashed app him for his services, and then told him what I wanted him to do.

SYMBA

"I hate coconut," Jameson said when the waiter brought our dessert.

He was coming back from the bathroom just as I hung up on Dominick. Mm, his name alone makes me once again look down at my thighs. It's insane because we haven't been face to face since the club. That was some time ago, and I still was enjoying him. He was keeping my interest. I don't even move like this; excuse me for sounding like a hoe but within the second week of knowing a guy we've already had sex.

Hell, day three is when I get the dick and determine if it made me proud or disappointed me. It's a way for a girl to live her life discreetly, tastefully and still remain a lady, still keep the pussy lips neat, pretty and clean. My point is, I haven't touched Dominick yet and he still had me into him…hot for him and loving saying his name as if I've explored his body. His voice was deep mixed with a sultry that I wouldn't expect from a white guy.

He had *flava* to him, but you knew it wasn't a front, it was just in him. Anyway, back to earth, I liked him but I was still me. Symba doesn't get questioned and I sure in hell don't get told what to do. Him telling me not to hang up and threatening me wasn't it. I do what I want unapologetically because I'm always honest; I told him nicely I was busy and I'd talk to him tomorrow.

Now, the other day he did pull the same thing on me. I wanted to talk but he was busy with his boys. I wouldn't say I was mad but I was a tiny bit irked only because I had got all comfy in bed all set to talk to him. But that was different, he can't do what I can do so I had to show him who the hell Symba was.

"Don't talk about my coconut cream pie, you know you want some," I flirted with a seductive smile.

"That ain't the cream I had in mind that I wanted to

taste." It was all in his eyes how in heat he was.

Jameson was cool. I've known him for about three months; he had good dick, but he just couldn't eat pussy right. Let me change that, he couldn't eat it without me directing him the entire time. But he was cute, had his own money from his good job, but I told him I wasn't going out with him until he got his own car. He thought using Uber was the way to go, a way to save money. That's all good, but if you wanna take me out you need to have your own wheels.

I've always had my own car even, when I had a beat-up, put-put of a car, it still was mine. Dick riding is not a form of transportation, won't get you nowhere, so I made sure I had a car. If I was looking for a boyfriend, I wouldn't pick Jameson. Not because of the pussy eating though, but because he was too friendly. My nigga gotta be stiff on hoes, I ain't with none of that friendly, smiling-in-everybody face shit.

I like book and street smarts, and Jameson as shot on the street part. Tonight was chill though; he asked me out to dinner, and I accepted. The conversation was nice, and I was enjoying him. I was ready to go home, get comfortable and talk on the phone to Dominick. It was going to be fun explaining to him how it goes when fucking with me. As fine as he is, I wasn't losing sight on the fact that I run shit. *Period.*

I licked my lips because the sweetness of the pie hit my taste buds. "You and I both know I don't cream, Jameson." I gave him a sly smile.

He looked at my face and I knew I turned him on even more. Jameson waved his hand over for our waiter to come back. "We'll have our desserts to go and the check, please."

I giggled lowly when he said that.

"Actually sir, your bill has been taken care of," the waiter said.

Me and Jameson looked confused.

"Oh really, by who?" Jameson asked.

The waiter looked at me and handed the black

checkbook that waiters carry the bill in. "I was told to give you this. You guys have a great evening." He walked away with a closed mouth smile.

I opened the checkbook, even more confused and there was our paid bill of $93.05 and a $100.00 tip for the waiter. Then there was a written note behind the receipt.

Never underestimate me, you have no idea who

you're fucking with.

-Dominick

I read it three times and would have read it more had Jameson not called my name.

"Symba, who paid our bill?"

I looked up at him smiling, immediately playing it off. "A courtesy from the owner, that was sweet." I put on a believable front.

Jameson bought it and shrugged his shoulders. "Cool, I won't complain over a free meal," he said, putting his dessert in the to-go container.

I boxed my dessert up as well and then we both got

up, ready to go. While Jameson and I walked, I looked around the restaurant searching for a sign of Dominick, but I didn't see anything. How the hell did he know where I was? This is Las Vegas; a million restaurants were here. Actually, fuck that! How do you narrow a person's location down?!

I know for a fact he wasn't following me or had me tracked. Hell, we haven't seen each other since the club. His note gave me chills and it made me really want to know who exactly it was I'm fucking with. Low-key, I was turned on, but I can't let that cloud the fact that this man really found out where I was.

"You ok? You been quiet the whole ride." Jameson asked me as his car stopped in front of my house.

I had planned on running in the house and making me an overnight bag since I don't let niggas in my bed. But now, I was completely turned off by the idea of going back to Jameson's crib. Dominick had me on edge, which I think is why he didn't reveal himself. He wanted me to not know where he was.

"Actually, I'm feeling a little off. I think my period is about to start, can we reschedule?" I half smiled, asking him as if he had a choice.

"Of course Symba, just call me when you feel better." He told me as he was about to get out to walk me to the door.

"It's ok Jameson, you don't have to walk me to the door." I kissed his cheek and got out.

He didn't pull off until I was inside. As soon as I locked the door, I took my heels off, left them in the hallway and went straight to my room. Taking my jeans and bodysuit off, I kept my thong on and put on a black bralette and my UGG slippers. I grabbed the scrunchie on my dresser and put my now straightened hair in a low ponytail. I still had my Bluetooth around my neck, so I grabbed my phone and headed to the kitchen.

Opening the bottom cabinet, I grabbed my crockpot and plugged it up. I opened the refrigerator, grabbed my bag of greens and all my other ingredients in the spice cabinet. I was annoyed as hell, had questions and wasn't about to give

Dominick the satisfaction of calling him. As a matter of fact, if he calls me, I'm not answering and I'm not seeing him tomorrow, either.

I'ma make his stalker ass wait to see my pretty face again. Making some good ass greens was about to calm me down. As I cooked, my Bluetooth vibrated hard letting me know my phone was ringing. I looked on the isle where my phone was sitting and saw Dominick's name on the screen. Whyyyyy did I immediately answer as if I didn't just say I wasn't?

"Did you bring me a doggy bag back?" He taunted as soon as I answered.

"Yup, I made sure to lick all on it, too," I said with a chuckle.

"Mm. I like my food sweet."

This damn man. "You're an asshole, Dominick." I had to cover my mouth to prevent my smile. Ugh, he was annoying. "How did you know where I was? Are you on some *Joe Goldberg* type of shit?" I asked, referring to the

Netflix show *YOU*.

He did a low cackle and said, "You underestimated me, simple mistake. You live and you learn, gorgeous."

"That's not how it works when you fuck with me. That's a quick way to get dropped," I said while stirring my pot.

"You dropping me is the least of my concern and what I'm not about to do is give you what you want right now."

I stopped stirring and put my hand on my hip. "And what is it that I want, Dominick?"

"To know how I found you and who I am. The only way to answer that is for us to keep getting to know each other. We need to learn each other the same way you just learned not to fuck with me." I hated how I got turned on by his deep voice.

"You're crazy," I said, focusing my attention back on my greens.

"Naw, I just like you, that's all."

I decided to fuck with him. "You do understand I was on a date with a fine guy who's just as crazy as you?" I was smiling big because all men hate competition, especially when it's for my affection.

Dominick laughed. "There isn't a crazy bone in that little toddler's body."

I squinted my eyes and scoffed. "How do you know?"

"Because he didn't do shit when he found out someone else paid the bill. I know I would want to know who had the balls to pay my bill *and* send my woman a note. He didn't do shit but accept it, that's a punk ass toddler you had sitting across from you." His tone and laughter was irking the hell out of me so I turned into a smart ass.

"Well you fucked up my dick appointment."

He laughed even harder. "I see you tryna get a reaction out of me, so I'ma break it down for you. I don't care who's had you before me. I'll wash that pussy off, kiss it up to God and murder it as if it was untouched. Now that we got that out the way, why don't you go get comfortable in your bed and talk to me."

I couldn't even hold my laugh in when he said that. "Did you just kiss my kat up to God?! Who does that!?" I was actually cracking up, turning my crockpot on low and walking out the kitchen to my bedroom.

"I does that," he joked.

I turned my TV on but put it on mute, hit my light switch off, took my UGG slippers off and climbed in my bed so we could talk all night.

**

"Nine-Bina get the hell up and get dressed. I knew you would try this shit, get up!" I pulled at her arm, trying to drag her off the couch.

Today me, Christian and Nina were going to meet Dominick and his two friends. Nina had been staying here with me and Christian and sometimes at her mama's house. Since her break-up with Marlo, she's determined not to go back. Me and Christian wanted her to move in with us permanently, but she didn't want to. That's what made me and Christian nervous; we felt she would go back to Marlo. Today, however, she was getting her ass out of bed and coming with us.

"Stop, auntie," she whined to me. "You two go ahead and have fun. I'm about to eat some of your greens you made and order me some sides and chicken from *EllaEm's Soul Food*."

I rolled my eyes at her then looked at my other niece, her sister, Christian. "No Nina, come on. We both promised Symba we would go. You were all in up until now. If it's lame then we will all leave." Christian said and I nodded my head in agreement.

Pretending to pout, Nina sat up in her bed. There wasn't any change in her aside from her breaking up with Marlo. We still couldn't get her to laugh, joke or even enjoy herself. She was never mean or rude, but she was like a soulless shell of a person. Her beauty was still very visible, but you knew the first few minutes of talking to her that she was troubled.

It still broke my heart even after all the time that has passed. Nina felt there was nothing beyond her past, that she was being punished by God or something for the loss of her son. Myself, Christian, my mama and my big sister, their mama, have told her over and over that God doesn't work like that. Whether we drag her, or she come voluntarily, she was coming with us today.

"I thought you were mad at Dominick?" She asked me.

"I was, but we made up." I covered my face so I wouldn't blush. "Look, just get the hell up and get dressed. It's a chill meet up so you don't need to go all out. It's hot as hell outside so throw on a cute maxi, some sandals and comb those wavy bundles down to ya' ass," I joked.

I didn't have on nothing extra either, just some jean shorts, my over the knee strappy sandals and a simple hot pink crop top. Christian had some cute light wash jeans on with a bandeau red top and some red wedges. Her pretty jumbo twists were all to the side showing her gorgeous baby hair.

"Ok. Ok, I did promise, so I'll go. Give me fifteen-minutes," Nina said.

Me and Christian jumped on her while she sat on her bed, kissing all on her. "Eww, get off me!" She laughed and rushed to the bathroom.

"I swear these niggas better look good. Oh, scratch that, I mean these white boys better be hot." Christian said from the back seat. I laughed because she put on her California white girl voice when she said the word 'hot'.

I was driving my car and they rode with me, just to make sure we all held up our agreement. If Dominick's friends were some hella ugly, then all of us were leaving. Me and Dominick would have to see each other after I drop them back home.

"Could you please not embarrass me?" I looked at her through the rearview mirror.

"If these men look like something I shit in a toilet, bitch call me Bozo cause I'm putting on a show." This bitch plays all day and kept me cracking up.

"They live in our old area," Nina said.

I turned the corner following what my GPS was saying. We were about fifteen-minutes from where we grew up at. Now I love me a hood guy, but I don't remember seeing no white boy around when we were younger. Dominick is six years older than me though, so maybe he flew past me. Either way, his expensive watch and diamonds in his ear didn't have me thinking he lived in the hood.

Mm, he just won some more points with me. I slowed down when the GPS said my destination was coming up on the right. I parked in front of a nice complex that looked like it belonged in the upper-class part of Nevada. It had midnight black out windows with navy blue chrome lining it. I picked my phone up and made sure the address Dominick gave me matched what I put in my GPS.

"Symba, tell me this isn't the right address?" Christian asked me.

"It is, I just checked, don't act bougie Christian. We

are right around the corner from—"

"Bitch no, it's not that." She sat up and pointed to the building. *"The Law* owns this building."

"The who?" Me and Nina asked at the same time, looking at her.

"Ugh, swear you two don't know shit. Remember when the rec center was closing, the one we used to go to every day after school? The owner of the building, that white guy from the hills turned up missing. Then the building was turned over to the city and an anonymous person bought it and kept it open. Remember a few years back I used to talk to Tank? He ran with Glenn heavy ass crew.

"They were troublemakers to the core, drug dealers and was running the city in the ground. Well Tank, Glenn and the rest of them just disappeared. Nobody gave a fuck though because of how much trouble they caused. It's more people I can name, just wiped off. I mean not kids or women, but still. No bodies, no trace, just gone."

Nina looked at me and then at Christian. "I do

remember Tank and when the rec was closing, but I didn't know the details. Who told you this?"

"What do you mean, 'who told me this'? It's just known." She laughed and said.

"I've heard shit about some guys called The Law, but... I mean... I'm sure it's not Dominick, he would have told me." I looked at both of them and Christian started laughing.

"Aunie Sym-Sym, why would he tell you something like that? Ok look, we have a choice. We can leave or go in and see what's up," Nina said.

"I got my gun in my purse if anything is off." I assured them. "Plus, Dominick is so fine y'all—"

"Oh, lawd! We about to die because this bitch want her coochie stirred!" Christian fell back in her seat, acting wild and making me crack up. Nina was just shaking her head watching both of us. I miss when she would get silly and play with us and I couldn't wait until she was back to her old self.

"I'm not! All I'm saying is, maybe he just lives here."

"Symba, years ago this used to be a run-down apartment building. I know you remember that?"

"Yea, I do." I answered Christian.

"Ok, well since Mr. Grimes sold it, have you seen residents living here? Buy yet, look at the upgrade." All three of us looked at the building.

"I don't know much about The Law, what they look like or how many of them it is. I don't even know what it is they do," Christian said.

Me and Nina looked in the backseat at her. "Well girl, what the hell do you know?!" I asked her.

"The little I have heard is what I told you, people disappear and it's because of The Law."

We were quiet for a minute, just staring at the building. To go in or not to go in, was the question. I might sound stupid, but Dominick's fine ass kept coming to my mind. Those eyes looking at me while he played guitar, his voice, our all-night talks.

"I'm going," I said, taking off my seatbelt and grabbing my purse. "I'd rather meet him with both of you than by myself. Get y'all scary asses out and live a little. Swear, I'll start shooting if anything is wrong," I said while texting Dominick that I was outside. He text back quickly and said Lori would escort us to him. Who the hell is *Lori*? I thought but I didn't say anything to them. They got out the car then and I hit the alarm on my ride.

"This shit better be worth it," Christian said, putting her phone in her back pocket.

We walked inside and the outside didn't do it justice. I remember being fifteen and talking to this little knuckle head boy that lived here with his parents. The lobby looked nothing like what I was looking at. Back then it was run down, carpet filthy, walls filled with chipped paint and mildew spots in the corners. Now, it was all marble floor, black leather lounge love seats in the corners. Glass table in the center and some low jazz music played all around us.

"Hello, I'm Lori. Which one of you are Symba?" This

pretty older girl asked, coming from behind her long-curved lobby desk. She wore an expensive two-piece pants suit with her hair in a bob.

"I'm Symba." I held my hand up slowly.

Smiling she said, "Follow me."

We followed her down the hall and she opened this steel door. That's when I noticed all the closed doors were huge and steel. Nothing on them, no apartment numbers or letters. Once we went down the one flight of stairs, the room looked like a sectioned off storage in the back with an enormous walk-in safe. Like the ones you see in banks. There was a desk in the left corner. *J. Cole* was playing loud enough for us to hear it, but not to the point that you couldn't hear yourself speak. One speaker in the right corner and the other on the side of the stairs

The desks were very nice with big leather desk chairs. Down the hall I could see three other big steel doors; they were closed. Down here was just as nice as upstairs. The TV mounted to the wall was movie theater size big, carpet was clean and soft even with shoes on. Walking further towards the left, there he was, Dominick. Looking just as good as the time I saw him in the club. Oh my goodness!

He had a man bun in his head, shaping that face making that honey color beard blend with those same color eyes. When he saw me, he did that squint and that's when I saw that light green mix in his eyes with the honey color. He was holding a guitar, but not the one from the club. He wore another crisp white V-neck T-shirt. Those black diamond studs were in and he had a black diamond Rolex watch with a burgundy face. Lori walked past us and back upstairs.

"Ladies." Dominick spoke first and walked towards us. "Thanks for stopping by. Names?" He looked at my two nieces and asked.

"I'm Christian, nice to meet you."

"I'm Nina, nice to meet you."

They both held their hands out to him and he shook them one by one. He looked at me and that squint in his eyes came back. "I'm sure y'all know I'm Dominick. This is my brother Quest, my other brother is in his office taking a shower. Work made him a little dirty, so he had to clean up."

"Oh shit!" Christian flinched when a knife literally went flying past us and close as hell to where she was standing. It hit the center of the board. "What the hell, nigga? You could have taken my head off!" She fumed at Quest, looking like she was ready to cuss him out.

Even though I was laughing on the inside because Christian's loudmouth ass looked shook, I made sure to keep my hand on my purse where my small handgun was.

"Calm yo' ass down. I never miss, and I wasn't about to hit ya chocolate ass. At least not hit you in that way," He snickered and threw another knife in the same spot.

Christian flinched again. "Hell naw!" This girl took her phone out her pocket then took her long strap purse off her shoulder, sitting it on the long leather couch behind her. "Stand yo' ass right here and let me throw knives through them big ass holes in your ears. See if I miss or hit the target."

Nina leaned her head on my shoulder which was her way of laughing and being embarrassed. Me, I let my laugh out because my niece was a firecracker with no chill. Quest had some medium earring gauges in his ears. He had a white beater on so you could see his muscular arms, tattoos all over. He didn't look like the type to have ear gauges, but it worked for him with that chest length full beard. Quest held the end of the knife in his hand, looking Christian up and down slowly like he wanted to hump her leg.

"He got a thing for chocolate girls." Dominick whispered to me.

"The only thing you can throw at me chocolate mama is that ass in a circle."

Even Christian had to laugh at how smooth and on point his clap back was. "We can work on that later, right now I want you to show me your circus act."

I covered my mouth laughing, and Nina was shaking her head. Christian was always blunt and lived up to what she wanted. That's where I got my bluntness from, but she had me beat. She walked over to Quest. Standing in front of him he put his hand on the front of her stomach, gave her a knife and started showing her how to throw them. I can't lie, they looked sexy together. I noticed he wasn't wearing a ring, but I don't think Christian cared.

"Come on over to the bar with me so we can make some drinks." Dominick said to me. It was weird having that voice in my ear face to and not over the phone.

I looked at Nina.

"Go ahead boo, I'm about to sit right here and watch my sister's crazy butt." She sat down and folded her legs. I loved how pretty she looked today with her black wavy bundles down. She wore a black spaghetti strap tube top, with some fitted black liquid leggings and some Steve Madden black platform sandals. The full bar wasn't anywhere but across the room, but I still wanted to make sure she was ok.

"Dominick took my hand and walked me over with him. "So Symba, what's up?" He asked me once we got behind the massive bar. He leaned on the counter that held all the brands of liquor, wine and champagne. I was in front of him leaning against the bar's actual counter. His big arms folded and those eyes were fully on me.

I made sure to look at him with a smirk too, just so he wouldn't think I was on some shy shit. "Nothing. I finally decided to bless you with my presence again," I joked.

He did this addictive laugh and one of his gigantic hands pulled on his beard. "You were going to do that anyway, or I was coming to you," he said with so much confidence. "And before you start that whole *you don't know where I live* shit, we both know I'll find out."

I swear I wanted to drop my mouth, but I wasn't about to give him the satisfaction of knowing I was appalled. "Speaking of you being a stalker—"

"Determined." He corrected me.

I just chuckled and continued. "Stalker." I re-corrected him. "How did you know where I was last night? You do know that's a red flag for me to get the fuck on, right?"

"Now we both know it's too much lust, curiosity and fondness for either of us to get the fuck on. Come here real quick."

I gave him an 'as if' look and arched my eyebrow. He clinched his jaw and his eyebrow did the same as mine. There was an 'I won't ask again' expression on his face. My feet said fuck what I was saying and made their way over to him. His hand went on the small of my back and he leaned forward, so close to me. Damn, he smelled all man and I shivered when his nose brushed across my neck. He took a sniff and his lips lightly brushed my ear and he said, "You smell so good. What is that?"

I couldn't even swallow. His deep voice and him being so close to my spot was everything. Oh, my goodness, I was about to pull this man's dick out in front of my own family. "Um, Burberry Her; it's my favorite," I answered, fighting not to close my eyes.

He leaned back with those burning eyes of his

penetrating my eyes. "Now it's mine." When he said that, his hand pressed firmer on my lower back, mushing me closer to him. As much as he was luring me in even beyond his touch, I still felt the need to make things clear.

"Dominick, I like how we vibe and all, but you'll never have me like you're used to with other girls. Honestly, you'll never have me at all. But we can have fun and chill. If you're wanting or looking to make this more, you will be greatly disappointed."

His eyes went to the left for a second; that muscular jaw of his clenched a little and I knew he was about to give me attitude like all men did. No matter the race, guys can't take rejection of any form from me. Y'all remember Ricardo's stupid ass snatching his chips back from me over me hoeing him. Dominick was no different, so I was already prepared to laugh. His eyes wandered back to mine and that hand slid slowly off my back.

"What's your preference, gorgeous Queen: dark or white?" He asked, taking out six glasses.

I was a little mixed up in emotions because it was as if I didn't lay shit out. "Oh, I uh... prefer white. Cîroc with lime juice," I told him, and he started making mine.

I knew that Nina wasn't drinking alcohol so I made her a cranberry juice with non-alcoholic margarita mix. Christian liked her Bacardi on ice with a lemon slice.

"We can have a drink with them and hang, but I want private time with you," he said, handing me my drink.

I didn't like how he wasn't responding at all to what I spoke. Sitting the drink down, I put my hands on my wide hips and asked. "Did you hear anything I said earlier?"

"I heard the hot air you were spitting out." Dominick responded, putting a cherry in his mouth and making drinks like he did this in his spare time.

"I get you heard me, but did you *comprehend*?" I questioned him again while sipping on my Cîroc and lime.

"Symba, I'm far from slow. I heard you and I comprehend what you said. Now like *I* said, I want private time with you after we have our drinks and hang with them for a minute." He put the drinks I made for Nina and Christian on a tray and gave it to me, biting his lip.

"Do you comprehend me?" He asked with those blazing eyes piercing back into mine.

"Yea, I do." Did I just fucking answer him!? Oh no, no, no! I'd have to make things clearer when we were in private. Dominick was too cocky for *my* own good. He needed to be knocked down a few notches. I gave Christian her drink who was still flirting and throwing knives with Quest. Nina was on the couch looking like she was enjoying watching them, even though she still wasn't smiling. Giving her the cranberry drink, I took the tray and walked back to the bar where Dominick was, just as someone came from down the long hallway.

"Who is that?" I asked Dominick.

"That's my other brother, Angel."

Angel was brushing his hair looking at all of us, but he stopped when his eyes landed on Nina.

NINA

I was actually having a nice time being out of the house with Nina and Christian. Being around them every day reminded me of when we were younger. The drama with Marlo disturbed me so much that I thought about it more than I did Nicholas. I went from thinking about how I felt knowing he was fucking my best friend Talia, to how I felt seeing that he was fucking her brother, *and* she knew.

What I can't wrap my mind around is why she wouldn't tell me. Talia hated Marlo from the beginning. Why would she not take the chance to expose him? Another thing was her brother Tino. They were not that close, in fact, she only lived with him because her dad said he would pay the bills if Tino let her move in with him. Tino wasn't gay at all; he was a troublemaker who hustled and fucked every bitch in his reach.

I guess all of that was a front. His big burly ass likes taking dick. It made me sick to my stomach because him and Marlo have been friends for years. I kiss Marlo on the mouth, fuck him raw, suck his dick from time to time…I threw-up three times just thinking about him out here sticking his dick in niggas' hairy ass shitholes. I just knew for sure I was going to have some kind of STD. Yea, I know it would be the same thing if he was fucking a woman, but I don't give a damn. This was much more gross, knowing he's been on some down low mess.

Since I have been sixteen, I've never been away from Marlo this long. I went to work and told Burt the details of what happened. It was something about him and his wife that always gave me so much comfort. I let them know that Marlo might show up a few times. Mary, Burt's wife, was on it. She gave me her Camry to drive since she didn't drive it.

I parked my car in their garage in the back of the funeral home. Burt told me Marlo would come by one time, he'd let him know that I was working and that would be the end of it. I think Burt's African accent made him come off as intimidating. Grandma told me Marlo came to her house a lot, but once she pulled her gun on him, he has been keeping his distance. I moved around the city like I was in a *James Bond* movie, not wanting to run into him or have him catch me.

Anyway, I agreed to come with Symba and Christian on this set up, but I honestly didn't mean it. I was just caught up in the mayhem of receiving negative test results from the doctor. Symba wasn't trying to hear it, so here I am. The sun was out bright, and I really didn't mind getting dressed. I came along, but I had no intentions on talking to whoever was set up for me. I really just wanted to be around my sister and auntie and see them have a good time.

Nothing much changed about me and how I was on the inside. Discovering the truth about Marlo further made me know that God was still angry with me. I failed Nicholas, failed to protect the most precious gift God could have ever given me. Everything about me was damned and felt like a curse. Like every day, God needed to remind me that I would never be forgiven. Still, I refuse to take it out on the world or my family. I enjoyed seeing them smiling, having fun and living.

I took a few sips of the drink Symba made me. It was good and sweet. I never, ever let alcohol touch my lips or any kind of drug. I missed nothing about it and honestly, probation helped me with that. I didn't want to go back to jail once I was out, so I abided by all the rules of my probation. Marlo didn't care about his probation rules. I had many, many dark times when I wanted to say 'fuck it' and indulge in all that he was doing.

I wanted to get that feeling back from the first time… the numbness, psychedelic feeling. I wanted the trip. As soon as I came close to not caring, I get a call about a possible job from Burt. That took up a lot of my time to sit and just live in guilt, regret and pain.

I roamed YouTube, marking the videos I planned on watching later. I looked up when I saw someone come from the long hallway. When the person's face was revealed, I held my breath for a second.

He was definitely surprised to see me too, only he played it off better. Once again, his style stood out, like he refused to dress like a 2020 man. His bowlegs looked good in the navy-blue Dickies pants he was wearing, with an over-size black button-up top. He had it open, revealing his sexy chest with that paragraph tattoo showing, I'm dying to be up and close to him so I can see what it says.

The Balenciaga gym-shoes he wore matched perfectly, but what made you know he wasn't a low poverty man was his jewelry. The big ass rocks in each of his ears, the bracelet that shined brighter than the Las Vegas sun outside, and his pinky ring that was bigger than a baby's little fist... that's when I felt those puppy doe's on me. He wasted no time walking my way.

"Small world, huh, chicken nugget?"

"Chicken nugget?" Christian asked, looking at me and Angel with a smile. "Y'all know each other?"

I stood up with my body full of nerves and butterflies. It felt so weird because I haven't had any emotions but blandness in so long. My insides literally were like a blank canvas, and now I'm feeling *things* in my stomach. My heart is really racing and I even felt a tickle in my throat.

"I met him at Burt's a few times," I answered nervously, but tried to play it cool. When he smiled big at me, I almost lost my shit.

Symba and Dominick came over to us, sitting on the love seat in the left corner. They looked good together and Symba seemed smitten by him. I made a mental note to tease her about that later. I was about to say something to Angel when a damn knife flew past me and hit the board on the wall behind me. I flinched a little and looked at Christian.

"Really?" I stared at her with an attitude.

She was laughing. "I'm sorry Nina-Bina, he's a terrible ass teacher. He's all beauty and no brains," Christian taunted while pointing to Quest, who stood behind her.

"Naw, you a terrible ass student with a shitty vibe.

You need to let me take you to my office so I can eat that pussy and adjust that attitude," Quest told her and I swear, they were a match made in heaven.

Christian was cracking up and nudging him with her elbow. She whispered something in his ear and he actually was squeezing her ass while she whispered. Before I could blink, he was licking his lips, grabbing her hand and they were walking down the long hall.

"Oh my God," I whispered and shook my head.

"Fucking freaks!" Symba yelled at them while laughing.

"Let them live their best lives." Angel spoke, looking at me. "Ain't shit back there but each of our private offices."

I nodded my head. "We don't have to talk or anything, I mean if you don't want to. I was fine sitting back chilling." I didn't want him to think he was obligated; sometimes Angel would show up at Burt's and act as if he didn't see me. He'd speak, but it wouldn't be very welcoming.

He watched my eyes move. He wasn't discreet about it either, so of course with us finding out we were each other's set up, I didn't want him to think he had to entertain me.

Instead of him responding to me, he just sat down on the couch I was sitting on. "Sit down." He instructed me with a serious tone.

I guess I didn't move quickly enough because he put his hands on my waist and gently pulled me down on the couch cushion next to him. When he placed his left arm on the back of the couch, I got a good whiff of his cologne.

"Next time, do what I say."

I looked at him with my eyebrows furrowed. "Your bossy behind didn't give me a chance to sit down."

He chuckled. "Bossy behind. That's some shit my Moms would say. She swore I was bossy as hell."

"Well, she does know you best, so it must be true. Tell her I agree, you're bossy." All my nerves went away and there were only butterflies in my stomach now. I was comfortable sitting this close to him… smelling him and feeling the heat from his body to mine.

"I would gladly tell her that if she was alive; she'd like you right off rip." His smile was placed back on his face and those puppy doe's lit up.

"Oh." I looked down for a second, thinking about what he said. Then I looked back up at him with sincerity and remorse. "I'm sorry, Angel."

"It's cool, you didn't know and you didn't say anything disrespectful. I haven't heard anyone call me bossy on sight in a while, it was refreshing." He had a calmness to him, like he reminisced about his mother just that quickly.

I nodded my head while putting some of my hair behind my ear. I knew grief and how one little thing could remind you of what you lost, but I wasn't about to speak on any of that.

"So, *Nina-Bina.*" He repeated the nickname Christian called me.

On the inside I was smiling and giggling. But my face

wouldn't let it form, I did, however, feel my cheeks flush.

"Christian used to pronounce my name *Bina* when we were little. As we got older, she added the Nina, now all my of family calls me that from time to time."

"Really, tell me more." He grinned and actually got comfortable, waiting on me to finish talking about my family.

I kept it light, told him about Mama and how hard she worked to take care of me and Christian. I told him the many of jobs she worked, then I told him about Grandma and Symba. I told him I was in school, my passion for cheerleading and the plans I used to have. I made sure to not hint about being a teen mom, Marlo, or the death of my son.

"You seem to have had a pretty decent childhood, you're beautiful as hell and have a good support system." He moved his finger to Symba and then pointed down the hall where Christian was. "Yet, I have never seen you crack one smile, not even a smirk. But them eyes hold all your emotions. What's that about?"

I caught my breath when his hand that was stretched on the back of the couch started messing with my hair, and then his fingers brushed across my ear. My God, I don't know what he just did, but the butterflies were gone. I now felt warm all over. How is it something so small could have such an effect on me? Why was I now breathing in short spurts, but my heart wasn't racing like earlier? It was now at an even beat.

"I don't smile." My voice was low and soft, but I knew he heard me. I shrugged my shoulders after I said that.

Angel nodded his head and went back to messing with my hair and ears. "We'll have to change that, Nina."

I sat up and turned towards him. "Why do you care?"

His forehead developed wrinkles. "Why wouldn't I? You know, since you ran into me, I been feeling you."

And there it was…those words that I secretly wanted to hear come from his mouth.

"But you don't act like it. I mean you speak to me dry and you don't say anything after that." I wanted to know what his game was. Let's be honest, this is *indeed* a game. No way in hell would a man who looked like him be perfect. No way in hell do I deserve perfect, so I wanted to know his angle.

"That's just me and how I act, but I know you see how I watch you. The fact that I speak to you at all is proof that I am, indeed, feeling you. I know you got some layers, I could see that shit from the first moment I met you. But it's cool, chicken nugget, I got all the time in the world. I don't just watch you in lust, Nina. I watch you in awe. Somebody made you stop smiling and after I put it back on your face, I'ma torture that muthafucka, make him apologize to you, then I'ma kill him."

My mouth dropped a little because I couldn't believe what he was saying. I waited to see if he was going to at least turn his words into a joke or show some form of humor. Once I didn't see any sign of it, I had to straighten some things out.

"Angel I—"

"You can't change my statement, Nina. It's done, I've already decided. Come on, sit back and finish talking to me. I like your voice." As he spoke, he gently pulled my arm, making me sit back. His hand went back to messing with my hair and ear while we both talked.

We were so wrapped up in our conversation that I didn't notice Symba and Dominick sneak out. When Christian and Quest came back in, the four of us talked and had a nice time. I was enjoying myself and the company. Symba and Dominick came back like an hour later. She looked the same...didn't look like she had just given her pussy out like my baby sister. I say that with humor. I in no way ever judged either of them. Had I not been so in love with Marlo, I would have been living my life like the two of them.

I was doing things I haven't done in years! Hanging out, shooting pool, listening to music...I watched them laugh and joke and we even played cards. What was supposed to be an hour turned into six and us ordering food. It was different.

I felt different around Angel, and even Quest and Dominick. It didn't seem like any of us were there by force. The laughs I saw Symba and Christian share were real. No fake giggles, filters or any of that stuff. They enjoyed the guys and the guys enjoyed them.

Angel stayed close to me whether we were sitting down, standing or eating. He kept me in reach, literally elbow to elbow, and I didn't stop him. I needed to… I know I should have, but I didn't want to. Have you ever felt certain about something so fast that it scared you? That's how I was feeling now, but the other voice in me was saying to stop being foolish. Even if Angel is the real deal, why on earth would *I* deserve him?

"Join me for breakfast tomorrow?" Angel asked as him and the guys walked me, Symba and Christian outside. I was about to put some of my hair behind my ear, but he beat me to it. Like he learned my movements just that quickly. "Don't tell me you have to work because we both know you don't."

He's smart because I was about to lie, but since he called me out, I figured I'd tell the truth. "I'm going apartment hunting tomorrow morning. Gotta get off my sister and auntie's couch."

He nodded his head slowly. "It's a date for the next day then."

"Asking or telling me?" I asked him with curiosity evident on my face, and my voice filled with sarcasm. I already knew his answer but I wanted him to know I caught it.

"You know the answer to that." He opened the passenger door for me. "Don't get in this car without giving me a hug."

I knew he was going to ask for one, I had already mentally prepared myself for a quick one-arm hug. Angel was so much taller than me, even on my tiptoes he'd still have to bend over for my arms to wrap around his neck. Why did he have to look so good as I got closer to him? His eyes were circling around my body slowly and he licked his sexy lips. The one-arm church hug went out the window as soon as his arms wrapped around my waist. My feet literally lifted off the ground about an inch. Both of my arms were wrapped securely around his neck and he held me with the best squeeze. I was secured and tucked in perfectly. I felt our bodies intertwine together and I knew his scent would linger on me, and mine on him.

"I'll call you, ok?" He said to me as he released me so that I could get in the car.

"We didn't exchange numbers," I reminded him.

"Burt gave me yours yesterday," Angel admitted with a smile as he closed the door.

I wasn't even mad… more like surprised that he even asked for my number. I guess I would have heard from him whether this happened or not.

"Sooooo, Nina-Bina!" Christian's loud butt yelled my name all in my ear. She leaned up and grabbed the back of my chair. "Why haven't we ever heard about Angel?!"

Symba looked from the road to me, smiling widely.

"Spill the tea ma'am, because what we just saw back there was a whole 'nother Nina."

I rolled my eyes and put my hair behind my ear. "It's nothing to tell. He comes by Burt's to do business with him and I ran into him one day. That's all there is, nothing more, nothing less."

"Girl bye, that was a lot more and wasn't shit about it less. He's into you Nina and you're into him, even though you still didn't smile. It was pretty clear," Symba suggested and Christian agreed.

I didn't want to get into this with them, so I changed the subject. "The real question is, what happened with you and Quest? You know he isn't married, right?"

Christian started laughing loudly, yelling like she was Cardi-B's twin. "Quest is definitely an exception of my married rule. And as far as what we did, a lady never kisses and tells."

Me and Symba smacked our lips and looked at each other like Christian was so full of shit. "What about you

IN LOVE WITH A LAS VEGAS OUTLAW 2

auntie Sym-Sym, where did you and Dominick go?" I asked her.

"Nowhere, just to the back seat of his truck to talk and kiss a little. I swear to y'all, that is a black man with no pigment. Whew!" She joked and continued. "But he's used to being in charge. All of that will change though when I fuck the shit out of him. Mark my words."

I shook my head. "I'm ashamed to be related to the both of you freaks." I joked, and Symba came off the freeway.

"Can you drop me at your sister's house please?" I asked her.

"Sure, everything ok?"

"Yea, it's only nine o'clock. You know she's still woke, I just wanna see her."

She complied and I sat back looking out the window while the two of them talked. My phone went off and I unlocked my screen to see what the alert was.

702-018-0324- I know you have a picture of you

smiling. Send it to me.

This was a new phone and a new number, so I didn't...Oh, I know who this is. I looked at Symba out the corner of my eye to make sure she wasn't watching me. Going to my gallery, I went all the way down to selfies I had from New Year's 2014. I still looked the same, but you can tell that it's a throwback picture. I sent him two where I was smiling and looking really cute.

702-018-0324- A fucking diamond.

His response gave me goosebumps because I could hear his voice saying that. I decided to respond with a smile emoji.

"Are you staying the night?" Christian asked when Symba pulled in front of Mama's house.

"Yeah, I'll be back in the morning to shower and go look at apartments." I laughed to myself because they both pouted every time I talked about my own place. I closed the door and walked up on the porch. I had a key but because Mama was still dating her men, I never just walked in.

"I knew you were still up," I said to her when she opened the door.

"No work tomorrow and Symba got me hooked on that S*candal* show on Netflix so that's what my night is looking like." She hugged me then locked the door.

I took my sandals off and hung my purse on the hook. I could smell cinnamon, so I headed to the kitchen.

"Oooh, these look like Grandma's." My mouth watered when I saw the hot fresh cinnamon rolls.

"Yea, she came over to see me today. I just heated them up in the oven. You staying the night?" She asked me while taking a knife and saucer out for me. Our relationship picked back up after I had Nicholas and she came to the hospital to see him.

"Yup. I have plans in the morning, so I'm leaving early." I washed my hands when she gave me a kiss on the cheek and rubbed my back. It was just me in the kitchen so I ate two cinnamon rolls and some ice cream.

Even though this was our childhood home, when

mama became a RN she upgraded the house. The kitchen had new a new stove, refrigerator and floor tile. The outside was painted black and white and the living room had new furniture and a television. After I ate, I washed my plate, fork and knife and went to my old room. Mama kept the sheets changed but other than that, everything was the same. It was like that with Christian's room as well. I took my clothes off and went across the hall to shower.

Three women and one bathroom used to be a battle between us. After I showered, I dried off and put on some linen pajama shorts and a black sports bra. My long bundles were wet, so I put five braids in them so it could be curly in the morning. My real hair left out blended perfectly with it, so I just let it curl up on its own. Putting my silk scarf on, I walked out my room and knocked on Mama's door.

"What season of *Scandal* are you on?" I asked her while I took my slippers off and climbed in her bed.

"Season three. That damn Columbus Short is so fine, I don't know how I watch *Grey's Anatomy* and never watched this."

Mama was sitting up in her bed up under her covers. I sat on top of them and folded my legs, looking at the TV. I had this saved on my list on Netflix so I could get into it too. Christian has sworn by it for years. I was a fanatic of *The Walking Dead*. Like, I re-watch that show so much and don't play about the new episodes. I looked at the TV, but I wasn't really watching. My mind was preoccupied. The word 'MUTE' appeared on the screen, breaking my daze and forcing me to look at Mama to figure out what she was doing.

"What's on your mind, Bina? You looking straight through that screen. Not only that, but you popped up over here unannounced. What's the matter?"

I looked down at my fingers for a minute, trying to collect my thoughts. When I looked back up at her, my tears poured down my face, non-stop.

"Aww Nina, what is it? Do you miss Marlo?" Mama asked with sadness in her eyes. Usually when we broke up, I would come in her room crying about how I missed him. But we all know that was *not* the case right now.

I chuckled a little and shook my head. "Trust me Mama, I do not miss that man."

"Then what is it?" Her voice was laced with concern.

"I'm scared, Mama." I couldn't even get my sentence out without my voice cracking and more tears pouring out. I cleared my throat and spoke part of some truth.

"Someone likes me and I like him, but I don't trust it. It has everything negative written all over it, but for some reason, I don't care." With tears still falling, I stared off and continued. "He put his arm around me, touched my hair and played with my ears. The six hours I was just with him we talked, he made my plate first when we ordered food...it sounds so small but I've never experienced that before. His eyes. Mama. Puppy doe's I call them...are so big and they stare so deep into mine to the point where I can feel them digging. He asked me out to breakfast on Tuesday and I'm actually going."

"Nina." Mama called my name, snapping me from my thoughts again.

I looked at her she had tears in her eyes. "You're smiling."

When she said that, I slowly touched my face. I could feel the small creases in the corners of my mouth. Mama got from under her covers and hugged me.

"I love you, Nina. I know I hurt you when I put you out for being pregnant. I was just angry at myself for failing you. Yea I talked to you girls, but I worked non-stop and I lived my life before spending time with you and Christian. I never should have told you to leave. I am so sorry for that." Hugging me tighter, she kissed the top of my head.

Mama never apologized with her words; I would cherish this moment forever. After we finished our moment, I watched two episodes of *Scandal* with her. Once she fell asleep, I covered her up and went to my room. It was a little after one in the morning and I was tired. Closing my bedroom door, I put my phone on the charger right when I saw that I had a text message.

702-018-0324- I know this is all new to you but for future references, unless you're lying next to me, I need to hear your voice at night. Sweet dreams chicken nugget.

I felt a small smile form as I put my phone down and got under the covers. I laid down and prayed I didn't have the same nightmare I've been having every night since Nicholas died.

I was sleeping so well until I heard a scream. My eyes squeezed together tightly because I hated when I had this dream. A loud bang and thud sounded off next and then it hit me. I wasn't having a nightmare at all. That was Mama screaming, and things were getting broken.

"Don't you touch her! Nina, run!"

I jumped up when I heard her call my name. Running bare foot to my door, I turned the knob but the door wouldn't open. Looking down at the knob, I turned it over and over again and it still wouldn't turn. I could hear what I knew was Mama being knocked around from wall to wall. There was glass breaking, her screaming and the entire house felt like it was shaking.

"Ma! Mama!"

I banged, kicked and even picked up one of my cheerleading trophies trying to break the door down. This door doesn't jam, never has. And I never close it all the way... Mama didn't play about me and Christian locking doors in her house. We always left our doors cracked. Someone or something was blocking the door. I was in a panic. Looking around I spotted my window that led to the side of the house. I took the trophy in my hand and broke it so that I could get out.

Once I cleared all the glass, I climbed through with no shoes on, completely immune to the glass I was stepping on. It was harder than it looked climbing out of a window. As I got both of my legs out, I saw two black figures run from the house. I was all the way out running to the front when an all-black crown Victoria pulled off with no license plate. My trophy was firm in my hand as I ran through the front door that they left open.

"Oh my God! Mama!"

I ran to her body lying on the floor. The emotion I felt was all too familiar... the feeling of helplessness, loss and guilt. Why the hell couldn't I get out the damn door!? Why didn't I just sleep in her room like I started to!? How could I not hear anyone come in the house?! As I had a million thoughts going through my mind, Mama opened her one good eye. The other one was swollen shut from being hit.

Her lip was busted and I saw her panties ripped up on the floor. I rushed to the end table and grabbed the cordless phone. Mama and Grandma were the only ones in the world with a Comcast land line. My hands were shaking as I called 911 and told them to bring help in a hurry.

"Mama, Ma listen to me. I know who the hell did this. It's Marlo and I swear to God—"

"No." She said in an almost inaudible tone. "No. It wasn't Marlo; the two guys were big and solid, t-t-this wasn't Marlo."

I looked around at the mess. It appeared as if Mama was trying to fight back. I didn't want to touch her too much, but I did go to the bathroom, wet her rag and wiped her face. "Are you able to sit up?" I asked her, still crying.

She inched up a little and then cried out in pain. "I can't. I can't."

"It's ok mama—" I stopped talking when I heard sirens and saw the flashing lights. I ran to my room and put my house shoes on then went to the front door.

The only reason I was able to think straight was because Mama was awake. Although she was beat up and in pain, she was still alive.

The emergency men came in and tended to her. The police came shortly after as well and wanted to question me, but I asked if they could do it once we got to the hospital. I rode in the back of the ambulance, holding Mama's hand.

I did make sure to grab my phone and her purse because I knew her insurance cards were in there. Thank God it was summertime because I literally had on a sports bra, some linen pajama shorts and house slippers. After we got to the hospital, I spoke with the police while the doctors took care of Mama. I told them everything that happened from the beginning to the end. I was all out of tears. Now, I was so angry because Mama said that it *wasn't* Marlo.

That meant it was a random act of violence... but why the hell was my door blocked? Come to think of it, there was nothing blocking my door when I went to get my cellphone and house slippers, to me it meant someone was holding my door shut. If this was random, why wasn't I harmed?

"Is she ok?" I asked the nurse when I came back in Mama's room. She looked like she was passed out.

The nurse gave me a light smile while she adjusted Mama's fluid bag.

"The doctor gave her a strong sleep medication for her pain. He wants to keep her two days for observation because of the contusion on her head, but she'll be fine. The good news is she wasn't raped. Those scumbags probably spooked off when they realized she wasn't home alone. Good thing you were there." She patted my arm then walked out.

I breathed out and kissed Mama on her cheek. The medication had her knocked out. Her eyes and lip were purple. Her ribs were bruised, but not broken. Tonight could have gone a whole lot worse. I stepped out the room with my phone so I could call my family.

"Nina?"

I looked up when I heard my name.

"Angel?" I was surprised to see him here and I'm sure he felt the same way about seeing me. Ugh, I look a hot mess! Scarf on, jumbo braids hanging out and some dorky slippers...

He walked towards me quickly while looking at my attire. "What are you doing here at three in the morning with nothing on? You ok?" As he was talking, he unzipped his hoodie and took it off. He then put it on me without even asking if I wanted it. The muscle tank he wore displayed the sides of his chest. He even zipped the hoodie up, his face still fixed in a serious expression.

"My mama was attacked in her house. It all happened so fast." I blinked my tears away.

"Is she ok?" He asked me with so much concern on his face and in his tone.

"Yea, bruised ribs and a black eye. Thank God nothing major." I looked up at him. "What are you doing here?" I rolled the sleeves on his hoodie up because it was so big on me.

"My worker's mom was attacked in her home too. Beat up pretty badly." As he talked, his nostrils flared and he seemed to be fuming. Was there some crazy person out hurting old women? What the fuck was really going on?

"Do you think it's connected? I mean this is crazy," my voice cracked. "Someone held my door shut so I couldn't get to her. I had to break my window out… all I heard was her screams and her calling my name." I cleared my throat and blinked my tears away again.

"Listen to me, Nina." He used his index finger and

made me look at him. "Don't worry or cry about this. I swear on my life, nothing else will happen to your moms. Who else was there with y'all?"

"No one, just me and her. I was about to call my family and let them know." His finger was still on my chin. He used that same finger to caress the side of my cheek. Why did these tiny gestures mean so much to me?

"Ok, I'll post with you until they get here," Angel assured and went to the nurses' station to speak to the one on duty.

I was surprised and didn't understand why this man was so into me. He admired me, touched me and took care of me as if we have been together for years. It's like he can see into the future and just knows him investing interest in me will have a happily ever after.

I made the call to Christian and she didn't answer, so I called Symba and told her the important details. She said she was on her way and about to wake Christian's hard sleeping butt up. I told her not to tell her mama, Grandma,

111

until later in the day. I didn't want her getting up at three in the morning.

"Everything good?" Angel asked when he walked back to me.

"Yes, my sister and auntie are on their way up here." I watched the two nurses come over towards me and head into Mama's room.

"They are moving her to her own room," he said as they wheeled Mama out and into the elevator.

We followed behind them but it was too many of us to get on the elevator, so they went first and we caught the next one while they waited for us.

"I'm sorry this shit happened to you and your moms. I ain't gone lie chicken nugget, this shit got me tight as hell. Same thing with my two workers and their moms. I don't play that shit about mothers... women in general. With mine being gone, it's a sensitive spot for me." He stood in front of me, gazing into my eyes. "I don't mean to come off so strong but then again, I do. I want'chu bad as fuck, Nina. I'ma get you to see what I see, don't even trip about it." The elevator door opened and we both finally broke eye contact.

The nurses were waiting for us as we got off, so we continued to follow them. I noticed the walls were different from where we were. They were fancier with more art on them. Even the vending machines had different types of choices. A Starbucks vending machine and a damn Barilla vending machine were also in the vending area. I had never seen either of those in my life.

We got to my mama's room and it was fancy, just like a hotel suite. Her bed was placed in the middle and there was a sitting area in front of her. A 50-inch TV was mounted on the wall; there were two pull-out couches and two love seats in the corner. After the nurses set her up, they left out the room. I wasn't crazy, I knew Angel did this.

"You didn't have to do all of this. I mean thank you, but I know this is super expensive." I looked around the room.

"Money is not a problem, Nina. There is always more

113

money." Angel sat down on the couch and shrugged as if it was nothing. The man was so nonchalant about money like he knew how to make it. "Come sit next to me. I know when your people get here I gotta bounce to give y'all some privacy, so let me soak up our time while I can."

I sat down next to him and we watched TV until my eyes got so damn low, I couldn't take it anymore. The last thing I remembered was putting my feet up on the couch and lying on Angel's chest.

**

"Well good morning, Sleeping Beauty." Symba and Christian were smiling widely in my face.

Between the bright sun and their stupid grins, I was so annoyed. I have never been a morning person.

"What the he—" I stopped cussing when I saw my grandma in the corner knitting and the look she gave me was '*don't make me fuck you up*'. "What are y'all doing? Move." I sat up looking mad but my mood instantly changed when I saw that Mama was up.

"Hey Mama." I smiled and walked over to her, hugging her softly. "I am so sorry I couldn't get to you. I don't know what was wrong with my door, but I broke my bedroom window out and climbed—"

"Nina." She cut me off because I was talking so fast and even started crying. "Calm down Nina-Bina, it's ok." She smiled and even with a messed-up eye and lip she still looked like a beautiful mixture of me and Christian. Rubbing my back while I laid on her shoulder, we watched as the nurse came in.

"Ms. Curwin, the police are here to take your statement. Is it a good time?" She asked Mama.

"Yeah sure, let's get it over with." Mama responded, and two black officers came in.

One was trying to be professional, but his eyes kept shifting to Symba. Her nasty ass flipped her hair and gave him a flirty smile. Grandma popped her on her thigh twice and made her sit down. As Mama retold what happened, it was worse than what I imagined. When she told the part about the guy ripping her panties off, I think all of our stomachs turned. The other guy yelled at him to do what they came to do and nothing extra so that's why she wasn't sexually assaulted.

Then she said the second big guy stood in front of my door holding the knob. That's why I couldn't get out; someone knew I was in the house and wanted to make sure I couldn't get to her. Mama was clear that it wasn't Marlo. I wouldn't have ever in a million years thought Marlo would do something like that.

But since seeing him give dick to a whole nigga, I don't put anything past him. Talia's brother wasn't a big guy. He had muscle, but Mama described the two men as solid and fat, and they had black masks on.

"Officer please get these disgusting ass filths off the streets before me and my rifle do it," Grandma said and it made all of us laugh. She was little bit about that life.

"We will do our best to personally catch these fools. We had another similar case last week, we are not trying to have a third." The cop who was sneaking looks at Symba spoke.

While they talked to Mama and Grandma some more, Christian and Symba pulled me in the hallway.

"Bitch, what the hell was Angel doing here?" Christian questioned. Her and Symba had those silly grins, again.

I folded my arms and realized I still had his hoodie on. I forgot he was here with me. "How do y'all know he was here?"

"When we came in here you were knocked out on him sleeping your best sleep. He laid you down all gently then kissed your forehead. Nina, the man is gone over the cliff for you. He asked us your clothes and shoes size," Symba revealed.

"Yea Nina, he's gone girl, and the nigga had the nerve to look at us and say, *'Let her sleep'*. We were like well damn, ok." Christian made me giggle when she put on a deep voice trying to sound like Angel.

"He's just being nice. Nothing is going on between me and Angel." We all turned around when we heard heels click-clacking hard on the floor.

"Hello, Nina. I'm Lori, we met when you all visited." The lady who was at the large, round desk at the guys' apartment complex was walking towards us with a smile. She was definitely older and had a pure sophistication about her.

"Yes, I remember you. Hello." I was a little lost as to why she was here, but I gave her a tiny close mouth smile to hid my confusion.

"Mr. McKay wanted me to drop some things off for you." She handed me two Nordstrom bags and one Gucci bag that had two shoe boxes in it. Then she passed me a Target bag with personal and hair products in it.

"Oh, and one more thing." She then gave me a manila folder.

"What's this?" I asked looking form her to the folder.

"A list of luxury apartments, condos and townhomes. All of which you have automatic approval for which ever you pick. Just make the call, tell them your name and the keys will be ready for pick up. Have a good afternoon, ladies." She nodded her head, smiled and then walked off in her expensive heels.

I was stunned as hell looking at this stuff. Symba stood in front of me with a smirk and her arms folded. "This doesn't look like someone who is just being nice, Nina."

"Shut up, both of you." I bit the skin on the inside of my cheeks to hold my smile in while I walked back into the room.

ANGEL

"Mrs. Newman was attacked in her house a few nights ago. Shane texted me and told me so I went to go see her last night. I had them move her in a private suite and covered her bill. While I was there, I saw Nina. Her mama was attacked in her crib, too."

"Oh shit, that's the girl you won't shut up about, right?" My pops snickered when he asked me that. He was being funny because he already knew the answer to that.

When my baby brother Axel died and then Moms, I made sure to take care of Pops. We grew closer. Every day I checked on him and twice a week we had dinner at his house. Of course, once I made money, I moved him out the hood. He picked a nice ranch style home with a barn and a lot of acers. He was a man who believed in working with his hands.

He was able to plow, plant livestock and he had a few

animals. Two dogs, horses, cows, chickens, a rooster and some ducks in the pond on the land. He wanted to move outside of Las Vegas, so I took him around for hours until he found his perfect house. He had the life him and Moms talked about, animals, acres, a garden, and a small pond.

I didn't care how much it cost me, money wasn't shit. It was always more money. I knew I couldn't fill the void of my brother and Moms being gone, but I could at least give him something to look forward to every day. He liked cooking for me, having a half glass of Highland Park scotch and good conversation.

"You got jokes, senior citizen," I joked while putting some potato salad in my mouth.

Pops sat dead smack in the sun. The only shade when you went outside was under his two big apple trees and in the barn. So, I let him know if he wanted me to visit, he had to get some A.C. installed. He only turned it on when I came over so I could be comfortable.

"I know why you have a spot in your heart for

protecting women, but you can't help them all son. Don't get killed being a hero. You still have the right to look after you. What good are you for that young lady if you're dead?"

He was right on a few levels; I couldn't go around trying to save the world. But he was wrong because I couldn't let this go. Mrs. Newman's two sons have worked for me, Dominick and Quest since the beginning. They introduced us to more of their doctor contacts who wanted to make some side bank. Written prescriptions, hospital supplies, and the fact that I trusted them made them like family. Then add Nina's moms in the mix... naw. I had to get to the bottom of this shit.

When I saw her at the hospital, I knew something wasn't right because she was half naked and looking panicked. I didn't like that shit; I was ready to pounce once she told me what was up. Since the moment she ran into me at Burt's, I wanted her. I could look in her eyes and see pain, grief and an unworthiness she felt about herself. I wanted to change that. Her insides needed to match her sexy ass outsides. I went to *Eternal Peace*, Burt's funeral home, every day just to see her.

But I didn't hold conversations with Nina. I spoke, did business with Burt and I watched her every move. I don't know if she knew I was watching or not, but my eyes were on her. When she would work, her face held a solemn expression... Like she was dedicated in making the dead look good, as if she owed them something. I remember the little girl she had to make look presentable. The child's mama was so messed up she couldn't even tell Nina how she wanted her to look.

I watched Nina hold that same vacant face but held all her emotions in her eyes tell that woman to not worry about it, that she would make her look perfect. The next day I came to *Eternal Peace*, and Nina was sewing the little girl a pink tutu. That's when I knew her heart was perfect, it was just broken and bruised. You can learn a lot about watching your mate or potential mate, and that's what I did. I came to the conclusion after about three weeks that I wanted her, and

I was going to have her.

I was blown away when she was one of the chicks Dominick was trying to set me up with. Nina's whole family was beautiful, Quest loved chocolate girls so I knew he had nut on her already. That was our way of saying we called dibs, but I wasn't tripping because when I saw Nina, it was over. The coincidence sealed that she was meant to be mine. Her falling asleep on me at the hospital was everything. Her little slim-thick set body was warm, and she slept like she hadn't slept peacefully in a while.

Even when her family came and I moved her, she still didn't wake up. I wanted her in my custom California king size bed, laying on my $2000 Charlotte Thomas bed sheets. That light honey skin, those thin, almon slanted eyes and perfect downward-turned lips I wanted to wake up to. I noticed lately she had been driving Burt's wife's car instead of her Versa Nissan. I wondered what happened to her ride. It bet' not have shit to do with some punk ass nigga taking her shit.

"I know Pops, I promise you I'm not about to dip out on you early." I looked up at him from my plate.

"That's all I ask son, remember, I want you to bury me, not the other way around. That's why I'm for you pursuing Nina. See if she's that one; give her the world and then the moon when you fuck up and then I was you to give me some grandkids. That way when my time does come, I'll know you won't be alone." He looked at me and held his closed fist out for me to pound it.

I pounded his fist and we finished eating and talking. When we finished, I went and messed with his horses for a minute. After helping him out around the house for about an hour and I headed out. Pops stayed strapped with guns and he was more of a soldier than I was, so I was cool leaving him alone. Plus, if I even tried to move him under me he'd kick my ass. I had a few hours of driving ahead of me, so I decided to see what Nina was doing.

"Hello." Her addictive voice swayed through the speakers in my car.

"You must not have my number saved," I suggested while sitting back in my seat once I merged into my lane.

"Yes, I do, Angel. I wouldn't have answered if I didn't know who it was. I have a new number and only a selective few have it." There was some confidence in her voice when she said the last part. Like I needed to be lucky to be one of the few. Confidence was sexy to me.

"You gotta come up with some cute name for me, then. I ain't feelin' that dry ass hello when I call," I teased.

"Oh really? What about *pookie* or *sweet cheeks*?" Her voice was hinted with humor, but I still didn't hear that sweet laugh that I knew she had.

I laughed. "Oh you got jokes. Naw chicken nugget, you gotta come up with something better than that."

"Well give me a few days and I'll get back to you." I knew she was playing but little did she know I was going to hold her to it.

"How are you today, Nina? How was work?"

"I'm fine and work was pretty good. I'm surprised I

didn't see you there, today."

My eyes bugged open in shock. "Damnnn, look at'chu lookin' for your man. You missed me?"

"I do not miss you. I was curious, and you are not my man."

"Lying isn't a good start to our relationship, Nina. It's just you and me here so gone and be honest, you miss me, bae?" My voice was low, and I would bet everything I had that she was turned on. Her silence for a few seconds told me I was right, so I decided to press some more. "Come on Nina, tell me you miss me."

I heard her breathe in like the truth was squeezing out of her, like she was closing her eyes. "I miss you Angel, where were you?"

Fuck. I have never had a woman make me feel like a bitch before besides my Moms. Nina's voice was small but sexual, and it was longing for me. It made my ravening heart skip beats and feel all warm and shit.

"I miss you too, chicken nugget. I had to visit my

Pops, spend some time with him." As I spoke, my other line beeped but I didn't know the number, so I ignored it.

"That's so sweet, you're an only child?"

Even though I told her about Moms, I never told her about Axel. No reason, I just didn't want to lay too much on her that day. My other line beeped again with the same number, but I ignored it again.

"I had a younger brother but he was killed."

"My goodness, I am so sorry, Angel." Sadness was laced in her tone.

"Thank you, Nina, but it's ok. That was years ago. I've learned to live with it. The only thing I'm having a hard time with is knowing his killers are still out there. But in due time, something will come up and I'll get'em." I admitted out loud. I hunted the streets down even as a teenager for the killers who took my brother from us. It may have looked like I've stopped, but I kept my ear and eyes out, always.

"Wow, you lost your mom and brother and you still manage to live, smile and not hold on to grief." She actually sounded surprised.

"I mean the hurt never goes away; sometimes I'll even tear up thinking about them. But I can't let it consume me. They wouldn't want that and it's no way to live. Death is a part of life, even if it's unexpected or a tragedy. You mourn, keep them close and figure out a way to gain some happiness and peace, then you go on."

"You would have come in handy a few years ago." Even though she held humor in her tone, I knew she was for real.

"I can say the same about you, Nina." We both were quiet for a minute, then I broke the silence.

"How is your Moms? Is she recovering ok?"

"She is... oh, and you just reminded me. Me and her want to thank you so much for her room at the hospital. Her home too; you really didn't have to do all of that Angel, but we are so grateful."

I smiled when she thanked me. Politeness went a long way with me. "It was my pleasure. Everyone deserves to feel safe at home."

"Yea but I know all of that stuff was super expensive. The clothes and shoes your assistant brought me too; a lot for a girl you've never had a date with. Is this how you get what you want?"

"I can't even feel some kind of way about you asking that. Actually, I'd feel a way if you didn't. But understand this, Nina. All I have to do is tell a woman I want her and I'll have her naked in a hotel suite within minutes. Everything about you just grabs me; I can't even explain it to myself. But I'm not fighting my instincts, it's in my nature to want the absolute best."

"And how do you know I'm the best?"

"Because you don't think you are." I knew I had her when I said that. My line beeped once again with the same damn number. "Chicken nugget, let me hit you right back. Don't go to sleep on me."

"Ok, I won't." As soon as she hung up, I clicked over.

"Yo' who the fuck is this?" I bellowed intensely

because I was irritated to the max that I had to hang up with Nina. Swear to God, if this was a telemarketer, I was hunting their ass down and ripping their eyes out. Y'all know I ain't lying.

"Calm down homie, it's just a businessman trying to reach out to another businessman." The shallow, raspy voice didn't sound familiar.

I turned my Bluetooth off and put my phone to my ear with my nose, making sure to speak in a harsh but serious tone. "Whoever this is, I'm warning you to stop playing with me."

They laughed. "Relax Angel, I ain't tryna have no problems with The Law. All I'm tryna do is conduct business with you."

I turned my nose up with a tart expression on my face. "I don't talk business over the phone."

"Neither do I, but it seems to be no other way to get your attention. I sent my guys to you and Quest threw a knife in one of their arms."

I knew then who this was so I laughed. "The struggle pimp from ashy ass Philly." I laughed harder. "I don't eat boy pussy, my nigga, so why the fuck you so pressed for me?"

He took an aggravated deep breath. "My boy told me you don't play nice—"

"I don't play at all and yo' boy returning with a hole in his arm should have told you what happens when you try to play with any of us." I was dead ass.

"The disrespect is unnecessary, I actually got a lot of respect for you—"

"Where you wanna meet? I ain't got time for no damn *'Lean on me'* speeches." My patience was wearing thin.

"Ok, we can meet in the open because I know you won't trust one of my spots. I'll text you the address." This clown ass bitch had the nerve to hang up in my face like some angry hoe.

I immediately called Quest and Dominick to tell them what just happened. I forwarded them the address the pimp sent me. Once they gave me the OK, I called Nina back and talked to her the rest of my ride back to Las Vegas. Once I arrived, I went to the outside spot Philly pimp said to meet.

I let my boys know how far out from the location I was. When I pulled up, I saw a red 2019 Ford Expedition truck parked. I was in one of my cheap rides, a Chevy Silverado 2500 HD. I parked it directly in front of his truck, bumper to bumper. I left my head lights on, shining bright in his face. As soon as I got out, he did as well. It was dark outside and there were no streetlights in the park we were in.

"I feel like I'm in the presence of royalty," he said with a slick grin. He had some Nike shorts on with a sleeveless vest and a pair of low top Nikes were on his feet. There was a toothpick hanging from his mouth, resting between his bottom gold grill.

I leaned on the end of my bumper and just looked at him.

He held his hand up. "Ok, ok I get it, you want me to get straight to the point. Well, it's no need to say what you already know. I'm Gunna, from Philly and I want to go into business with you. That whole big complex is more than enough for my girls to occupy some rooms when needed. I make a killing; on my worst day I still see a grand."

Now that made me laugh, "My nigga, a grand is how much it is to just get my contact information. Seems like you were blessed enough to skip that process and got a freebie. Let me cut it short. That building belongs to The Law and it ain't for sale or rent. You do yo' hoeing business and we'll do what we do. I got no beef with how you live; this is Vegas, hoes are everywhere.

Make yo' money how you make yo' money but you will not do it in the complex. It's not up for discussion. Now that you heard it straight from the stallion's mouth, we shouldn't cross paths anymore." I never turned my back on anyone, that's a quick way to get killed. I looked at him with a piercing stare and waited to see his move.

He wasn't happy, he sucked on his teeth. "I don't work alone, I work for someone over me. He paid for a high lawyer and got me out of jail. I owe him, he runs all of Philly and when he suggested Las Vegas as a place of new residency because of the money, I hurried and came but one of his demands was that I get in good with The Law.

The way you have this whole state in your back pocket, the way I have friends in high places who love buying pussy... the partnership just makes sense. We could own Philly and Nevada. I know more than you think I know, Angel." Headlights came on from another car parked in the pitch black. The door opened and one of his guys he sent to talk to me and my boys earlier stepped out, holding a pistol in my direction.

"My boss doesn't take 'no' very kindly," Gunna said to me with that slimy smirk again.

I stood there looking at him, still unbothered. "You couldn't know too much," I told him, pointing to his chest.

He looked down and saw three red dots on him. Then he looked at his clown ass guy and saw three dots on his chest. His guy looked at his own chest in shock. They stood in their same spots but were looking all around them, trying to see where the dots were coming from. There was nothing but pitch black around us, except for our headlights.

"Now like I said, the answer is no. Accept it and move the fuck on."

That slime's smirk wasn't on his face now, he looked like he was ready to charge at me. "You're making a big mistake."

I nodded my head. "You and your so-called boss will make a bigger one if you try me." We had a hard stare down for a few seconds before he whistled to his boy to leave.

Once they both pulled off, I headed to my ride and waited 'til Quest and Dominick pulled up on the side of me.

"I think I found out who sent y'all the little notes. Nigga said he has a boss he answers to," I told both of them when they got out of their rides.

"But why only us, why didn't you get one?" Quest asked me.

"Because I got my threat face to face. Look, whether

Gunna was lying about having a boss or not, they know deep secrets and know our families. Who else would have a reason to come at us this hard?" I was guessing and hoping that Gunna and his boss were the ones sending out these messages because we would be back at square one if it wasn't.

"So, what's our move? I personally don't like to leave enemies breathing long," Dominick stated, getting frustrated.

"If we kill Gunna, his two cheerleaders he has and even all his hoes, we still leave his boss out there unidentified and ready to strike. Y'all know there is no safe way to do this. If we draw his boss out, this could get nasty." I looked at both of them so they knew I was for real.

"I love getting nasty," Dominick's cat colored eyes were glowing and looking all evil and shit. Swear muthafucka was Michael Myers.

"Hell yea, I ain't never been scared of death. I'd be more scared of us giving in to some goofballs. We The fucking Law. Not them." Quest spoke, and we all nodded our heads in agreement.

"For life." I held a closed fist out to them. We hit our knuckles together and got ready for all that was about to pour down on us. We were fa sho' coming out on top.

**

It was seven o'clock in the morning. I stepped out of my shower ass naked and dripping wet. Grabbing my navy-blue, jumbo-size bath towel, I wrapped it around my waist and walked out the bathroom and into my bedroom. I loved my house because I had the say of the build of it from the ground up, which I took pride in, from the custom bullet proof diamond shape windows all around, to the high suspended ceilings.

I had custom soft wool, chocolate brown carpet going all throughout every room except the bathrooms and kitchen. This was my five-bedroom, eight bathroom haven that sat nicely on the hills of Las Vegas. Beautiful mountains behind me… and at night I loved to look out my enormous bedroom window at all of the Vegas lights. I walked in my closet that was the size of another room and dropped my towel.

Pressing the button on my magnetic drawers, I grabbed some boxers and a pair of white socks. I didn't have anything planned till later tonight when we were meeting the Africans at the warehouse. Ever since we got on the Black Market selling these organs, business increased. We had an Indian buyer coming through tonight, two million cash for two organs. Sounds easy, but you never know who to trust in this field.

The FBI and Homeland Security try every day to crack any sellers and buyers of the Black Market. No matter what was for sale, it was a supply and demand field. Money can buy just about anything; even the right cure to diseases you always thought had no cure. Me and my brothers have seen it all firsthand. It's a whole other world out there. Politicians and any world-renowned doctors don't want that shit getting out.

What do you think pays for their lifestyles? The money you pay for all the prescriptions you need for the diseases *they* have diagnosed you with. One taste of what me and my brothers did or what we knew and the men in suits would have our asses at the Pentagon so fast, our damn heads would spin. That's why it was a risk selling to anyone, whether Burt's contacts knew them or not.

But money will give just about any smart adult motivation to take the risk. This world went around because of crooks, so me, Quest and Dominick had no remorse for our line of work. Money was the root that grew power, and respect was the flower that grew from both. This was just how we got ours.

Anyway, since I didn't have plans till later, I wore a pair of grey Old Navy sweatpants and a black muscle tank. I brushed my waves, put on my Armani deodorant and then I put my black Panerai watch on. Leaving out of my room, I went down my curved staircase while dialing a number on my phone.

"Mm, hello."

"Now that is a sexy sleepy voice," I said when Nina

answered on the fourth ring. "Good morning, chicken nugget."

"Angel, I am not a morning person. What do you want at seven-thirty in the morning?"

I laughed because I could tell she indeed wasn't a morning girl. She just had that look. "I want yo' grumpy ass to get up and come join me for breakfast."

"Did you not just hear me when I said I *wasn't* a morning person?"

"I heard you, but did you hear me when I said I want you to join me for breakfast? What I tell yo' ass about doing what I say?" As soon as I walked in my kitchen, my sensor lights came on.

"And what did I tell you about being bossy? Actually, That's my nickname for you, Mr. Bossy." She snickered through her nose.

"Naw that don't work for me, try again. But for right now, tell me. Do you prefer cheese in your eggs or no?" I wasn't taking 'no' for an answer, so she might as well stop

141

fighting me. Little did Nina know, in a snap of a finger she could have me gone off her. I would be at that woman's beck and call, giving her all of me and the world as a bonus.

"Angel—"

"You need me to send a car for you or would you prefer I come get you myself? It makes me no difference. Look, you ain't gotta put on shit special. Hell, come as you are, morning breath and all. I wouldn't give a fuck, as long as you're here, Nina."

Her groans were cute as hell. "Text me the place."

I smiled when she finally gave in. We hung up and I texted her my address, which I knew she would be surprised once she realized we weren't meeting at a restaurant. I grabbed all the ingredients that I would need out of the refrigerator and cabinets. The fridge had a touchscreen on it and it showed me when I was out of my favorites. I was making banana and walnut pancakes with cheese scrambled eggs, some turkey sausage and hash browns.

I also was cutting up a nice big bowl of kiwi, berries,

mango and bananas incase Nina enjoyed fruit like I did. The pancakes alone took time because I don't make them from a box. Moms used to cook them all the time for me, Axel and Pops so I learned how. As I made each dish, I sat it outside on the back patio dining table. I had a lid over the food and warmers under them to keep it nice and toasty. I sat a tall glass pitcher of orange juice and raspberry tea out as well.

I would always see Nina drinking a can of the tea at work so I knew she would appreciate that. My doorbell rang just as I sat the silverware out. I walked back inside and headed to my front door. I was taken back at how gorgeous Nina actually was.

"Good morning. How the hell can you look like that and *not* be a morning person?" I asked her while letting her inside.

The smell of her fresh Dove soap permeated my senses. I could see that the ends of her hair was curly and damp. The strapless maxi dress she had on hugged her C-cup titties and was loose at the bottom, stopping just under her knees. I peeped her pretty feet in the Gucci Bloom slides I bought her when she was at the hospital with her moms. Nina's face was bare, but got damn, if it wasn't perfect and pure.

"Good morning. This is your house?" I could tell she was surprised by the way she was looking around the foyer.

"Before we answer each other's questions, let me get a hug." I grabbed two of her fingers, pulling her into my embrace. My height always made it so I had to bend down a little, but when her arms went around my neck, it was easy for me to love the tight squeeze I had around her waist.

"You want a tour before or after we eat?" I asked, putting her hair behind her right ear like she always does.

"After. You got me out my bed, the least you can do is feed me." The humor was all in her voice and eyes, but still… no smile.

I laughed and led her to outside where the food was set up.

"Oh my goodness, Angel, this is beautiful." Her eyes

lit up when she saw the mountains and the Las Vegas city view.

My pool was built in the ground on the edge as if it was coming from the layout of mountains. The bricks and stones that surrounded it and the clear water inside completed the patio. My favorite time was at night when that crisp black sky and stars were out and the water turned an aqua blue. I stood back and let Nina take in the scenery. It was nice seeing her take a deep breath, like she was releasing a little tension and soaking up the beauty.

"Thank you, I'm glad you like it."

"I love it, I don't see how you leave it every day. I wouldn't be able to tear myself from all of this. The sky, the mountains... and I know at night when all the city is lit up it is just stunning." Finally, she walked back to where I was at the table and sat down.

It's funny because she was admiring the view while I was admiring her. "Any time you want to see, come over and just be up here, you can, Nina. Day or night. You are allowed over here for whatever reason." I told her honestly while taking the lids off the food.

"Wow, this looks better than any restaurant." She glanced at me with her lips turned up. "Do you have a cook or is this catered?"

I laughed and shook my head. "Woman this is all me. Breakfast used to be a big deal growing up. My Moms and Pops would go all out so naturally, I picked up some skills. Now anything beyond breakfast, then that's when my cook comes in." I picked her plate up. "What all do you want?"

Just like when we were at the complex chilling and I made her plate, she gave me the same taken aback look. "Um, a little of everything please, especially that delicious looking fruit." She answered.

I nodded and made her plate and I asked. "Why are you always so shocked when I make your plate?"

"I don't know I just…I don't know." She stared off for a second and then shrugged her shoulders.

"I thought I told you that lying isn't a good way to

start our relationship." She may have thought when I told her that the first time that I was playing, but I wasn't. My expression told her that right now.

"Angel, you don't want to know about me; it isn't shit pretty."

The sadness on her face made me feel some type of way. I sat her plate down then picked up the bowl on the side of her plate and put some fruit in it. "I want to know everything about you, from you telling me and the rest from just learning. Now how you want all that to happen, I'll let you decide."

I commenced to picking up my plate and putting food on it before placing the butter style syrup in front of her. When I had my food, I sat down and grabbed her hand so we could say grace. I was glad she obliged because that would kill everything if she wasn't a praying woman. Yea, I did what I did for a living, but show me a person without sin and I'll show you bullshit.

"I have…had a boyfriend… the only one I've ever

had. I was sixteen and he was nineteen when we met; he fell in love and I fell in a trap." She put some pancakes in her mouth and stopped talking. "Holy shit, these are good."

I laughed because she was dead ass. "Get used to that taste," I told her and she blushed.

"You do things, Angel... things that I didn't have when I was with my ex. Making my plate is one of them. I know it sounds immature, but when you have had something one way for so long, new things seem foreign. You do and say things to me like it's so natural to you."

I watched as she put some hash browns in her mouth then look at the view while she chewed her food. The sun was shining, but my patio had a visor so that it wasn't beaming in our faces.

"In what way did he hurt you?" I inquired.

She looked at me and said, "Mentally in the start, and then emotionally."

I sat back and took in what she said, trying to control my anger. "When a man physically abuses a woman, the hits are quick, unpredictable and eventually kills her. I believe those type of men deserve a quick bullet to the dome. Maybe pull a Quest move and slice open his throat. But..." I looked at her and finished. "To emotionally and mentally hurt someone, that takes time. A sick muthafucka gotta take enjoyment of watching him suck the soul from a woman. They know the hold they have over'em and a lot enjoy it. I believe those type of men deserve a slow, torturous death."

I knew that was a bit much, but I was being honest. Like I told her earlier, lying wasn't a good way to start our relationship. Her face told me she was a little shook. "Um, Angel, what do you do for a living?"

Usually, I would tell a woman to watch her tongue before I remove it. But not Nina. She was different, so I remained honest. "I kill who needs to be killed and recycle their remains." I laughed when her fork hit her plate in surprise.

Clearing her throat she said, "I'm sorry. What does that mean 'recycle their remain? How do you recycle someone's remains?"

"You know when you get a new driver's license and they ask if you're an organ donor?"

"Oook, so you take them and what, keep'em for good luck?" Her smart tone led me to believe that she either didn't believe me or thought this was a game.

I put some fruit in my mouth then sat back in my chair. "Nina. Listen to me carefully because I'll only repeat this once. Me, Dominick, Quest are The Law in Las Vegas, hell Nevada. The name stuck because we've been outlaws since we were kids. In and out of juvie and jail, we stumbled across a way to not become rich, but wealthy. I know you've heard of us, I'm not here to put any rumors to rest. Whatever you've been told ten out of ten times I can assure you, it's true. That complex is where we do business. We don't answer to anybody but ourselves. Me and my brothers will be the most notorious, but also the best thing in you and the girls' life."

She just stared at me after I was done talking, like she

was really processing what I just told her. Then, she took a sip of her raspberry tea. "So basically, what you're telling me is, I need to get up from this table and leave?"

I chuckled and put the last of my eggs in my mouth before responding. "You could try."

"See, when you say things like that, it makes me think you're crazy," Nina challenged and once again, that 'call my bluff' was in her tone.

"Oh, I'm bat shit crazy, chicken nugget, but if it makes you feel any better, I'm the sanest out of the three of us." I grinned widely. "Let's change the subject." I said and she agreed.

Let's be real; Nina could have dipped. I mean it's not like I could tie her ass up and make her be mine. The thought crossed my mind but I wouldn't, I wanted her to want to be mine on her own. She knew that I was the real deal, that's why our vibe was flowing just like it did at the complex. We talked about movies, TV shows; that's how I found out that we both fucked with *The Walking Dead* heavily.

I had a dishwasher but we decided to do the dishes by hand, and even that was nice.

Her eyes man… they held all the joy that her face wanted to show. I don't know how the hell a person can go through life and not smile or even laugh. I don't give a damn if you're the meanest son-of-a-bitch walking, you still will crack a smile or even a damn chuckle every now and then. It's like Nina programmed herself not to do it… like she feels she doesn't deserve it.

It's deeper than just her ex nigga; something else happened to her. I had a feeling that it would take an army for her to open up to me on that level, but I was already at the front line ready for the battle when it came to her. It was crazy as fuck how she had me like this so soon, but like I told Nina, I'm bat shit so I wasn't out my element.

"This refrigerator is hella sick, I've never seen one like this before." She closed it after grabbing a bottle of water.

"Yea, it keeps me on my toes when I run low on shit.

I shop weird as hell," I joked.

"Oh goodness, don't tell me you are one of those ones who goes to the store almost every day instead of just making one big trip?"

I cracked up because she just read my ass. "Hell yea, don't nobody got time to be in a long ass line with a basket full of shit. My cook already knows when she comes over to go shopping first." We walked out the kitchen and I began giving her the house tour from top to bottom.

"Oh my goodness, look at this view from your bedroom." She stood amazed in my master bedroom, looking out the massive bay window.

We'd just gotten from downstairs where I showed her my entertainment basement. Nina of course shook her head at the stripper poles. Hell, I was a man first. We then visited the gym with the sauna inside, my multi-car garage, the guest rooms, bathrooms and finally, we were back where the king lays his head. I was enjoying the hell out of having Nina here. I had women come over but they were getting on the pole and dipping out. My basement has seen its share of parties and my boys have definitely taken women to a guest room and handled their business, but no woman has been in this room, even if we were together.

I stood behind Nina and put my arms around her waist. Her body froze in place and on God, I could hear her heart speeding up.

"I never had a woman react to my touch the way you do. Why is it everything I do you feel like you don't deserve it Nina?" I whispered in her ear and noticed how she closed her eyes. She didn't answer me, but she breathed in and exhaled.

"Turn around," I told her and she did what I said. I picked her up and sat her on the edge of my bay window so we could be face to face. This woman was gorgeous beyond words. I needed to make her inside match her outside.

What she did next blew my cap all the way back. Her small, soft hands went on both sides of my face and she brought her lips to mine. I put my hands around her slim waist and brought her so close to me, we shared one soul. Nina's lips were so soft and when I put my tongue in her mouth, hers welcomed it. Our mouths wrestled as if we were teens. Tongues making love to each other, I'd suck lightly on her bottom lip and she would do mine.

I hate to admit it, but she made me let out a low moan; that's how good it felt kissing her. Fuck my dick being hard because that was obvious… this girl had my entire body set ablaze. My hands went up the small of her back and I smiled to myself when she dipped it in.

"Wait, stop." She pushed me off of her and hopped down. Her back was to me but her hands were on her hips and she held her head down. When Nina turned and looked at me, I could see her eyes changing, filling with fear and sadness.

"What the fuck are you, Angel?"

"Come again?" I was confused as hell by her question.

"What is all of this? I mean you ask me to your

155

enormous ass house, cook for me and do all this shit that makes you perfect. What is your angle because how the hell do you have what you have, look the way you do yet you're still single? I don't need this." She started shaking her head.

I folded my arms, not out of frustration, but I always did that when I felt my back was against the wall.

"I've only been in this house for a year. It takes time to have your dream home built. I was in another crib just as nice while this was being built. Ain't shit about me perfect, Nina. Hell, just look at what I do for a living. But my dick and I have been smart enough to not leave any kids behind. I've had my share of relationships; some I was faithful but majority of them got cheated on.

"Like you said, I have what I have and look the way I look so I was a dog but, in my defense, the type of bitches I had as girlfriends weren't here for the right reasons, anyway. I didn't care because I was looking for the wrong shit in women: the party goers, you know the Instagram hoes who shake they ass for the camera. I don't know what the hell you want me to tell you, Nina. This ain't no fucking movie, this is the real deal and I want you."

"Why!? Why do you want *me*? I'm messed up and I have so much shit I'm holding on to. God—"

Her voice cracked and she continued. "He wouldn't give me someone like you; he's too angry at me."

That shit broke my ass. I'd never seen a woman so messed up. Walking up on her again, I grabbed her waist, pulling her to me and I just hugged her. I walked her towards the side of my bed where my nightstand was. I had a lamp and my Alexa speaker sitting on it, so I turned it on and told it to go to Pandora. Looking at Nina, I pulled my shirt over my head and sat her on my bed with me, between her legs. The music started and Alexa must have known how I was feeling because it hit it on the nose.

I've finally found the nerve to say
I'm gonna make a change in my life
Starting here today
I surrender all my love

I never thought I could

I'm giving all my love away

And there's only one reason that I would

And baby it's you

My man *Jesse Powell* was speaking to her with his voice and I was speaking to her with my actions. The daylight was all through my room and I was loving it. I wasn't a man who could only fuck at night. I leaned in Nina's face and kissed her lips while wiping her tears. After I kissed her, I went to her neck, licking and sucking on it like I was marking it with my name. While I stayed on there, I slowly pulled her dress up.

Nina didn't stop me either. Once I pulled it over her head, her sexy body glimmered in nothing but a thong. I went back to making out with her while laying her back on the bed with me between her legs. Her skin on my chest was so soft and it felt good, but it was nothing compared to the heat coming from between her legs. I sucked on her supple titties and pulled lightly on her caramel nipples. Her hands were on the sides of my face as she moaned while I worked my way down to her thighs.

I kissed and licked all around and sucked a little when I got between them. Nina's pussy was a fucking sight; there was a little bit of hair on it. Just a little, you know that five o' clock women get just before you shave... that shit was sexy. Using my fingers, I opened her thin pussy lips, exposing that clit. It was just sitting there, all pink and wet as fuck. Licking my lips I dove in, tongue kissing it slowly. Nina tasted like she looked: sweet, savory and good. I sucked lightly and that drove her wild.

"Oh shit Angel, oh shit, oh shit." Her voice was higher than normal and I could tell I was getting her right.

I used my index finger and went inside her while I kept swirling my tongue around her clit. Got damn Nina was tight; I never had a bitch pussy grip my fucking finger. Her walls were soft, squishy and as soon as I sucked on her again, that pussy surprised me. It coughed up all in my mouth. I caught every bit while she shook and moaned out. My nasty ass held her juices in my mouth while I pulled my finger out.

I spread her legs wider, showing that kat's fullness and I let all the juices pour from my mouth to her pussy. When I was empty, I went back in face first, licking her good. I even fucked her hole with my tongue while my fingers massaged her clit. She came again and I caught it all, this time letting it slide down my throat. I kissed my way back up to her titties and sucked on them some more. Nina was breathing hard and her face had ecstasy all over it as I took off my sweats and boxers.

Her hands went back on the side of my face and we kissed deeply again. Nina was feeling my naked body on top of hers; Her arms went around my neck and she wasn't trying to let me move. I didn't mind, though; I could tell it had been a while since she's had this level of intimacy. I finally sat up and just looked down at her naked, sexy body on my bed. I was between her legs with my hard dick literally poking her wet pussy.

Her smooth legs were rubbing the side of me. I

kissed her knee and grabbed her pretty feet, putting them on my chest. Taking the tip of my dick I soaked it with her juices, then I stared in her eyes as she nodded her head 'yes'. I wasn't this reckless, I used condoms, but I ain't gone lie, I didn't want to now.

I sucked on her toes while I inched my dick in her gripping pussy. I was eggplant thick with inches for days. I knew I was about to do some damage on her little pussy, but in a good way. Once I got in, it was over. I let Nina's long legs fall on the side of me as I slowly started grinding.

"Fuck Nina, I knew you would feel good, but damn." I grunted in her ear and then sucked on it. After a few good grinds and working that pussy, I wanted her from the back. Turning her over, my dick was so wet that the tip of it had her juices dripping.

"Oh shit, look at'chu ready to get fucked." Nina moved herself to make a perfect arch. I didn't have to position her or nothing. Her round booty looked ripped so I licked both her cheeks and pushed my way in.

"Ooo Angel…Uhhhh…Argh, yessss."

I had to think about something else aside from her cries and how good her pussy felt. I wasn't ready to cum yet, but she was making it hard. The grip was real and every time my hand went trailing down her back, she would gush. I knew something about that back made that kat cough up just like when I suck on that clit.

"Aight, now fuck me back. Come on Nina, I know you got it in you," I taunted, biting my lip. I wanted her to come out that shell, throw that hand full of booty she got back on this dick. "Yea girl, like that." The slapping sound, her moans and that loud pussy tipped me off. I pulled out, squeezing them ass cheeks and shooting all on her back.

"Ugh, fuck!" I held my head back while I came hard as hell.

I stood on my feet, pulling her to me as I picked her up, even with my soldiers all on her back. I walked us to the bathroom so we could shower and of course, I fucked her again while we were in there.

Now, we were dry and lying under my covers.

"You know, I didn't plan this part. I really just wanted you to come eat with a nigga," I confessed while I played with her ear as she laid on my chest.

She lifted her head up and laid on her side while looking at me. That 'I just got fucked' face was pasted all on her. "So, now what?" She asked.

I turned my head, glancing at her while remaining on my back. "What do you think, Nina? You are a smart girl, you tell me what you think. The way we vibe and after what we did... and I'm not even just talking about the sex. From the moment you walked in my house till now, what do you think this means?" I wasn't mad, but she wasn't about to act like her head was in the clouds.

"I mean, friends have sex all the time."

I felt my eyebrow rise. "Girl, I will beat yo' ass if you think we still friends."

"Well damn, you'll beat my ass?" She asked with a shocked and slightly scared demeanor.

"Fuck yea, the B is silent though." I joked and she did something that stopped my entire life... she laughed. I mean she was cracking the hell up. And it was so fucking beautiful. The way her cheeks creased on the sides of her jaw... those pretty, white, straight teeth and her laugh itself was soothing to hear.

"Oh shit, look at my chicken nugget laughing! Wait a minute, I need to capture this shit!" I rolled over and picked my sweats up from off the floor. Grabbing my phone, I hit record and she covered her face.

"Naw, hell naw Nina. Show me that smile again. Don't get all shy when we both know you far from it." I laughed and kept knocking her hand down.

"Angel, stop! I don't wanna be recorded, stop!" She tried to yell but she was cracking up and I had all of it on video. "I'm naked!"

"I don't give a damn; ain't nobody about to see this but me. As a matter of fact, let me see them titties." I bit my lip, looking at her in my phone.

"No, you perv!" She joked.

"I done seen, licked, kissed and touched every inch of your body. You betta take that sheet down and let me see." I licked my lips when she did it. I squeezed lightly on her left titty and played with the nipple.

"Mm, look at it getting all hard. Do me a favor and look at me."

Her pretty eyes looked at me and I fixed my expression.

"Your mine. My woman, my pussy. That's what happens next. We move forward, and you keep letting me into your life. We don't play games and we never lie to each other, cool?"

"Ok, cool." She agreed.

"Good." I stopped my recording and put my phone on the nightstand. "Now, come put that warm pussy back on my mouth." I said as I pulled her towards me.

I demolished her ass good for another two rounds and now she was knocked out in my bed, like I always imagined.

I laid there watching TV and watching her sleep. I couldn't believe how good she was sleeping and it wasn't just from the good dick or my expensive bed. This was a peaceful sleep, like all her other ones before this were torture. As if she never got more than an hour of it at a time. Even when I moved her hair, kissed her lips and kissed her shoulder a few times, Nina didn't move. I went downstairs to get something to eat.

She caught me on a good day because my cook was here yesterday, and she did some heavy grocery shopping, so I was stocked up. I looked at my watch and it was going on nine o'clock. It was almost time for me to head out and meet my brothers at the complex so we could meet with Burt's boy and the Indian buyer. I got upstairs and put some of my Old Navy sweatpants back on. I went in my closet and grabbed my Steph Curry Golden State Warriors jersey and then put it on.

I already had on some white socks, so I put my feet in a pair of grey Air Max 90s gym-shoes. Putting my keys, wallet and phone in my pocket, I walked out my closet to Nina sitting up, going through her phone. It was cute because she had the sheet wrapped around her like she was embarrassed.

"I am so sorry I slept so long. Give me like five minutes and I can—"

"Whoa, whoa." I stopped her when she appeared scared and tried to get out the bed.

"Nina, why the fuck you jumpin' up like a nigga got beg bugs or something?" I snatched the sheet down, exposing them pretty titties. "Get the fuck back in my bed and wait for me to come back. Matter of fact, you can roam all over this muthafucka as long as you in one of these rooms when I return." I had wrinkles in my head, annoyed because of how she was acting. Once I saw her face, it softened me up. I sat on the side of the bed, putting my arm across her. Nina sat up so we were face to face.

"You staying the night with me so I can let loose in that pussy and have breakfast with you in the morning."

Her eyes got wide. "Umm, so you wouldn't call what we did earlier getting loose?" Her expression was laced with so much concern.

I chuckled and kissed her deeply. "Make yourself at home chicken nugget; give me two-hours." I walked out the room and down the stairs. Poor thing didn't know they type of nigga she had. I was nasty as hell, especially with my woman. I wanted to sixty-nine with her and blow in that pretty asshole while she sucked my dick good. Mm!

CHRISTIAN

"Your favorite person is here today." Molly, my co-worker/homegirl, whispered in my ear and said.

We were in the employee lounge on the tenth floor drinking frappes and eating plain donuts. I didn't like too much sugar in the morning, but I needed my caramel frappe with an espresso shot. Work has been going pretty well; I still hadn't given my boss no pussy and he still flirted with me every day. Today everyone who works in the office can dress casually, but the realtors had to still dress in business casual office attire.

I had on a pair of black skinny jeans with an olive-green Calvin Klein buttoned-up blouse that I tucked in, and some olive green Nine West pumps. Per usual, I rocked my jumbo twists. They were lying to the side, showing off my pretty baby hair. Today was Friday and Monday my work schedule changes because I start classes for my real estate license. I wanted Molly to do it with me, but she said she wasn't ready.

"Who are you talking about?" I asked, putting my napkin in the trash. Before Molly could respond, the person walked in the room, giving me my answer.

"Morning sugar lumps. How are things from down below?"

Kamila, with her long straight hair, designer pencil skirt and fitted vest always had some smart shit to say. Her designer heels always were at least six inches high and she was as bougie as they come; at least that's what she had these bitches in the office thinking. She was one of Kelin's Reality top five realtors and the bitch acted as if her shit didn't stank. Her main problem was with me because she assumed I was fucking my boss because of how he treated me.

The only reason the hoe was so bothered was because *she* was fucking him and I never denied or confirmed if I was or wasn't. Molly always asked me why not defend myself because it was my reputation on the line. But honestly, I didn't owe not a soul in this building shit. The funny thing is, if Denny, my boss, was indeed getting this pussy, he wouldn't be able to work with me ten feet from him every day. But Kamila's funky ass didn't care; she believed what she was going to believe.

"Things are pretty good, thanks for asking. I feel like I should take a picture of you for photographic memory. It's rare I see you without Denny's balls in your mouth." I smiled widely at her. "It's like seeing the zoo animal finally come from behind the rock."

Her attitude kicked in and she turned her nose up and flipped her hair. Kamila was beautiful; I'm no hating bitch, I give props when due. But she was no me, and her inside made her ugly as fuck.

"It's always the dark skin girls hating on a hot Puerto Rican. You already have the good hair, I can't do shit about that skin color." She giggled and bit into her donut.

"Girl, fuck this hating bitch." Molly rolled her eyes.

I laughed. "Girl, I love every drop of chocolate on me, but you..." I pointed to her face. "Didn't I tell you to stop putting make-up over them bumps? Damn face look like a Nestle Crunch bar." I took a sip of my frappe with my eyes bucked, walking out the employee lounge.

Molly was cracking up following on the side of me. "She is cussing your ass out in Spanish."

I waved my hand. "Fuck her Taco stand ass, she get on my nerves. You wanna do lunch at one?" I asked before we each went into our offices.

"Yup, let's go to *8 Kitchen*," She suggested and I nodded my head ok.

I closed my office door and sat my frappe on my desk. My office wasn't anything fancy, about the size of a bedroom in an apartment. But my window had a nice view and of course, I made the office pop with my taste. My colors were white, grey and pink and I had a cute glass desk and chair that Denny bought me. I may have not been fucking him, but I would accept a gift from him any day.

I was getting to work when my phone went off.

Quest: Sugar tits, what's the deal?

I laughed because he called me that since we were at the complex when we went to his office. I let him suck on my titties and he got a lil' taste of my sweet pussy. We didn't fuck though because he needed to work for that. But he claimed my nipples had chocolate coming from them. Quest was so damn fine; I thanked my auntie Symba every day for hooking that up. He wasn't even married and I still was interested. He did, however, tell me he had a bitch he was ending things with.

We all know how that works; that was code for I have a woman, but I cheat. I didn't care because I wasn't looking to be with him. I was looking to make him one of my fuck buddies, probably give him Friday nights. Who wouldn't want to lay under that sexy nigga after a long week of work? I already knew his dick was big because he showed it to me; I stroked that thick bitch for a few minutes in his office. I responded while still laughing.

Me: You're annoying lol. I'm not doing shit, just working.

He responded immediately.

Quest: You know Imma get yo' chocolate ass pregnant.

That text actually made me laugh out loud.

Me: And Imma kill it but wyd? (What are you doing?)

My phone rang and I giggled when it was him.

"I'm trying to make a living," I joked when I answered.

"Girl, I will pay you an hour the same amount that you make in a week." I loved Quest's voice because it was scratchy, but deep as well.

"Nigga I make about $3,000 every two-weeks."

"That's change to me sugar tits, but let's talk about you killing my baby."

I cracked up. "Swear, I'd turn lil' homie to mush. And who the hell says they wanna get somebody pregnant and haven't even taken them out, yet? What kind of flirting is that?" I sat back in my chair, turning it in to face my window.

"Flirting is childish as hell, we grown as fuck. I'ma tell you the truth, I wanna titty fuck you while I delete all the niggas' numbers out ya' phone."

I swear I laughed so hard, my cheeks were hurting. He was laughing, too.

"I do wanna take you out tonight though, you down?" Whew, that voice got sexy and low.

"Yea we can do that, what time you want me ready for you?" I was biting my lip just thinking of seeing him again.

"Six is good."

"Ok, I'll text you my address." I put the top of my pin cap in the side of my mouth.

"No need boo, I'll see you, six sharp." He hung up and I was sitting there, looking stunned as hell.

It made me think of the rumors about that complex. The Law; I heard it was three or four guys who were on a new level of killers. They were in the dictionary after lunatics. I had to ask Quest tonight if he were he a part of that, or if they were just rumors. After talking to him, I had to push him out of my mind so I could get to work; that shit wasn't easy.

**

"Hey, Mama." I kissed her jaw when she let me in her house. Since the attack, Angel had a black aluminum fence built around her house. He also had center-block windows placed around that could only open from the inside, in case a fire took place. Angel even replaced the front, back and side doors with iron and marble doors. Mama's house looked completely different in a good way and it stood out form the other run-down homes. After work, I went over her house to see her and get a slice of peach cheesecake she made yesterday before—

"I knew yo' big booty ass would be here! I didn't even see your car outside!" I pouted when Symba was sitting at the table eating what I knew was the last slice. It was all big, too!

"I know damn well you ain't cussing in my house." Mama popped my arm. "I told you to get here before her and Grandma," Mama said as she went in her room.

When she closed her bedroom door, I put my purse down, washed my hands and grabbed a clean fork. "Hell no bitch, you about to give me some." I sat next to Symba and dug in.

Symba was laughing but I was real life mad; I had been craving a slice since work. "You mad or naw, niece?" She joked, laughing harder.

I rolled my eyes and put some in my mouth. "You need to give me the rest. It's all gonna go to your booty, anyway." I was big mad, especially with her still laughing.

"Here, greedy bitch." She handed me the plate with the rest of the slice on it. "That was my second piece, anyway." Sticking her tongue out at me, she started twerking.

I poked her booty with the fork. "Oooh, you know I like it rough, hoe."

I laughed this time because I swear my auntie was aggy.

"DIDN'T I TELL Y'ALL TO STOP FUCKING CUSSING IN MY HOUSE!?" Mama yelled from behind her closed bedroom door.

"That's your child being all mean to me!" Symba yelled to Mama.

"No it's not ma—"

"I DON'T GIVE A DAMN WHO IT WAS. WE SERVE THE LORD IN THIS HOUSE AND I DON'T WANT NO FUCKING CUSSING!!"

Me and Symba fell out laughing because Mama's mouth was the worst and she always wanna talk about the Lord.

"Thank y'all for waking me up from my nap." Nina came in the kitchen looking like she just woke up.

"I didn't know you were here," I said putting the now empty plate in the sink.

"Of course, you didn't; you came straight in tripping

over some cheesecake, greedy butt." Nina played, sitting on Symba's lap.

"That's right niece; she's so mean." Symba teased and put her middle finger up at me.

Sometimes those two got on my nerves because they liked to double team me. "That's why I got a date and you rotten nipples are sitting at home." I don't care that I was being a brat.

"A date, with who?" Nina asked.

"With Quest." I licked my lips just saying his name.

"Wait a minute bitch, wasn't you the first one who warned us about messing with them? All those urban legends about The Law and that complex. Now you just about to go out with the could-be-dangerous killer?!" Symba snickered.

"I said I *think* they might be The Law, I will find out tonight." I responded.

"Well, be careful. You know they say you attract what you fear," Symba warned, looking for real when I knew for a fact she was still messing with Dominick.

I thought about how fine and delicious Quest was and said, "Well ahhh! Big dicks, ahhhh! So scary, please help."

Nina shook her head; me and Symba broke out laughing. A knock came to the door and since I was sitting closest, I got up to answer it.

"You have got to be fucking kidding me," I said out loud when I saw who it was.

"Christian, may I please speak to Nina?" Talia stood on Mama's porch with the nerve to look all sad. That eye was still very dark from where Nina said she punched her, so that made me proud.

"Hell no, bitch, get the fuck outta here." I turned my noise up and scoffed at her.

"Who is it?" Nina asked as her and Symba approached the door. When she saw Talia, her entire expression changed.

"Get the hell on Talia. You're lucky I only hit you once." Nina scowled at her.

Talia started crying. "Nina, please. I swear I wasn't

trying to hurt you. But…but he's my brother and—"

"Fuck your brother! This wasn't about him! You're my best friend and my nigga was doing me wrong. Where is the loyalty to me? Do you honestly think this shit stops at him?! Then he's out her fucking in shit holes raw! I could have caught any type of disease!"

Nina was in that bitch's face tough. I think she saw Marlo in Talia, that's why she was so emotional and pissed.

"I swear, I wanted to tell you so many times, but you know my brother. He doesn't play about his reputation in the streets. I didn't set them up or anything; Marlo and his crew would come over and they'd be in the kitchen talking about robberies and their next hit. One night I was supposed to stay the night with this guy, but plans fell through.

I came home and walked in on Tino and Marlo in the living room. My own brother grabbed me by my neck and threatened to kill me. You know we have never had a tight relationship, but he's always protected me, not hurt me. I looked in his eyes and he was serious; I feared him more than

I feared losing our friendship. I apologize, if I could take it back—"

"You said he'd do anything to protect his reputation in the streets. Does that include sending me a message through my mother?" Nina asked her.

Me and Symba looked at each other and Symba snapped. "You stupid bitch! Did your brother send some people here to hurt my sister!?" Before I knew it, she slapped Talia and I was pushing her inside.

"I don't know what you're talking about!" Talia held her cheek, crying hysterically.

"Yes, the fuck you do! Tell your brother to bring that shit my way; I'm telling everybody who will listen that he takes dick better than I do!" Symba was shouting at her, making me laugh because she didn't give a damn.

"Auntie! Shut up!" I yelled while cracking up.

"What the hell is going on?!" Mama came out her room holding her rifle that was the same as Grandma's.

"Nothing Mama, it's fine." Nina said to her with her

eyes big, looking at Mama's rifle. Then she turned to Talia and said something I never knew she had in her.

"Get the fuck from over here and you better pray that your brother had nothing to do with what happened to my mother. If he does, then bitch, you better run and hide because I'm coming for you *and* him."

The look on Talia's face was similar to mine, Mama's and Symba's, except hers held more fear in it. Still holding her cheek and crying, Talia walked off the porch and out the gate that I realized I left unlocked.

"Damn, Nina." I said when she walked past us, back into the house.

**

"Oh yea, you are definitely giving Quest some pussy tonight wearing that dress." Symba stood at my door, looking at me while I was standing in front of my full-length mirror.

"Shut up." I laughed and checked the back of myself out. I did look good as hell. My jumbo twists were in a low bun with a pair of gold hoop earrings in my ears. I didn't put on any make-up because I didn't know if we were going to be indoors or out. Even though summer was almost over, Las Vegas was still humid. I wore a navy blue bodycon dress that stopped mid-calf. The front had a heart-shape right between my breasts, but the back was my favorite.

It was shaped like a V, exposing my entire back all the way till you got to the top of my butt. My round booty looked good as I slid my pedicured feet in some gold heel thong sandals. I put my gold charm bracelet on and just some gloss on my lips. My eyebrows were beat and I knew Quest was going to be all over me, which was what I wanted.

"You look gorgeous, sissy." Nina came in my room and sat on my bed.

"Thank you Nina-Bina, what are y'all doing tonight?" I asked her and Symba.

"Facials and hair; I need to take this sew-in out and let my real hair breathe for about a week," Nina answered.

My phone tweaked and I saw that it was Quest texting me, telling me that he was pulling up.

"Ok ladies, I'm about to head on out." I picked up my mini purse. They walked to the front with me and we all heard a car pull up.

"Holy shit, girl." Symba exclaimed, peeping out the blinds.

"What?" I hoped it wasn't anything bad.

"That nigga pulled up in a Lamborghini Sian; that's a three-million-dollar car."

"Yea, right." I peeded through the window, watching Quest park. He couldn't see us so that was good.

"Trust me, I'm not... I mean I knew they had money based on the dates Dominick has taken me on, but damn." Symba said.

"What does his house look like?" I asked her.

"Shrugging her shoulders she answered. "I don't know I haven't—"

"Bitch, I know damn well you're not about to tell us you haven't broken that white boy in yet." I was in so much shock.

"Awww, honey, you really *do* like him." Nina placed her hand over her mouth, shocked as well.

"No, the hell?! I just don't know if I want to go there with him, y'all know I'm racist."

I laughed because I swear she was silly as hell.

"Maybe they don't have bank like that; his car might be a rental." I looked out the window one more time when I saw Quest open his door to get out.

"Naw, they got bank like that." Nina chimed in effortlessly while looking at her phone.

"How the hell do you know?" I asked, looking just as curious as Symba.

Nina cleared her throat. "I'm just guessing because of the way they fixed the apartment complex up."

"Well, I'll let y'all know when I get back tonight if they are the real thing or not." I opened the front door.

"Have fun, do everything this one wouldn't do." Symba joked, pointing at Nina.

I laughed and closed the front door. "Hey,

handsome."

"Mm, got damn, sugar tits. You look so fucking good." He approached me with a hug like this was our twentieth date. The man smelled of expensive cologne and the way he looked was a whole other story. He had on a short sleeve Valentino Polo shirt that was red and navy blue, like he just knew what color I was wearing.

I could see the nigga's hard abs through his shirt and the jeans he wore on his bowlegs draped off of him perfectly. None of that tight legging shit these 2020 men wore; he wore red and blue Jordan's. I loved the gauges in his ears because it gave him an edge that mad you not look at him as a pretty boy. Finally, that beard. Whew, it was so long, black and full. His gingerbread complexion and medium shape lips made my mouth and pussy water.

"Thank you, Quest. You… I like how you decided to copy and wear my color, tonight." I teased when he opened the passenger door for me.

"Get'cho fine ass in the car; ain't nobody tryna be

like you." He laughed and closed my door.

I put my seat belt on and looked around the two-seater car. It was dope as hell and the dashboard looked high-tech, like a car in a video game. I was surprised Quest's long butt could fit in the car, but when he got in, I saw he indeed had room.

"So, where are we headed?" I asked as we pulled off.

"Ever been to *Sinatra's*?" He asked, driving all sexy.

"Nope, I have never even heard of it."

"Well, it's good. Dominick rented it out for his pop's birthday and I've been meaning to go back since. You'll dig, bae, don't trip. I got'chu."

I wish y'all could hear how good he sounded saying that to me. As he drove, we had small talk, both making each other laugh. I told him what happened at Mama's house, leaving out some key detail because I didn't want to spill all of my sister's business.

"I like how you and your family have each other's backs, especially because it's all girls. Like that shit that

IN LOVE WITH A LAS VEGAS OUTLAW 2

happened with you and Nina's mama...it really got to Angel. He hates knowing about women or kids being physically harmed. We all do, but he really hates that shit; he was about to fuck shit up when he told us about y'all mama."

"Yea, it was scary as hell for us, too, especially for Nina because she was actually there. But your brother is really sweet for how he fixed up my mama's house."

"Yea that's how he is. That's why me and Dominick got so much love for that nigga. He'll give you the shirt off his back if he felt you needed it more. He's head over heels for your sister. I'on know what she did, but that fool *ga-ga-gone*." We both laughed.

"He better be good for her or me and Symba on his ass with a rifle." I may have seemed like I was joking, but I was so serious.

We got to the restaurant and it was very nice. Five-star luxury nice. Quest had valet park his car, then we walked inside. I liked how he opened the door for me. I haven't been on a date since my ex, Tucker. Y'all remember my first love… the won who I took a baseball bat to when he cheated on me because I got sick? Yea, him. I haven't been on a date since then. Hell, I fuck married men left and right, not date them, so this was really nice. Once we got inside, we were seated and given some menus. The waiter came back with a bottle of wine and took our orders.

"This is so damn nice. I never even knew we had a restaurant named after Frank Sinatra. My Grandma would leap for joy," I stated while looking around.

"Yea, it's dope. My pops used to listen to him and the Queen of Soul, Aretha Franklin, a lot when I was younger. He would have dug coming here."

"Would have?" I asked him.

I could tell by the glint of sadness in his face that I maybe shouldn't have asked. "Yea, he uh… died of liver failure some time back."

I put my menu down and put my hand on top of his. "I'm sorry Quest, I couldn't imagine."

"Thank you, but it's cool, I've adjusted. So what

about you? I know your Mama is around; what about your pops?" He inquired, taking a sip of his water.

"Me and Nina have never met him; don't know anything about him, either. Only that he bought our mama the house she has. I personally don't think me and her share a dad, but Nina gets pissed when I say that. We look a lot like Mama, even got her pretty hair, but I mean the obvious is our complexion, and Nina is so soft while I'm hard."

Quest laughed so hard, I kind of got mad. "Ain't shit hard about you but your dome. You may think that because you got a slick mouth, but that's because the right dick ain't been in it."

"You know, this would be the time when I would throw this glass of wine in your face and storm out," I admitted, waiting to see what he was going to say.

"But you won't because you know I'm right. Let me guess; you had a dude, but he played you so now you're all tough. You started dating hood niggas till y'all up boxing at two in the morning because he tweakin' off a perc."

As much as I didn't want to, I cracked up. "You are hella annoying, Quest. Part of what you said was right. I did get hurt before, so it changed me. But hood niggas haven't been my thing since high school. A lot of shit broke my heart but fixed my vision, so I haven't done a relationship since. I fuck and keep it moving." I arched my eyebrow and took a bite of my shrimp. The food slapped hard, I can admit that.

"You fuck enough and eventually, you'll catch feelings." Quest said and then he put some steak in that sexy mouth of his.

"Not if you fuck a man who already has a situation," I spoke honestly because I wasn't ashamed at all with how I rolled.

Quest put his fork down and took a swig of his wine. "Oh I get it. You fuck married men. That's smart."

I sat back in my seat with my wine glass in my hand. "What about you? Did you ever break up with that girlfriend you claimed was done?" I already knew the answer, but I wanted to see if he was going to lie.

"Naw I didn't; we got five years on each other. Some good, some bad, and a lot toxic." He surprised me when he told the truth.

"Since you called yourself reading me, let me return the favor. You basically just told me y'all both have cheated on each other. If I had to guess, I would say she cheated first, which is why you won't let go... because you feel like you gotta prove to yourself you won't be caught slippin' and let another nigga in her again. But, now you're a dog to her and of course, she isn't about to let go because I mean, look at you, Quest. Sooo, you two go back and forth, she probably fights hoes over you and you beat niggas asses over her. How'd I do?" I put my wine glass down so I could finish my food.

He was now looking a little thrown by what I said. I laughed to myself when he rubbed the end of his beard.

"Some of what you said is right." He confessed. "But I do want out, it's just hard to break habits." He quickly licked the corner of his mouth while he ate. Quest knew he was sexy and turning me on; he knew it and he liked it.

"I wish you the best in that." I responded in a low tone.

"Damn, you act like you about to dip right now." He chuckled and looked at me.

"Not at all; I don't give a damn about her or y'all's situation on any level. All I care about is how you treat me when we have our time." Under the table, I was using my foot to go up his leg.

"I can dig that." Quest licked his lips again.

We finished eating our dinner, ordered dessert and talked. If I wasn't making him laugh with some of the crazy shit coming out my mouth, he was making me laugh with his non-filter having ass mouth. After dinner, we got back in his whip and rode around the city. It was a good night to take advantage of the Las Vegas lights. After that, we went to his house.

"Wow Quest, this is just...Wow." I stood in his backyard by his massive in the ground pool. He had it shaped like a giant T and it was gorgeous. Once we got here, Quest showed me around his seven-bedroom mansion. I could tell he had a woman and I liked that he didn't hide it.

Her clothes, shoes, and hair products were in his bedroom. It was obvious she didn't live here, but she definitely made her mark. I didn't care though because guess what, I was here now. Quest had a basketball court, individual patio canopy sofas on the side of his pool... the outside of his house was white and steel grey with square windows all around. It was stunning and I knew then that him, Angel and Dominick had real deal money.

"I appreciate it, Christian. It's not my dream home, but it'll do." He was standing on the side of me.

I turned and looked at him. "How the hell is this not your dream home?" I asked with an open smile.

"I mean its dope and sexy but naw, I picked it because I can afford it. It's not a home." He looked straight ahead at the city with a serious expression.

"Damn, I wouldn't have thought you felt that way.

Well, I bet your dream home is just as perfect, better even." I said, trying to lighten the mood.

"Come on." Quest grabbed my hand and we walked back in his house.

We went to his living room which was grey, brown and white with a zebra print rug. I noticed on the wall were many gold swords. It looked like some shit you would see out of a medieval movie. He had gold and chrome knives as well. It was so dope how he had them hanging.

"You really love this type of shit, huh?" I asked while still admiring the display.

Quest came behind me with his arm around my neck, putting a glass of wine in my face. "Yea, that's my shit. Any kind of knife, sword, massive blades...it all interests me. That's over half a million worth on this wall."

"Well, I know what to get you for your birthday," I joked.

"I know what you can get me now." He took the wine glass out my hand and sat it on his fireplace. Then, he put his arm around my waist and we kissed. This wasn't our first one, but it sure as hell felt like it.

"I've been wanting to taste you again bad as fuck, Christian." His sexy voice vibrated in my ear and he kissed my neck.

"My turn this time, bae." I put my hand on his chest, walking him backwards to his couch. Once he sat down, I stood between his legs, bent over and undid his jeans.

While I did that, he pulled his shirt over his head. Goodness he was beyond perfect. His hard abs, tattoos… and I loved that he had an outie belly button. I couldn't help it; I had to run my hands down his chest. When I did, his eyes followed my hand til' I got to his unbuttoned jeans. I helped him out of them and out his boxers. His dick sprang out like a hydraulic car. I got on my knees between his legs and took that big, wide dick in my hands.

I used my tongue to tease the tip and then I put some in my mouth slowly. I knew I wasn't putting it all in, but what I could fit, believe me, I was sucking good. My mouth was getting wetter because of how sexy his dick was. It was neat as hell; there were two veins on the side and he had hair. Yea, I know you bitches frowning, but I don't give a fuck. I love hair like Quest's: soft and odorless. My pussy was so wet which made me suck his dick even better.

"Shit Christian, suck that dick, girl." He moaned out and I don't know how, but in one smooth move he took my bun down, releasing my jumbo braids.

"Fuck, all this pretty ass hair." He roared out while playing in it. I loved the fact that his stomach was going in and out fast, and he was grinding his hips a little.

I finally came up for air with wet lips. I used my right hand and grabbed his balls, sucking on them. Getting them nice and wet, I was doing shit that I don't do on men I've been fucking for months. Not everyone gets this treatment, but Quest turned me on so badly. I just hope that he knew how to use this big dick. I showed TLC to one ball, licked it good, got saliva all on it and then I did his other one. I smiled to myself because I was fucking him up and I loved the fact that he had a girl.

I bet she doesn't do what the hell I do, make him feel the way that I'm making him feel. I planned on having Quest gone off me and when the time is right, I'll drop him, leaving him with nothing but a memory. I'll always make sure I do the hurting before any man hurts me ever again.

Once I was done with his balls, he stood me up between his legs. He raised my dress up over my ass and licked his lips.

"Missed this pretty ass pussy," he practically whispered, but it was loud enough for me to hear. Then, he started kissing it through my thong before pulling them down.

I stepped out my thong and pulled my dress over my head at the same time. I didn't have a bra on because the dress didn't call for it. Quest pulled me on his lap, making me straddle his naked body. I threw my head back when he grabbed my left breast and started licking and sucking on it. Gosh, his tongue felt so good on my nipple. His soft beard was tickling my stomach as I held my hands on the side of his neck. He repeated it with my right breast as well, getting my nipples harder than his dick was. I was grinding a little in his lap, just enjoying him suck on my breasts. I never had a man take such time in something so basic. I mean, I had his lap drenched and he hadn't even fucked me yet.

"Mmm Quest bae, damn." I moaned out and I was embarrassed because this wasn't shit. I had been getting my breasts sucked on since eighth grade and her I was, actually cumming over this.

"Ssss, shit Christian. Daddy fucked you up that bad that you came? Mmhm, I like that." His scratchy heavy voice bellowed.

I finally lifted my head forward, glancing at him with a smirk. I pulled his beard in so I could kiss him. While we made out all wildly, he leaned up, holding me in place so he could get his jeans. I knew it was for a condom and I was cool with that. I had a few magnums in my purse if he didn't have any. He opened the foil and put it on quickly before we went back to kissing. Lifting up, I grabbed his dick and slid down slowly while leaning him back on the couch. I put my hands on the back of it, gripping it as I slid all the way down his shaft.

"Hell fucking naw, girl." He grabbed my jaw and made me look at him. "You mean to tell me this pussy this tight and snug?" He asked like he was really ready for me to answer.

I just smiled and started snaking all on his dick.

"Ugh Quest, whew bae! Ughhh." I was moaning all in his ear while we were fucking. The size was fitting snugly now and this was amazing. He felt so damn good inside of me. I sat up and put my hand on his knee while still grinding. Quest licked his sexy lips while squeezing my breasts and nipples, driving me wild. I put my other hand on his other knee, dropped my head back, closed my eyes and got wrapped up in his dick. I felt his mouth back on my breasts, sucking and biting on my nipples, making me cum a second time.

"Ahhh…argh Quest, Daddy I'm cumming!" My damn head was jerking and I felt like his dick was kissing my stomach and humming on my clit. I gripped his knees so hard I thought my nails were going to break. Finally, the high slowly came down and I was able to salvage some dignity.

"Told you yo' ass wasn't hard," he said in my ear with a chuckle.

I was still out of breath, but I was able to talk shit. "Shut the hell up, that always happens the first time."

"Oh, yea?" He grabbed me by my jaw again and shoved his tongue in my mouth while standing us up. Laying me on the couch on my back, he pulled the condom off and told me he would be right back.

I nodded and laid there, looking at his high ceilings, ass naked. I felt so good that I could probably run Nipsey's Marathon. Quest came back with a rag with soap on it in one hand and another wet one wet nothing on it. He cleaned me up and got me together, throwing the rags on the floor.

"I hate that condom taste," he told me before getting

on his knees on the side of me and without warning, he just started eating me out. His tongue swirled all around the inside of my pussy lips slowly. Quest held one of my legs back by my knee and the nigga was digging for gold.

"Ugh….Sssss, shit, Quest." I looked down at him and it was picture perfect. The nigga was concentrating so serious on the task.

He sucked the perfect pressure when he had a hold of my clit. Those lips of his were so soft, just like they felt when they kissed me on my face. Once he made me cum, He stood up and put on another condom. I was spun from cumming, but he didn't give a damn. Climbing on top of me, Quest kissed me passionately as he pushed back inside of me. He draped my left leg on the back of his couch and he put my right one on the floor.

Then he laid his hands flat on the side of my head and started fucking the shit out of me on his couch. I couldn't believe how he had me moaning and crying his name out. This was hands down *the* best sex I have ever had in my life.

There was no comparing or debate. He sucked on my breasts perfectly, knew when to kiss me, and when to talk all kind of shit in my ear.

I knew then that I was fucked; for the first time ever, my plan had backfired. It wasn't him that was going to be gone over my pussy, it was *me* that was going to be gone over this dick... over this nigga. Once he made me cum for the I don't know how many times, he came once, and we passed out on his couch.

BANG! BANG!

We both were startled by the loud pounding on his door. We were like vine, wrapped up naked on his couch, sleeping good as hell. It was still dark outside so it had to be around three in the morning.

"What the fuck!?" Quest was pissed off. He picked up his shirt and put it on me, then put his boxers on.

I stood up because I knew this must be his girlfriend, and y'all know I live for shit like this. I'm never scared and will drag that hoe all through this mansion. The way he just

IN LOVE WITH A LAS VEGAS OUTLAW 2

fucked me, oh, hoe we about to be sister wives in this bitch.

Quest grabbed one of his knives from his display and walked to his door. *Damn, he was about to slice the bitch up,* I thought to myself, following him to the door. I gave him his space, but I wasn't about to wait in the living room and this bitch try to sneak up on me. He yanked open his large brass door like it was as light as a feather.

"Ma!?"

Ma!? I shouted loudly in my head, because the *last* person I was expecting to be at his door was his mother.

QUEST

I was having some good ass sleep with Christian's warm body wrapped up in mine. Her soft skin felt bomb as fuck, but nothing was compared to how her mouth and pussy felt. That shit was so damn lit, and her head had me squirming like a bitch, but I'on even care. I'm all man, but that chocolate princess had me hitting high notes when she made love to my balls with her mouth. I wanted to give her ass everything I had. Seeing her cum on my dick back to back made our session increase in ecstasy.

Her moans, groans, the way her face would look... I just knew I was the best she ever had. Did y'all see that shit she tried to spit about her first nut was always intense? Like I wasn't about to have her like that each time. I proved her wrong. Each time Christian came was better than before. Once I had her cumming over and over, I finally came, and it took all of my energy. I grabbed her and we wrapped up tightly, naked on my couch, until sleep came.

Now I was forced out of my slumber because someone wanted to bang on my door like a fucking cop. I knew it was Kamila, no question about it. I just hope Christian can hold her own because Kamila was wild as fuck. I wasn't going to let either of them go too far, but you know how y'all women get. If you wanna get at a bitch, then that's what you'll do. I brought Christian back here because this was my shit, and mine alone.

Yea, Kamila had some stuff here, but she didn't live here. I wasn't about to get a hotel room like I don't live alone. I've done it before, but I really wanted to show Christian how a real nigga should be living.

After I was decent and she was too, I grabbed my knife with the trailing point. Whoever this was, heart was about to be in our freezer at the complex. If it was Kamila, then I was probably about to cut one of her fingers off, no lie, cause I'm tired of this popping up shit.

"Ma!?" I was blown the hell back when I saw my mama standing on the other side of my door. "What the fuck are you doing here? How did you get here?" I asked, pissed off and pulling her inside, closing the door.

She didn't look beat up or harmed at all, in fact, she had on some leggings, a PINK shirt and a pair of Pumas were on her feet. Those were all clothes I bought her, I made sure Lori made her way up to the rehab every other week with new clothes and shoes. Ma's long hair was in a low ponytail and she looked beautiful, like nothing was wrong. But when her eyes went on Christian and she spoke, I knew she was far from ok.

"Oh, my goodness, Quest, she is beautiful. Way better than that other girl you are always with." Ma ran to Christian and hugged her so tightly, you would have thought they were long lost family members.

Christian was surprised as hell, but she hugged Mama back and smiled. "Thank you so much. Nice to meet you, I'm Christian," she said while Ma was still hugging her.

"Ma, let the damn girl breathe and come tell me how the hell you got here?!" I was more annoyed at the facility because I pay bank for my mama to have the best care, including security, food and just her overall living quarters. Ma is schizophrenic with mild bipolar disorder, and I have her staying in a treatment facility. I didn't want to do it, but years of trying to have her live at home failed.

When my dad passed away, she couldn't take it and fell off bad. She stopped taking her medication so after I spent unlimited money on helping her, a judge finally signed the right papers saying she's a threat to herself and others. I was able to pick out the absolute best rehab treatment facility for her. I loved that place because it was upscale, had the best psychiatrist, activities for her and her room was better than any five-star hotel suite. I visited her a lot and so did her sister, Naomi.

Ma finally let Christian go. Her smile was so wide on her face that I had to hide mine because I was supposed to be mad. However, I haven't seen her smile like that since I was around five, and I remember her sitting on the porch swing looking at the sky with a kool-aid grin.

"I don't know why he thinks I'm his mama; probably because I raised him better than my no-good sister. I'm his favorite auntie, Alanna. Nice to meet you, Christian."

I dropped my head and put my knife back on the display. Christian looked at me confused, but when she stared at my beautiful Ma and her innocent face, it's like she pieced it together and fell into role.

"Well he has had a little wine and you know how that can be," Christian joked and they sat down on the couch. "Alanna is a very pretty name but if you don't mind me asking, what you are doing out so late?" I was glad she asked because someone was about to tell me something.

"Oh, I put my sleeping pill in Edith's coffee when she went to the bathroom. Then I paged for security from her phone while she slept. While they were off their posts, I slipped out. It was so easy, girl." Ma confessed as if she was slick, then she picked up the four gold Magnum wrappers off the floor, giggling. "Oh shit, y'all been busy."

Christian's chocolate cheeks flushed, and I snatched the wrappers from Ma's hand.

"Ma, you can't be doing this shit. If they kick you out, you know we would have to send you out of state. I don't want that shit because me and auntie Naomi won't be able to see you as much. Is that what you want?"

"Quest, stop yelling." Christian snapped at me when she saw Mama about to cry. "Alanna, Vegas streets at night are no place to be for woman who is alone. Quest is just worried about you and always wants you safe." Christian had patience that, at the moment I didn't have, because I was so pissed off.

"Ma…I mean Auntie Alanna, how did you know where I lived?" I wanted all the details so if the muthafuckas at the treatment center tried to put her out, I could blame it on their negligence. Edith, Ma's around the clock caregiver, loved me and my auntie. She admired how we never forgot about Ma and how we would do whatever to help her. Also, she loved how much money I would donate to whatever the facility needed.

"I looked on the computer, silly. You know I'm a computer nerd. That bitch Sonequa is the dumbest bitch out of me, her and Naomi." She laughed like this was funny.

I was about to say something when another knock came to my door.

"Um, put some pants on." Christian said to me.

I looked down and forgot I had on boxers with my dick literally about to fall out. I winked at Christian, picked up my jeans and put them on. I could see the flashing yellow light and I knew it was Edith with a few orderlies coming to tell me that they lost Ma.

"Quest something has—"

"Come on in, she's here," I said, and they followed me inside.

Ma got up and ran to my kitchen. "No! I don't want to go back, I want to be here with my nephew!"

"Sonequa, you know that's not possible," Edith spoke

in a calm tone; she was really good with her.

"STOP CALLING ME SONEQUA! I'M NOT THAT BITCH! SHE KILLED HER OWN HUSBAND AND ABANDONED HER ONLY CHILD! I'M BETTER THAN HER!"

I swear I hated this shit, all of it. If I could find a cure or something to snap Ma out this shit, I would, no matter the cost. I wanted her normal, at peace and not battling voices all the damn time. I really hated that Christian was witnessing this shit, especially with this being our first night together.

"Auntie, please go back with them and—"

"NO!" She cut me off, shaking her head, screaming and crying.

"Is anybody hurting you at the facility? You know your nephew will handle it!" I asked her first, because she has never broken out. All she had to do was say yes and Edith and these orderlies were good as dead, right where they stand. I don't give a damn; this is my mother and no one was about to hurt her.

"No, I just want to stay here with you and Christian. If I leave, I won't see her again and you'll bring that other bitch up there to visit me. Sonequa likes her, not me." Her voice broke my heart, but I knew her going back was best for her.

"I'll come visit you, Alanna," Christian spoke up and we all looked at her. I was trying to come on the side of Ma so the orderly could sedate her because I knew she wasn't leaving here easily.

"You will?" Ma asked Christian.

"Yes, I promise." When she said that, Ma put that big smile back on her face and Christian returned it.

"Can you and Quest drive me back? I won't be a problem." Her voice was now soft and sweet.

Christian didn't know what to say, so she looked at me. I looked at Edith and she nodded her head.

"That's cool, auntie, we'll take you back." I walked on the side of her. The orderly was able to come on the other side of her and stick her with the needle in her left arm.

"Ouch, ouch!" She cried out, but I knew it was more of the shock that scared her.

I gave the other orderly the keys to my Lexus LX outside. "Lay her in the back seat and put a blanket over her," I told him and he did what I said.

"Mr. Foster, I apologize for this. I don't know how this happened. Five years your mom has been with us and—"

"I already know, Edith. She told us how she did it." I walked her to the door.

"I should have watched her take her pills like I always do. But she does so well, I thought I didn't have to anymore. I'll give her this month and next month rent free; this will not be documented, either."

"Thank you; let us get dressed and y'all can follow behind me," I said, letting her out. "You wanna stay here or come with me?" I asked Christian while I closed my front door.

"I'll come, I don't mind. It's almost daylight anyway, so you can drop me off after you handle your mom."

I nodded my head and she took my shirt off, revealing her sexy slim-thick body. My dick twitched and I had to remember I had some shit to do. Giving me my shirt, I put it on and it smelled like her sweet perfume. I watched her put that sexy dress back on and put her pretty feet in her heels. The braids she wore was her real hair, which impressed me because usually those type of braids be weave in bitches' heads. Her ass was perfect; not too big, but that fucker bounced back like the *Big Sean* song.

"Ready." She said, picking up her purse.

We walked out of my house and to my Lexus. The orderly did what I said; Ma was in the back knocked out with one of their blankets over her. I let Christian inside and then I jogged around to my side and got in.

The drive was pretty chill. We talked and listened to some music. With what happened with Ma, Christian kept the conversation basic. Either she was overwhelmed, or she didn't care because after today, she was done with me anyway.

I learned the kind of woman Christian was at dinner. Dating married men, fucking and leaving so she wouldn't get hurt. I respected that if that's how she rolled, but I knew I could change that, if I wanted to.

We got to the treatment facility and Edith got Ma prepared to return. Me and Christian stayed back while they did their thing.

Once she was in her bed, a female nurse went in her room and put her pajamas on while we stood outside of her room. I signed the papers saying rent was free for the next two months and Edith explained to me how she was going to make sure this doesn't happen again. Once we were done, I went in Ma's room, kissed her on the forehead and left out.

"Well, our first date was um, interesting." I said, joking with Christian when we pulled up to her crib. I had already let her out and we were both leaning against my ride.

"The fun part was when your mom showed up. I enjoyed her. Everything before that was blah." She looked at me, laughing.

"Ohhh damn, I see you got jokes." I pulled on my beard, smiling. "Naw, you can't fake the way I had that chocolate body." I licked my lips and stood in front of her. "Your skin turns me the fuck on. I got a chocolate fetish bad as fuck." I knew I had her pussy soaked.

"I turn you on that bad?" She asked me with that 'bullshit' expression on her face.

"Hell yeah, I love chocolate girls. Imagine fucking a dar… a dark sk… Shit, I can't even say it. I'ma nut." I was dead ass too, wasn't shit better than a chocolate bitch.

"I swear you are so wild." Christian smiled.

"Why haven't you asked me about my mother?" I questioned, because I was curious.

"I figured you'd tell me when you were ready. I have a friend named Molly and her dad is schizophrenic. I've seen him in his moments, so I knew that probably had something to do with your mom. I know that's not easy to talk about, so when you're ready, I'll be listening." She was sincere as hell and sweet about it.

"I appreciate that Christian, for real bae. That's dope of you, especially how you helped me with my mama. Thank you." I looked at her with a stern expression so she would know I was for real.

"No problem Quest, I really did have a nice time with you. It won't be the last." She kissed my lips and walked towards her house.

I watched her sexy ass go up the stairs and get inside her place. As I got inside my ride, my phone rang and it was Kamila.

"What?" I answered while pulling off.

"What'chu mean what? Why haven't I heard from you? And don't tell me no bullshit about you being stuck with work or your Ma because we both know that's a lie. Quest, don't make me flip out on you, what bitch you been with?"

"You ain't out of hot air yet Kamila; why the fuck you always calling me with bullshit? I ain't heard from you either, so whatever you been doing, I been doing the same." I shot back at her loud ass while I got on the freeway.

"I swear to God I will mess up your life—"

"Kamila, you know me and you know I don't play about threats. What the hell do you want?"

"*You.* I don't want to keep playing this game, Papi." She did that low Spanish talking shit that she knew got to me. Kamila and I were a mess; we needed to stop because it was all drama, games and bullshit. Has been since she first cheated on me. Five years to some may not seem like shit, but trust me, it's a lot of time to spend with someone.

It becomes about letting go and being at peace with letting go… closure. I always thought what if she gave another man the best of her once I exit out her life? That meant it was me; I was the problem. I hated feeling that way, so I always kept her. We knew everything about one another. All flaws, insecurities and we been through hell and fire. I know I'm being a greedy muthafucka right now, but I wasn't about to put both my balls in Christian's basket. Ya'll heard her when we were at dinner.

"You at home?" I asked Kamila.

"Yes." She responded with joy all in her tone.

"Aight." I hung up and put my blinker on so I could get off the freeway and head her way.

Dumb ass nigga.

**

"How is Mrs. Newman?" I asked Angel while me, him and Dominick were in our walk-in freezer getting three coolers. We had two doctors upstairs preparing for the two bodies we were about to bring them. They handled the removal of any organs and they also perform the test on them for health and blood type. Later tonight, we had another buyer who offered $10,000,000. That was way over our asking price, so the three of us knew off rip the request was going to be outrageous.

"She's fine; her sons put her house up for sale. Made her move out of Las Vegas and closer to them. Mrs. Newman wouldn't move in an apartment, so they got her a nice crib with a big ass garden."

221

"That's what's up, we need to find out who did that shit to her," I said, grabbing my big trunk from under the steps.

"Yea, I'm already on it. One of the idiots who was in her house ate some of her food in the kitchen. Left his DNA on some shit. I got one of my cop buddies handling it. He'll give me his information soon. You know he gotta make sure nothing traces back to us," Angel told us.

"Good, I bet those the same muthafuckas who fucked with Nina and Christian's Mama." Hell, we all had mothers so I'm sure we wanted to all get involved.

"What's up with you and Nina? Y'all chilled after the girls came here?" Dominick asked Angel. He was putting bullets in his 500-mag revolver gun; his crazy ass always had it on him but never used it. His big hands and knuckles were all the weapon he needed, but you know how pussy men out here always wanna shoot first, so I liked that he had it.

"Yea, we been together a lot. That's all me."

Me and Dominick looked at each other a little

appalled but with a surprised expression.

"Like official or like this nigga?" I asked and pointed to Dominick. Yea, I called him a nigga because the muthafucka was more like us than we were. "In his head, Symba's his but clearly, she ain't got the memo yet." I laughed. Watch how his ass flip out.

"I swear I will make your fuckin' eyeballs touch ya' stomach," he threatened, slamming his duffle bag on the table and walking to his office. His eyes were on me like I was a target.

I was cracking up.

"Why you keep fucking with him? You know how he is about her." Angel asked, laughing too.

"Cause the shit funny as hell; he know it's all love. So, you and Nina legit? That's what's up, bro. I like her for you," I told him honestly.

"Thanks, yea we legit. She been at my crib a few times, we go out and shit. It's another feel I get when I'm around her. I don't know what that shit about, but I felt it on first sight."

I noticed how he was looking when he spoke. I'd been with Kamila for a while and I know I ain't never looked like that when I talk about her. Even when things were perfect between us, I just never had the expression Angel had. "I'm here for it man, you deserve that happiness, and keep those feelings always," I told him on some real shit.

Dominick came back up front, looking pissed like a damn grizzly bear. I held my closed fist out to him. "My brother?"

Evil ass looked at me and then my fist for a second. That slick smirk came on his face and he pound my fist with his and said, "For life, bitch ass." We both laughed.

"Y'all ready to roll?" Angel asked us shaking his head.

"Hell yea, let's get it."

We got outside and headed to our blackout van parked in the back of the complex. We were in all black from head to toe with black skull caps on our heads. It was hot as hell outside, but our van had AC, and besides, when you're going to do some killing, all black is best. We also had on black leather gloves and black shoe covers over our gym-shoes.

"You got the file the doctor gave you, right?" Angel asked Dominick as he drove.

"Yea, it's five guys and only two are AB-negative."

"Cool, so we only gotta kill two. Short and simple," I said in the back while wiping my Latin machete off. This was my baby I got from Paris. Custom Latin blade that cut so smooth. The blade is made of carbon steel mixed with jade stone and rhodium. I used it one time to cut the limbs off this sucka ass nigga in Minnesota. That was two years ago and I needed a reason to use it again.

"We could kill just two, but this is a notorious gang. If we kill two, we might as well kill the other three," Dominick said to me and Angel.

I turned my nose up at him. "Man you just wanna do some killing, with'cho *Halloween* ass."

"Fuck you dummy, if the three of us in a house, do you think anyone stands a chance of coming in and killing one of us? Naw, idiot. They'd have better luck tryna take out the whole crew." Angel and I were quiet because he did have a point. "Plus, I'm in the mood to do some killing."

We chuckled and just shook our heads at him.

The world is filled with enemies, whether they are hating on you or just simply don't like your face. But if you don't have enemies or haters, then you ain't shit in life. Our job is to eliminate all ya' haters for a hefty amount. It didn't take long for our names to spread because we have had to handle some of the world's most important enemies.

We were like your lawyer, therapist and priest, rolled up in one. We're sworn to secrecy by what you hire us for and once our job is done, we part ways. It also showed us how fucked up people are. We get hits on all kinds of people. One Cuban dictator wanted us to kill his wife and brother because they were fucking around. So, y'all know what we had to do. Kill the brother and then the dictator. We don't kill women and kids of that nature.

Now a trifling bitch who was out here on some sick twisted shit will get got easily as hell. We killed so much it began to be like a sport, but we had to kill to keep our business going. The world wasn't about to miss any of these people, anyway. The gang we were about to kill now have been slipping through their enemy's fingers for a few years. Once we were told their names, we gave them to our doctors who were able to pull up their medical history and tell us their blood type.

You see, we never accepted a kill job unless it benefited our Black-Market business. We weren't hit men, which is why we didn't charge millions of dollars to kill. The killing was pocket change and our wealth came from the actual organs we got ahold of. The buyer we have coming later tonight wanted two AB-negative hearts. The rarest blood type, and they asses wanted *two* of them. We lucked up with this hit and was about to come into $10,000,000 easily.

"Even though it's five guys in this folder, how do we

know it'll be five people in the house?" I mentioned it once we pulled up a few houses from our mark.

"We don't, that's what makes it fun," Dominick answered with a big grin on his face while putting his brass knuckles on both his hands. Them bitches were heavy as hell and had sharp spikes sticking out of them.

Angel's eyes were beaming when he pulled out his two-ball flail. That's basically a twenty-inch metal pole with a chain coning out the top of it and two balls with blades sticking out all around. It was time to do some killing and the best part about our line of work is we pick the style. Nice and slow, quick and painless or a bloody mess... tonight we were going for a bloody mess. We walked down the street towards the house. The block was in a pretty decent neighborhood and the house was spacious as hell.

All the streetlights were busted but the one on the left end of the corner. We got to the side door of the house and the backyard was in sight. I counted five cars parked from the driveway to the grass in the backyard, so we knew then it was more than five people inside. Once Dominick unlocked the side door, we slithered in like mamba snakes in a field. The house was a two-story home and the side door led to the kitchen.

We decided to handle the first floor first, then work our way up. Our only rule was we never, ever split up. We got through the kitchen and into the round hallway that had the upstairs staircase around it. Angel put his hand up for us to stop walking. He looked at us and shook his head 'no' while putting the quiet signal up. That meant it was quiet in the house... too quiet.

"Corner, left!" Angel yelled and by the time we sprinted to the left corner for cover, the bullets started spraying out.

PHEW! PHEW! PHEW! PHEW! PHEW! PHEW! PHEW! PHEW!

We stood behind the wall while they fired at us. Still gripping our weapons, we each gave each other the 'ok', meaning we weren't hit. These dumb ass niggas were trigger happy because they kept shooting even though we were out of sight.

"It's only one way upstairs," Angel said.

"It's another, but that means we need to split up. I can get up there then you two take the stairs," Dominick suggested.

We looked at each other for a minute because this was going against our own rules. Even though all three of us were in charge, me and Dominick would look to Angel to make the final call.

"Naw bro, we don't split up. I got an idea. Quest, go to the right side of the wall. D, go in the kitchen. When Quest makes his move, then you head upstairs. We'll be behind you."

We moved on our marks and Angel dropped his weapon in the opening of the hallway. I knew what he was doing, making it look like we were down since the other wall was blocking me and Dominick. It was mad quiet, but we could hear footsteps coming downstairs to check on our dead bodies. I was in position, ready to use my lil bitch. Two guys stepped in the walkway and my machete went completely through the side of one of their necks.

I pulled it out smoothly as he dropped to the floor. By the time the other guy could raise his gun, Angel quickly picked up his weapon and swung it twice on top of his head, splitting it in two. We hurried behind Dominick, going up the stairs. Another shooter came at him and he hit that nigga fist first in his throat so hard that he opened it and exposed his Adam's apple. Three more came at us, but we were quicker.

Angel swung, hitting the guy in his stomach, then the front of his face. I brought my Latin blade down on the second guy's head, meeting between his eyes. Dominick high-kicked the third guy, snapping his entire neck around like that bitch from *The Exorcist.* We hit the rest of upstairs up and came across two more shooters. I took care of both of them with Latin straight through the gut. Once we cleared, we headed to the basement, which was empty, then we went around the entire house and checked their cars.

"That was fun," Angel chuckled and said after we pulled off with the bodies in bags and loaded up.

The drive back to the complex was the same as always. Music playing, we took our shot of vodka like we always did when we finished a job. My phone went off while we were on the freeway and I saw it was Christian. It had been a little over a week since our first date. What I'm about to say is going to make me sound vain, but I got no fucks in my fucks given department. Christian was going against all her plans that she had for me.

I knew the way we went rounds on my couch and how I had her body that she had met her match. Not even just that, I got texts and calls throughout the day checking on me and seeing how I was doing. Don't get me wrong, I hit her up first a lot of the time, too. But for a woman who claimed to be hard and always ten toes down, she was struck by me. Now we had some problems because I kept it real with her about Kamila and she claimed she could handle it.

But I get attitude from her, she snaps at me and

claims she's good, but I'm not stupid. I know what's up. I haven't left Kamila alone and Christian doesn't like it; the woman who claims she only fucks with unavailable men doesn't like that I'm unavailable. Ain't that shit wild? But I don't disrespect Christian. I asked her if she wanted me to fall back. She'd maintain her cool and tried to tell me I was being dramatic.

I wasn't trying to do this shit on purpose, which is why I haven't seen Christian face to face since. I didn't want to fuck my head or hers up even more. It was hard though, believe me. It was hard because I missed that body, skin, her moans, her kiss and the way she tastes. In a nutshell, it was all about when I was going to make my mind up and if I did, would it be too late.

Sugar Tits: Are you done being a liar?

I dropped my head and chuckled when she asked me that. Yesterday she wanted to go out and I told her I was working. I really was, but when I planned on leaving it was to Kamila's house. Truth be told, shit was going fine between us. I mean she was still her annoying self, but we were in a good space. I just couldn't let Christian go. It didn't sit well with me to even think about cutting her off even when I asked to.

Me: I'm a King, Daddy or even your everything, but I ain't no liar Christian.

Sugar Tits: Whatever, it doesn't even matter. I was just calling to tell you I have a date tonight so if you can't reach me than that's why.

Christian loved trying to make me jealous, especially when she would think I was with Kamila. Even though she'd be right, her way of showing she didn't care was by being messy. One day she sent me a picture of herself in the sexiest lingerie I had ever seen a woman wear. The caption in the text was 'I miss you, Blake'. I was fuming but what could I do? I had Kamila between my legs giving me head. I just texted back it was all good and was dry as hell with her. Christian had got to me, but not in a way that I would let Kamila go.

Me: Have fun

Christian: Just like I did with you 😊

Man, I swear her tarbaby head ass was about to make me flip. Christian's mouth was so fucking slick I hated that I loved it. I thought nobody's mouth could touch mine, but she had me beat. Even if I will shade her with my words, believe me, she was coming back later with a kill. Like, watch this shit right here.

Me: I miss you.

It took her about three minutes to respond so I know I made her smile. She was about to say she misses me too, but then she remembered how our relationship was, so she decided on some slick shit.

Christian: Come lick my booty then.

See what the fuck I mean? I was annoyed with a hard dick that I pushed aside everything I just said.

Me: Cancel that faggot date you got; I'm coming through.

Who was I trying to fool? I missed everything about

that pussy. I texted Kamila some bullshit real quick.

Me: Working late, I'll hit you up in the morning.

Kamila: It's cool, I'm going out anyway.

I was bothered but nowhere near as bothered as I was when Christian said she had a date. I didn't even text back, I just put my phone in my pocket and focused back on work.

We got to the complex and pulled in the back. As soon as we did, three of our doctors came out with gurneys for the bodies. I went to our basement and got the coolers; the fifth floor was where we did all the surgeries and any organ removal. The penthouse was where all anonymous clients came to get handled. STD testing, pills for if ya' piss burns and at the right price, abortions. On the fifth floor we looked at Doctor Lee unzip the bags of the three AB-negative kills.

"Would it kill the three of you to be a little cleaner?" He huffed when he saw the first guy with his neck open.

"That's his crazy ass," Angel laughed and pointed to Dominick.

"Fool, you got one in there with his whole face looking like shit in a blender," he joked back.

We played all day but when it came down to work, we didn't fuck around. The doctors removed all the organs that were saleable and placed them in coolers. The ones we weren't selling right now, me and Dominick ran to the basement to the walk-in freezer.

"Here you go." Doctor Lee came downstairs with three coolers. "Three fresh AB-negative hearts. Rare as hell, and you three have them on hand," he joked.

Angel came from his office with some black briefcases. "Here you go Doc, all paid up." They shook hands and he went upstairs to clean up and then leave.

Once they were done and it was only us and Lori upstairs, we each went in our offices to shower and change our clothes before the buyer got here.

"You good?" I asked Angel when we got back upfront, because he looked pissed.

"Yea, I'm just annoyed Nina fell asleep at her mom's

crib. I told her to just stay at my house after she got off work. Hardheaded ass, and now I gotta sleep alone."

Yo', me and Dominick were laughing so fucking hard we both were holding our sides. "You sound like a double bitch with a side of pussy." Dominick got out between his laugh.

"Fuck both of y'all. Act like grown men so we can make this money."

"Nigga how you gon' tell us to act grown when you just pouted for mommy's breast milk!" I joked, pissing him off more.

We roasted each other back and forth, laughing until Lori let us know a car pulled up outside. We went to the wall behind the stairs and looked at the surveillance. It was our buyers, Burt's friend. We put the three hearts on the Market and no one was offering more than $10,000,000. Before, when we were just selling our organs to a certain buyer, we would make a straight amount and that's it. Being on the Black Market was like eBay; people can bid each other until the highest won.

We look at the numbers and pick who wins. Once a bid is accepted, we have forty-eight hours to deliver or all bets are off and we are out.

Lori escorted the buyers downstairs and there were all serious faces. No TV, music, drinks offered or anything. Dominick grabbed the money and counted it in our multiple counting machines. While he handled that, everyone watched each other like a hawk and waited. No one moved, went to the back, hell, you couldn't even scratch your nose without shit going south.

It was tense every time because of how dangerous this shit was. Once Dominick was done and nodded, me and Angel handed the buyers the three coolers. It was a matter of trust on their part now. There was no way to know if they were really getting what they needed unless they risked killing the organ. We wouldn't play about this shit though because we knew everything we knew and loved would die. Once they had what they needed, we watched them on the cameras get in their ride and pull off.

"Who the fuck is this?" I said out loud while I looked at the cameras.

Angel and Dominick came back to look as well. Dominick's creepy ass started making this damn growling sound and getting that evil expression on his face. I got hype too though, and ready to spill some more guts. Two guys got out the pitch black and chrome 2020 Suburban truck. The first one wasn't recognizable but the second one was the one Angel met at the park one night… the nigga from Philly who sent his kittens to talk to us on his behalf.

"Let them in, Lori," Angel spoke over the speaker.

We didn't go get any weapons or anything; there was no need. If anything popped off, we know how we were gonna handle it. Lori came downstairs first with Gunna and the other guy following. It wasn't one of his other two guys he sent.

"My apologies, fellas, for us dropping in late at night, but when my associate told me I needed to come forward, then I figured why not now. So, here I am all the way from Philadelphia even though this is my birthplace." This muthafucka stood in front of us like he was a star attraction. He looked to be around our age group, maybe a year or two younger.

He stood the same, about 6'3 like me, but what got me was what this muthafucka had on. He wore black jeans with a neon red Gucci belt, and a leopard short sleeve button-up open with a white beater under it. He had a gold bracelet on and a gold chain. Now, this is Las Vegas baby, so style was a must, but this shit was gaudy as hell. The three of us stood side by side strong like always, looking at them with intensity.

"Maybe if I introduce myself then we'll be more comfortable. I'm Tucker. Gunna and I are business partners. I'm from here had a whole life and was about to put Nevada on the map with my football skills. Had the whole dream mapped out." He looked at me when he continued to speak.

"I even had the woman to prove it. But shit happened

and now I live in Philly, pimpin' hoes. My associate moved here cause the money is long and all we seem to hear about when we mention Nevada to any real niggas is *The Law*. Please excuse the first two dummies that came and talked to y'all." He pointed to Gunna who was looking at Dominick a little slick with a slim smirk.

"Those are his boys, so I can't vouch for them or anything you do to them. I'm here because I think you really need to reconsider my offer. Now if you say yes, then I'm on the next plane out of here and you won't see my face no more. You'll only deal with Gunna. Of course I'll be getting paid, but you won't have to see my fine ass face." He smiled.

"Tell me, when you moved to Philly did you pick up the same dummy skills as yo' boyfriend?" Dominick asked and Tucker's face changed, wiping that grin off. "We said no, so you hopped yo' ass in coach and flew here for the fuck of it. Go visit ya' old field or some shit because you ain't got a damn thing coming from here."

Tucker looked at Gunna and then at us, laughing. "I

know one of his parents is black because this scary looking nigga got soul." He rubbed his hands together. "Don't be a fool—"

"Man, get this *Cheetah Girl* the fuck outta here." I got pissed off because this shit was getting old. "Quit begging and get the fuck out while you still got limbs." I huffed at the both of them.

Gunna stepped close but Tucker stopped him. "I get it, you've had this entire apartment building to yourself. You don't wanna share... but you always eat better when you do it with someone who has something to share in return. Now, I'm more patient than my business partner so I'll let you marinate on it." They walked towards the steps and he stopped. "Please fellas, don't make me have to persuade you."

"If you gone make threats, could you at least be in tiger print?" I asked, picking my falchion sword from off the top of my desk. I was ready right now, but Angel stopped me as they left out.

"Let them niggas do their best. When we kill them, it will send a big message for anyone who tries to come our way. We making more money and building up a bigger rep, that means more problems." He looked at his watch. "It's still early, we about to build ourselves some insurance." What he had us do was smart as hell and it led to one in the morning, but our code was business first. It's what keeps everything else in our life rotating.

After I left the complex, I called Cyrus up. I gave him the access code to our surveillance; I needed photos of Tucker, Gunna and his two kittens who first came by. I was driving to my destination going faster than normal. I was anxious to get the answer that was about to change up this situation. In minutes, Cyrus sent me clear pictures of all four of these hoe ass niggas. I pulled in the parking space of my Ma's treatment facility. Security knew me and let me inside with no problem.

"Mr. Foster? Is everything ok? Your mom has been doing really well." Edith was surprised to see me this late.

"I know she's good, I actually came by to ask you a question." I stopped in front of her workstation and took my phone out.

"Ok, sure." She put her magazine down and gave me her attention.

"Remember when you said Ma had some flowers delivered by Same Day Delivery?"

"Yes, I remember. She hasn't had any attempted deliveries since, I know you said to inform you." It was funny because Edith as well as every other person who worked here was always nervous when talking to me. They knew I would flip quick when it came to Ma.

"That's good. I need you to look carefully at these pictures and tell me if any of these guys were the delivery guy who dropped the flowers off. Or if you have seen any of them in this building for any reason. Take your time, no rush."

Edith nodded her head and I gave her my phone. She took her time studying each picture which is what I wanted. I didn't want her feeling rushed or anything, I wanted her to think hard on it.

"No, I'm so sorry, but I have never seen any of these men. I thought maybe him." She pointed to Tucker. "But I think it's because he favors my friend's son. He used to play football." She laughed and said that with no effort. Tucker said he used to play football, that shit had to be connected.

I smiled when Edith gave me back my phone. "Ok, thank you so much. You were a big help. I'll be back up here Thursday to visit Ma. Have a good night."

"You too Mr. Foster, I'm sorry I couldn't be any help."

I waved at her and left out. She had no idea she just helped me a lot. Now, I was about to dig all into the life of Tucker.

**

"You're late."

"We never even picked a time, I said I was coming through and I'm here." I stood on Christian's porch while she stood on the other side of the screen door.

"Well it's too late. I already got taken care of." She gave me this sexy half smile that was poking me.

I pulled the end of my beard and took a deep breath because she was really about to send me on tip.

"Christian, open the damn door and stop playing with me." I looked at her and she knew I wasn't playing. As soon as she opened the door, I wrapped my arms around her waist and lifted her up. "Why you like playing so damn much?" I asked while admiring her chocolate beauty.

"Because you like playing and lying to me," she spoke in a hushed tone, biting her lip.

"Which room is yours?" I asked while we walked down the hall.

"Left door." As soon as she answered, her lips came down on mine. We were kissing so intensely that I swear my tongue was trying to dig for her thoughts. I laid her on her Queen size bed, which I was bigger than, but I didn't care. I lifted her little t-shirt she had on up and started on them sugar tits she had. Licking those chocolate Hershey nipples letting them melt in my mouth, like the first time, Christian was moaning and going crazy because I sucked her titties good.

"Mmm Quest bae, yessss." Man, she sound like a sweet song calling out my name like that.

I stood up and took her shirt off, revealing her naked body. I got undressed and put three Magnums on her nightstand.

"You like pissing me off, we about to fix that. But first, I wanna taste this pussy." I got on my knees and propped her legs up on my shoulders. Before I went in, I looked her in her eyes. "You may not be my bitch Christian, but you *are* my bitch." I'on give a damn if that didn't make sense to y'all. In my head it did, and I know to her it did too. I wasn't her nigga, but I *am* her nigga.

I opened them lips and attacked that sweet clit. After I ate her pussy good and made her cum a few times, I fucked Christian all over her bedroom till she passed out into a deep sleep. I was right behind her knocked the fuck out till the bright sun came through her light pink curtains. My damn phone was vibrating in short sounds, so I knew it was text messages. Unlocking my phone, I had ten texts from Kamila, all with the same bullshit. She was cussing me out and tripping about me being in some pussy. I shook my head and blacked my phone out, looking over at Christian sound asleep.

I slowly pulled the covers back. I moved carefully, trying not to wake her up. All the condom wrappers were on the floor so I picked them up and threw them in her garbage. Putting my boxers on, I began getting dressed when Kamila texted my phone again.

Kamila: Why are you doing this to me Quest? I thought we were doing good and starting over.

Shit. I felt bad as fuck because I could hear her tone and see her tears as if I was in her face. Kamila was right, we were good in our own way. Thing is, I would drop any hoe I'm talking to for her and play this good ride we would have for about three months. But looking at Christian sleeping, I don't know how I'll do that. It wasn't just the sex. I liked just being with her and I keep thinking about the way she had Ma smiling. I needed to get up out of here, so I turned around and picked up my shoes so I could put them on.

"Wow, you really was about to pull the asshole move and sneak out." Christian laid there with her eyes open. She sat up and grabbed her t-shirt, putting it on. "I been hearing your phone going off, I know it's her." Standing up folding her arms, she looked at me.

"Well then you already know I gotta roll." She chuckled and I swear it looked like her eyes watered.

"What was that bullshit you was talking last night, about how I'm yours but I'm not yours? That's not what the fuck we about to do—"

"Well then tell me how you want it, because you knew I had a girl."

Her mouth dropped and she looked at me like she wanted to fight. But I didn't give a damn because I wasn't the only one wrong in this.

"What the fuck you even complaining for anyway? Ain't this yo' thang? Niggas who belong to someone else is what keeps Christian hard, ain't that what you said?"

"Oh please, Quest. Don't try that bullshit on this situation. We don't even treat this like just a fuck and you know it. You tryna put all the blame on me to justify the fact that you are holding on to a toxic ass, hot mess of a relationship. You are acting like a little boy."

That ticked me off. "I'm a little boy because I won't leave what I know, for a woman who proudly likes being a side piece of ass? Tell me how I come out winning?" I regretted that shit when I said it. On God I did, especially when her eyes watered for sure.

Christian looked at me with hurt but then she blinked her tears away and shook her head, looking at me with disgust. "You lose either way Quest, because now I'm done and you're stuck with the bullshit you came in with. Get the fuck out, *little boy*."

Pulling on my beard I thought about saying

something else or grabbing her ass up but naw, I just opened her door. "Fucking bitch."

Even though we just said some harsh shit to each other, I knew we weren't done.

DOMINICK

"Ugh fuck, D! Oh my God!"

I had Anika bent over the dresser with her legs wrapped around my waist. I wasn't as deep like I wanted to go, but it was good enough. I wasn't even halfway through and I had her yelling. It was cool, the pussy was good like always. Me and Anika have been fucking for a long time, I met her about a month after my baby sister Denise passed away. I killed her doctor because of how heartless he treated me and my family.

This was the only chick I ever fucked with that wasn't black. She lucked up when she met me. I was in a dark place and only saw a cute face. The first year of Denise's death, I took it hard and went to a local bar to drink my pain away. One-night Anika was there, this cute Indian chick who looked like she was out of her element at a bar. But when she opened her mouth, I saw she could handle herself. So, we fucked that night and have been on and off since. No relationship, no love, we hang sometimes and fuck when either want to. Anika was single and so was I, so we weren't harming anybody.

To tell you the truth, today was the first time I was fucking her, and my mind was elsewhere. Even though we had some years of knowing each other, I still took her to my hoe house to fuck. I don't give a damn, my home was just that. My home, my peace. If you weren't my brothers or my cleaning staff, then you were never allowed there. Even my parents couldn't come because when I did let them visit, they didn't know how to respect my shit.

I keep this house clean as hell too. The maid comes and changes the sheets and to clean. It was furnished and comfortable, it was just obvious that this wasn't my main crib. Anyway, I was fucking Anika because I was horny as hell from my activities earlier. Now, before I tell y'all what type of shit I was on, don't go judging me. I think all the bullshit I was mixed with from my parents that got me acting this way. Jamaican and German people heads ain't right and I had that mixture along with some other shit in my DNA.

Let me get to the point. So earlier today, I watched Symba leave the house that she shared with Christian. They both were gone and after I gave it a while, I got out my truck and walked on their porch. It was easy as hell getting into their house and they were blessed as hell that no one ever tried to come in. They didn't live in a bad neighborhood, but the devil has no zip-code preference. All you needed was to unlock their top and bottom lock and you're in. They didn't even lock the screen door.

But it was women who lived here so it goes undone. This house, however, was protected. Every muthafucka knew not to come near it on no crazy shit or they'd have Tha Law to deal with, and y'all seen how we get down. Once I was inside, I went and looked around, and nodded my head with how neat and clean it was. You just knew women lived here because the colors and everything had fur or glitter shit on it.

There were throw blankets folded on their long sectional couch and magazines on the glass coffee table. I walked past the kitchen and dining room which was also clean. I knew the bedroom that belonged to Symba because I could smell it. She had a scent to her that I was addicted to. That Burberry HER perfume was infused in her skin, which was why anytime we hugged I had to take a big whiff. I opened her door and my dick woke up just being in a room that I knew was so personal to her.

Her walls were a dark grey and she had a gorgeous azure color Queen-size bed frame with a gold comforter on the mattress. Her bed wasn't made up, but I didn't care about that. Her bedroom was fixed for a Queen with gold and grey all over. There was even a big painting of a crown hanging up on her wall. I walked in her closet and this woman had so many clothes and shoes it wasn't even enough space. I chuckled and closed it back. Her room didn't have a bathroom in it so I went to her dresser and opened the first drawer.

"Bingo," I spoke lowly to myself when it was her panties drawer. I haven't gotten to see her in a pair personally, but I imagined it a lot. I picked up this one thong that was sexy as fuck to me. It had a thick band around it that said HOT. The part that goes between her fat ass cheeks and the part that goes on her pussy was sheer.

"Fuck." Speaking lowly I was on some creep, nasty shit because I licked the pussy part and put them in my pocket. I had to get out her pantie drawer because I'd fuck around and take every pair. I opened the rest of her drawers and noticed Symba was a clean woman... folded socks, pajamas separated by style. Her bras and sports bras were even separated. I dug it and was glad because I hate a trifling female. I could care less about what's folded or not, but bitch be clean.

Don't have panties with holes, fucked up bras, socks that should have been long gone. I hated that in a woman.

The top of her dresser had deodorant, perfume and that spray shit girls wear. I picked up her favorite Burberry bottle and saw she was almost out. Opening it, I smelled it and closed my eyes as if I was hugging her. I loved how the desk in her room had her schoolbooks on it. Symba took pride in her education and goals.

One thing I didn't notice was she didn't have any sex toys, unless she hid them well. I assumed all women had some kind of toy, unless she went acapella and just used her fingers. Either way, I was done so I closed her door and headed out. Getting in my truck, I was pleased to know Symba wasn't just a fine woman. She took care of herself on every level and didn't let her looks be all she had to offer. But now, I'm horny as fuck and who I wanted, we hadn't taken it there yet.

Being in her space was such a turn on. I don't know what the hell it was, but Symba had my nose wide open. I ain't never broke in a woman's house because I was so obsessed; I had to see how she lived. I damn sure ain't never took a female's panties or knew her scent from a mile away. We spent time together but the funny shit is, we both are so much alike that we make sure our plans are outdoor activities with a lot of people around.

When we make any kind of eye contact or touch in any way, it's so intense that I know for a fact if I was to fuck her on spot, she'd let me. I wasn't about to let Symba fuck me, no way. I was fucking her bent over, ass cheeks spread wide and her calling my name. She reminded me all the time that we were friends and nothing more. Yet the minute she doesn't get her way with me, she clowns. Like y'all know our thing is talking all night on the phone.

For the past two nights, I been cutting that shit out. Can't keep doing all this emotional shit and claim not to be mine. Man, this girl left me a long, nasty voicemail. She wasn't disrespectful but she for damn sure was heated. I laughed and replayed it twice because her voice was sexy pissed. I wasn't even busy, but I had to teach her that she was not about to run me and claim to be single. Naw, that's for them other boy-titty having men she fucks with.

I wasn't looking for a relationship either, but Symba

did something to me that had me obsessed and wide open. Anyway, I had a hard dick and no Symba, so I hit up Anika and here we are. Her being here helped me on about 20% on a 100% scale. The head was good and sloppy like I like. Pussy still felt good; she was soaking up the condom, moaning and all in. I was just on another planet.

"What's up, D?" Anika asked me when she came out the bathroom from her shower.

I was sitting on the edge of the bed looking at the turned off TV. I took a shower in the other bathroom, put back on my Balmain jeans and Balmain vest. I kept my arms out because it was too warm outside for a shirt underneath. I put my long hair in a low ponytail, and I had Angel line my beard up yesterday. I had my diamond stud screw backs in my ears and a Rolex on my wrist. I was meeting up with Angel and Quest after I leave here because Quest said he had some shit to talk to us about.

"Nothing, you cool?" I asked, picking up my Jordans and putting them on.

"I'm good, but I know you're not." She put her panties on and took the towel off her body. Anika was slim with some thick thighs and a flat stomach. Her booty wasn't as big as I liked and her weight wasn't up like I was into, but she was bad. Her hair was in the middle of her back and her Indian features made her stand out.

After I put my other shoe on, I looked at her, confused. "Ain't shit wrong with me."

"Yes it is, you weren't all the way here when we were having sex." After putting her bra on, she placed her hands on her small hips.

"Didn't I just make you cum a good six times?" I asked her.

"Yea, but I been fucking you for a while. I know you don't do the whole pussy eating thing because we're not together, but I know how it is when you're all in. Don't get me wrong, you were excellent like always, but I felt a disconnection." Her eyes searched mine like she was hoping she was wrong.

I just shrugged my shoulders and put my wallet in my pocket, then my revolver behind my back.

Anika chuckled and put her skirt on. "Wow, what's her name? Should I have savored this session of ours? Because whoever she is, she has you wrapped."

I looked at her and responded honestly. "Her name doesn't matter to you, so why are you asking? If you think something was off then those are your feelings. I'm not about to talk to you about my fucking love life, Anika." I don't share or talk about how I feel, not to anyone who wasn't my mama or brothers. I've never sat and opened up with any female because what was the point of that when I knew what we were?

"Well damn, did you forget I've been knowing you for years?! Whoever this woman is, she's new! I've always been here when you call—"

"And want to fuck!" I was pissed off because I don't play that yelling at me shit. "You're here when I want some pussy sprinkled on my dick. Don't act like we were anything but that, Anika. We will chill and then I take you home. Not to my crib, my parents or even where I work, I take you home or here. Why you gotta make shit weird? I just fucked you good and fed yo' ass. Shut up." I walked out the bedroom door and she followed, pissed off.

"You're a jackass if you pass me up and get into a relationship with any other woman." She kept it up all while we got outside. I was glad she drove her own car because I swear, I wouldn't let her loudmouth ass in my ride.

"You're just going to ignore me!?" Anika stood in the middle of the lawn, watching me hit the alarm on my car.

I had nothing else to say and I damn sure wasn't about to argue with her. I opened my door, put my revolver on my passenger seat and closed the door back.

"Dominick!?"

While she called my name, I pulled out the driveway and down the street.

"DOMINICK YOU SON OF A BITCH!"

I turned DMX up loud and headed to the complex.

DMX was my boy, I played his music like it came out today. *Belly* was my number two favorite movie. I had another one, but I'll die before I tell anyone that. Anyway, Anika blew my phone up so much I had her blocked by the time I got off the freeway. I think she felt because we had some years on each other that I was about to bend.

Hell no, that's some shit Quest does, I ain't the one. I love my brother, but he fucks with Kamila that hard because of the amount of time he spent. Time is precious, we as humans don't know when life will end so I didn't like wasting it. Our goal was to not waste more time than necessary. Once you realize a muthafucka ain't shit, then get the fuck on. I pulled up at Quest's crib and shot Symba a text.

Me*:* I better talk to you tonight.

Symba Baby*:* Talk to whoever you been talking to the past two nights.

I chuckled and took in the fact that she had some jealous ways. I liked that shit; her attitude was what turned me on too. It was fiery with a hint of sarcasm and humor; I couldn't come at her any kind of way.

Me: Don't play Symba, remember you tried that already and you lost. Now, I better talk to you tonight.

Symba Baby: NOOOO!!

I laughed and put my phone in my pocket; I bet I talk to her tonight.

"How the fuck you arrive on CP time when you ain't even black." Quest joked when I walked in his house. They always played about how late I am, saying I be on 'colored people' time. These fools always got some shit to say.

"Shut the hell up, clown ass, and you betta have some food cause I'm hungry." I laughed going in his basement where we always hung out at.

"Bro-Bro, what up!?" Angel stood up and we pound fists.

"Shit smooth this way, you good?" I saw the spread of food on the pool table and my stomach growled. It was pizza and tacos, which meant longer in my gym tomorrow, but I didn't care.

"Greedy ass muthafucka." Quest cracked sitting in his game chair.

I gave him the middle finger, grabbed a napkin and beer then went to sit down in his other recliner.

"So, what'chu gotta talk to us about?" Angel asked.

I folded my meat lover slice of pizza in half and took a big bite.

"Those Philly niggas didn't send me and D those notes."

That got me and Angel's undivided attention. I swallowed my food quick and wiped my mouth with the brown napkin. "Who the fuck was it then? I tracked down my parents' mail carrier and she didn't have shit for me."

"I don't know exactly who it is, but I know it's not them. I took their pictures to my Mama's facility and showed them to Edith. I watched her go through them carefully, she has never seen them at all. I even went to the guards and asked and they haven't, either. But that nigga Tucker stuck out to her; she said he looked like her friend's son who used to play football. I got all his information from Cyrus; turns out Edith was right, that is her friend's son. I told Cyrus to keep eyes on Edith and Tucker's people, just in case."

"Ok, so how do you know they didn't send us those notes?" I asked.

"Because they not keeping an eye on y'all family?" Angel questioned.

"Exactly." Quest agreed and went to explain. "You see how I told Cyrus to keep an eye on Edith and Tucker's people? No one is watching my Mama or your parents, D. I know because no one has seen them and no changes have been made. For instance, any new neighbors at the trailer park, new landlord or anything?" He asked me.

"Come to think of it, naw." I answered and thought about it.

"Right, not at Ma's facility either. No new staff member, tenant or unusual visitors. It's not Philly, though."

I looked at Quest's face. He was confident, and he

wouldn't have come to us if he wasn't. I was so damn livid because I felt like we had enemies right under our noses. "They'll slip, for sure they will slip. Whoever it is wants something from us together because ain't no damn way this is a coincidence. You just so happen to have an enemy the same time as me, and they both left us notes. Then the shit they know is personal as fuck," I took a swig of my beer.

"Angel, I swear if it's you playing nigga, I'ma fuck you up." Quest looked at him and said.

Angel is the prankster of the three of us; he plays jokes and records our reactions all the time. He been that way since we were kids. We've gotten him back a few times as well.

"Man, why they fuck would I take it to this extreme? This ain't shit to play about. Regardless of who it is, they begging to die. It doesn't matter that I ain't got no note, we brothers, in this shit for life. What y'all next move need to be is keeping a look out for slip-ups; I don't mean moving in fear, but I mean not letting nothing fly past you.

I also think we need to kill them Philly muthafuckas, let them make their first move. We already insured ourselves, but we don't wanna strike first because who knows what traps they've laid out. They want us to strike first because of our rep. Naw, we about to sleep on them and let them hit first. All this shit gone be over, soon." We all nodded our heads and agreed with Angel.

After we talked about that, we ate and played some NBA2K then we called it a night. As I rode home, I thought about what's all going on. Philly clowns coming in and demanding we partner with them. How the fuck you come on new territory and feel because of your line of work that it gives you access to roll with the best? The thing with us, money wasn't something we were in dire need of. We have stocks and investments that would generate even when we die.

That's what these Philly muthafuckas didn't understand. They felt because they offered us a fee that we should jump at it. Nope, being that money hungry will get you killed out here. I know how it is to be hungry and not know if you would have a roof over your head. My parents were drunks, gamblers and even some occasional pill poppers. Rent money, food money, the light bill money has been blown plenty of times.

Sometimes I had to steal me and Denise food either from the store or neighbors' mobile homes. That's why I was grateful when I met my brothers; we had each other's backs hard. I got into church because of Angel's mom. She would make me and Quest go with them. After a while, I learned so much and found myself even more. I know for a fact me and Quest loved her so much for that. We each had things that our parents taught us, like my dad taught Quest and Angel how to fish.

He always had some crazy ass story while we would be fishing, but it was enlightening. He taught us how to scale, clean and cook. Quest's dad taught us a lot about being a groomed man. Having nice things, furniture, suits, dress shoes, cologne and to always have a watch. Then Angel's dad, he had all the knowledge about love, family and money. How to invest or save every two dollars you made, they were all appreciated and where one fell weak, the other had strength.

My point is, Philly got the wrong ones if they thinks a few thousands would make us collide. Then this shit with me, Quest and the letters was annoying as hell; it was a lot of blood about to be spilled and I knew it wasn't going to be none of ours. Finally, this thing with me and Symba. Well, that's not even a problem because I was about to break that girl all the way down. She was about to be putty in my hands and I had a feeling that she was about to have me the same in hers.

If she did then that could be a good and bad thing because I love differently, I think differently, and I protect differently.

I got to my palace of a home and pulled in my large, round driveway. Parking my Lykan Hypersport next to my other rides, I got out. I loved the front of my palace because I had the builders make a beige stone color porch with an arch. It was like a tunnel that had warm light hidden inside with beautiful green leave vines all on the inside.

I loved the rustic log cabin style, so I had that going all through my entire home. That's why I don't let anyone come here but the people I named earlier because I made this my escape from all the bullshit. As soon as you walked inside, I didn't have walls; I had grey stones as if some shit out a castle. That style wrapped around the staircase and all the way to the ceiling. Even my chandelier was metal with candle shape lightbulbs coming out of it.

I took my shoes off and walked down the hall to the left where the living room was, which was the start of the house. My walls were white, but every window was lined with Brazilian cherry wood. I had a giant pebble style fireplace that had a 70-inch flat-screen mounted on it. My living room was beige, cream and chocolate brown. I had hickory wood all through the house. Every room, including my kitchen was luxury cabin style with brown marble counter tops.

Nine-bedrooms, eleven bathrooms, a movie room, gym, pool and jacuzzi outside. It was a lot of house for just me, but it's what I wanted. Once I made it upstairs to my bedroom, I took my clothes off and went to take a shower. The turbo shower head felt good hitting my body. I was tired as hell. Aside from work, I still went to fights that Mauwi, my dad's best friend, put together. I didn't do it for money, I just loved to fight.

I dug everything about it, especially the ass-beating part. My hands were so big and knuckles so large I could kill someone with one hit. If you get in the cage with me, then that was your own choice. I never took it easy on someone because of their size, race or situation. If you were fighting for money or trying to impress your girl, then I felt bad for you. Two hits, that's the most anyone has ever got on me before it was lights out.

I got aroused by that shit every time. Anyway, I'd been fighting and working so my body needed some TLC. A nice back rub, shoulders massaged, hell, even a foot rub. I made sure to keep my feet handled so touching them wouldn't sicken a woman. Since I didn't have that, this shower head and hot water would have to do. After I cleaned my body and washed my hair I got out and dried off. Throwing my towel on the love seat at the edge of my King-size bed, I put some deodorant on, pulled my covers back and got in. I sleep naked every night with the central air on. Cutting my TV on, I went straight to the DVD option and played my favorite movie, the one no one knew about. I always slept with it on, even though when I woke up the title screen would be on. Tonight, I put it on mute, grabbed my phone off the charger and laid on my back so I could call Symba. I was really hoping she wasn't about to have me leave my comfortable bed and hunt her ass down if she didn't answer.

"What, Dominick?" Her smart voice answered on the third ring.

Since she picked up, I opened my nightstand, grabbed

her thong I stole from her drawer and put it on my bare chest before I laid back on my fluffy pillows.

"Now, I never answer the phone rudely when you call me, so why I gotta get that?" I smirked because she let go of that very faint, low moan that she thought I never heard.

"My bad, I wasn't going to answer—"

"Stop fucking with me, Symba. I said I needed to talk to you." My tone got serious as hell because she was taking me there, talking about not answering.

"But you didn't need to talk to me two nights in a row, though. Who kept your attention Dominick? Don't lie. We're not together, so there is no need to."

"That right there is why you didn't talk to me. All you do is remind me that we not together. I know that, Symba. I don't need you telling me every damn day. Look, I'm not about to argue with you. I called to hear your voice and talk to you. Now, you can either tell me how your day was, or hang up." I was so damn serious with this girl and right here is how you are about to see Symba not being as tough as she pretends to be.

"My day was pretty good. I had school, work and then I met with my old homegirl from high school for dinner. With her five kids, she's really busy."

"Is she twenty-four like you?" I asked her, hoping she was about to say no.

"Yea, she is but she had her first child at fifteen and a half."

My eyes bucked out. "Well damn, did she even play with Barbie dolls? She went straight from pacifier to balls."

Symba broke out laughing which was such a sweet and sexy sound. "Oh my goodness, Dominick, don't talk about my friend that way. She is in a relationship with a good guy who fell in love with her and the kids in less than a week."

"A week?! If he moving that fast with her and she got five kids that man homeless and need a place to crash." This time we both cracked up and I continued. "Let me tell you how a woman can know for sure if she's his woman. If his

Mama don't call her when she can't reach her son, then he's not her man. Real talk."

"Dominick, I swear you got my stomach hurting." She said between her laughing so hard.

"I'm speaking big facts; you know I am. That's why I'm done with having *situationships*, either we together or a chick is one of my hoes." I chuckled.

Symba got quiet for a minute. "So, what am I?"

I knew she was about to ask me that. "You know where I stand with that, but you repeat every day that that's not what you want."

"I just don't have time for all of that. Fuck all that love and relationship shit." Those words left her mouth, but even I knew she didn't mean it. That was a cry for help because she was just scared.

"Naw, not fuck love and relationships. Fuck the person who made you think like that," I spoke true shit to her.

"I've never been in a relationship. I watched my

mama, sister and nieces fail at it, so I just decided I wanted no parts."

"Like I said, fuck the person who made you think that way."

"So basically, fuck my family?" She lightheartedly asked.

"Yup, because someone should have told you how *not* to take their experience and base your life upon it. You have the right to take notes and learn something, but you are taking it too far. Fuck what'chu doing to yourself; you are making me miss out on what was meant for me." I was for real as shit.

I could hear Symba's heart skip a beat and I swear when I closed my eyes, I felt her next to me. That gorgeous face, those prominent eyes staring in mine, that melanin brown skin, them juicy ass thighs that I wanted to grip, lick and suck on. *Shit.*

"Why you get so quiet?" Her voice asked in a soft, soothing tone.

"Thinking about you laying here next to me. You can't keep running from me, Symba. You'll drive me crazy and you don't wanna be responsible for that." I wasn't threatening her or trying to scare her, I was just telling the truth.

"Dominick." There goes that soft tone again.

"Symba." I called her name after she did mine. Hers was pleading for me to stop... stop making her feel like this was right. But she had me fucked up, I wasn't about to stop.

"I'm getting sleepy, I'll talk to you tomorrow, ok?"

Now normally we fall asleep on the phone together, but I knew Symba was having a wave of emotions, so I let her be. "Ok, sleep good Symba, baby."

"You, too."

After she hung up, I just chuckled and shook my head at her. I was breaking her down and she wasn't liking it. But this is just what it was, so she might as well let it happen. I put her thong back in my nightstand, charged my phone up and watched my movie until it was watching me.

"Yea, that diamond shape looks good. Go with those and keep the black trimming."

"Yes sir, Mr. Reed."

I stood outside, leaning against my Escalade truck, watching the window installation company I called do their job. I wasn't at my palace, I was at my hoe crib. Anika's stupid ass broke out every window on this house. Was I mad? Not at all, but now you see why you shouldn't let every person know where you lay your head. I ride past this house every day just to check on it and that's when I saw it.

I knew it was a woman and the only one who had beef with me at the moment was Anika. I've been cused out, slapped and even had an object or two thrown at my head by pissing a girl off. Especially in my early twenties; I was a dog of all dogs and I stayed ducking from a woman throwing shit at me. I don't hit girls because I'll break they face, besides, I had a lot of that shit coming with how I treated them.

IN LOVE WITH A LAS VEGAS OUTLAW 2

But, each and every one of them knew not to take shit too far. What Anika did wasn't shit. I had a company out here the next day working. But her ass knew not to try this with me again or I was stepping on her damn hands.

"What the fuck you keep calling me for?" I answered my phone, annoyed as hell.

"D, I'm sorry. I was just mad, I'll pay for the damages."

I laughed when Anika started pleading and begging. Why do y'all women do this, act out of emotion then when reality hit you wanna cry sorry? "$7,000."

"What?" She asked.

"That's how much it cost to fix what the hell you did. Didn't you just say you'd pay for the damages?"

"Y-Yea but—"

"Then you need to make your way over here with either your debit card or checkbook ready." I hung up the phone, cracking up.

See the thing about me, I'll call a muthafucka's bluff

because ya' grown ass shouldn't be trying to play games. Anika got the money; she always talked about her wealthy ass parents. Her car stayed up to date with the year as well as her shoes, clothes and purses. I've bought her a bag or two, but she had her own bread.

After I hung up, I went back to watching the people work. I don't care what it is, I never left before a job was done.

Companies slack off when you leave them alone. Dumb fucks will go eat, drink and pussy foot around on my dime. Naw, get this shit done and get gone so I can go about my day. It was only seven in the morning, but I had plans later and didn't want this to take all day. It was coming along good so I didn't think it would. About an hour later, Anika's silver BMW pulled up and she got out. I stayed leaned against my ride with my blue tint Tom Ford sunglasses on, blocking the brightness.

I had my hair down today with a burnt orange Polo shirt, some light faded distress jeans and a pair of Air Jordan

1 High Tops. Aside from my diamond studs, I decided to wear my platinum chain-link bracelet. Anika walked in my direction looking good, which I knew she did on purpose. It was seven in the morning on a Saturday; wasn't no woman about to be all dolled up this early. Me on the other hand, I had shit to do and didn't want to drive all the way back home to get dressed after this was done.

"Are you for real right now, you're really about to make me pay for this?" She flipped her long hair and moved her Chanel purse to her other shoulder.

Anika had on this mini short dress with some heels and her titties coming out. She only had a B-Cup but they still were nice. Anika was spoiled. She had no job because she didn't have to have one; she went to school and did shit rich girls did all day. Social media, friends, shopping, traveling and staying groomed. She was twenty-seven, no kids and probably rebelled against her Indian parents. I didn't know much about her family because I didn't make it my business to.

"I'm not making you do shit, you offered and I'm taking you up on your offer. I don't get my check til' Monday so you just came through with the clutch." I kept my shades on because she wasn't that important to me for me to look in her eyes. Besides, I was talking bullshit anyway but she indeed was about to pay for this.

"Stop joking around, D, you know damn well you have it. Look, can we just talk, please?"

"Go pay them essential workers first." I told her with all seriousness in my voice.

Smacking her lips, she tried to stomp off but her heel got stuck in the grass. I saw her go over to the boss and say some shit to him while opening her purse. He looked confused and then looked up at me. I nodded my head 'yes' at him and he walked her to their company van. He had a credit-debit card machine with him. Anika swiped her card, signed it and he went to his other machine and printed out her receipt. She signed it and he gave her a copy. Making her way back over to me, she looked agitated.

"There, paid. Now can we talk?" Putting her hands on her small hips she stood in front of me.

"Humor me." I put my phone in my pocket.

This girl actually started talking. I laughed to myself because this was part of the reason I adored black women. I need that attitude, that fire and clap back that they had anytime they felt men had them fucked up.

"I'm done being looked over; I think me and you should be together. I've sat back for years and waited for you to come to realize that I'm the one for you. I love you, any flaw you think you have, trust me, I'll love as well." She was being real; I knew it from her eyes.

I took my glasses off so she could see I was about to be real as well. "Anika, me and you would never happen. Not because of what you did to my house, I could care less about that petty shit. But you and I have nothing in common outside of fucking and spending. You have no goals other than living off your peoples' riches and looking cute. You don't challenge me in any way. The growing up you have to

285

do is something I don't have time for."

Her face looked blown away, but I didn't understand how. Anika knew me and her would never be together.

"D." She smiled and walked closer to me then she wrapped her arms around my neck. "It's me; we have history. I'm not as naïve as you think I am. Whoever the bitch is, I swear she won't be better than me."

I looked past her and saw the workers doing their job. The driveway wasn't nearly as long as the one I had for my palace. I looked at Anika and turned us both around so her back was facing my truck. Her eyes were filled with hope and excitement because I was holding her close. My hands rubbed up and down her back as I looked down in her eyes.

"The workers are a few feet away from us and I didn't want them to hear me. Anika, you wouldn't even rank in the top five of women I would choose to be with. But most importantly, if you ever refer to her as a bitch again, I will rip this small spine of yours out through your throat. I let you slide with the act you did to my house. So, you owe it to yourself to walk back to your car, drive off and leave this be." I ran my finger through her hair and kissed the top of her nose.

Tears were falling down from her face and she looked vexed off and hurt at the same time. "D, you are making a big mistake."

"I don't make mistakes, I make decisions. Now get the fuck outta here."

Anika pushed away from me and ran to her car crying. I watched her pull off aggressively with her loud screeching tires.

It took about another hour for the house to be done; the manager said he didn't understand why they were paid twice. I told him to take the other $7,000 and split it amongst his four workers. I got in my truck, went to Denny's and picked up breakfast to go for me and my parents.

When I got to their spot, I paid more attention to the neighbors and any cars that rode by. They lived in a rundown trailer park with bad ass kids running around, barking dogs and ghetto behavior. They all knew me so any new faces I was making a note of. I even went to the leasing office and checked shit out. Everything was all good, so I went inside and chilled with my parents until one in the afternoon when my date was up.

"Hey, how are you?"

"I'm good, you know you were about to get left taking all damn day." I said opening the door for Tish. One thing I loved about being single was having a shit load of choices of women to choose from. Tish was a dope girl, twenty-eight, divorcee and has four kids. I wasn't playing stepdaddy to anybody, so I didn't care. What I dug about her was she wasn't looking for shit but fun and honesty. Her and her ex-husband got married when they were eighteen and he's all she knew.

Now that she's single, she was out here wild as hell, if you know what I mean. We fucked twice about five months ago. She hit me up last night and asked if I wanted to go to the mall and grab some food. I had a birthday coming up soon, so I needed to get some shit to wear for that, so I figured why not. I know y'all ready for me and Symba to get together, but I wasn't the one tripping, she was. I haven't talked to her in four days. I called and sent texts, but she wasn't responding.

Now of course, I would have popped up on her, but fuck that. Symba was used to men being in her ass, chasing her around and all. I did it for a while and it didn't work, now I'm about to do something that I know no man ever has to her. I'm falling back and leaving her alone. Was I giving up? Hell fuck no, but she wasn't about to keep playing me for a weak sucka. Women respond quicker to you when you ignore they ass.

So, I was back to my life as if she wasn't in it and it was working too, because I didn't reach out to her at all and this morning, I got a text from her. Nothing much, just a good morning text, but she only sent it because I didn't say anything to her yesterday. See what I mean? Games, but it was all good. She was about to see how I'm the MVP. Tish was bad, an exact twin of *Jordyn Woods,* except she was a little darker and she had a Cardi-B type of personality, but she knew to calm that shit down with me.

"My bad, I had to make sure I looked good for you." Damn girl was practically naked, but she wasn't mine, so I didn't give a damn. Muthafuckas knew The Law, so whether I was with a thot, a bop or a tik tok, I was to always be respected and who rolled with me was too.

"Did yo' kids see you leave the house like that?" I asked her as I drove off.

"Yea, but they know mama got a life. Fuck all of that, it's my time."

I just laughed, shook my head and turned on some music. In twenty-minutes we were pulling in the mall parking lot. It was pretty busy, nothing out the norm. We got out and made our way inside.

"So what are your plans for your birthday?" Tish asked me while we were in the Gucci store.

"I'm having a black-tie party, always wanted one." I

told her, looking at some shoes and belts.

"Cool, when are you going to have it?"

"The 24th. My birthday falls on a Wednesday, my party will be that Saturday."

"Aye! That's my son's birthday," She said proudly.

"That's what's up." I responded, putting the shoes down.

"You should let me be your date. I know how to get all fancy." Flipping her long braids, she was grinning and anticipating my answer. We didn't see anything in Gucci so we left out to head to another store.

"Didn't you just say your son's birthday is the same day as my party?" I looked at her, confused.

"Yea, so? He's eight years old, his daddy will celebrate with him. I'm tryna turn up." Fucking girl actually sounded like she didn't give two fucks.

"Naw Tish, I'm good. That wouldn't even sit well with me. You wanna do other shit besides be with your kid,, then that's on you but you won't be at my party." I meant that shit for real, how trifling can you be.

Walking to the third floor of the mall, I saw Footlocker which was my holy grail so of course I was about to go in there. They brought the space from the store that was next door, so it was split into three parts. Men on the left, women on the right and kids in the middle. Tish went to the women and I went to the men and that's when I saw Symba with a guy standing next to her. Not just any guy, but that corny Philly rat, Gunna.

I wanted to go over there, break his jaw and stomp on him over and over with my size 15 foot until I could see the floor through his chest. But because of who he was, I wanted to see if Symba was who *she* was. Meaning I was about to see if this whole time, she's been knowing me and being with me was bullshit. Was she setting me up? Was she the one who mailed the letter to my parents?

I didn't want to kill her, but I swear if she was, then I was going to make her death quick. Maybe snap her neck or use Quest's method and slice her neck open. I snapped myself out my thoughts and walked over there like the boss outlaw I was. The minute she sees me, her first three reactions will tell me everything I need to know. Whether I had to kill her or not, I wasn't about to do no lame shit and say 'hi', I can tell you that much. Her hand was on her hip and she was looking though her phone.

"You look bored out'cho fucking mind," I said to her.

Symba knew my voice, so she looked up at me with wide eyes. Gunna turned around from the display of shoes he was looking at to see who she was talking to. Now things were about to get interesting. My eyes stayed on her as I took in how beautiful she looked. Her attire was sexy, but not trying like Tish was, which made me glad because that told me getting fucked wasn't on her mind.

She had on some Puma stretch shorts that stopped above her knee and a tank top that had her sides out, showing the matching sports bra. The purple Pumas on her feet were cute. Her hair was straight with a part in the middle and that gorgeous face had little to no make-up on it. That glass shit on her lips and eye lid stuff females wear. Anyway, she was stunning; her expression when she saw me was expected. Now, I wanna see how she was about to act and what she was going to say.

"What are you doing here?" She asked me, still looking nervous, not a good thing in my book.

"It's a mall, Symba baby. It's open to the public." My eyes were still on her when Gunna stood in front of us.

"Can we help you with something? You kind of all in this lovely lady's face and I ain't feelin' that," Gunna said to me.

I didn't take my eyes off Symba and hers were on me, too.

"I text you this morning, but you didn't respond. Why?" Folding her arms, the attitude she displayed was cute.

"The same reason you didn't respond to my text and calls. Look, that ain't important." I used my thumb and pointed to Gunna, still looking at her. "Explain this shit."

"Aye my nigga or whatever you are, don't point at me

and not acknowledge me like I ain't shit." Gunna stood there, acting like a child.

I chuckled and shook my head at Symba. "You into this pouting cry baby shit?"

She scratched the back of her neck and tried not to laugh. "No. I mean…He's not a cry baby—" Seeing my reaction had her stuttering and breaking up her sentences.

I arched my eyebrow and furrowed them when she sounded like she was defending him.

"I mean, we are just friends, Dominick." I believed her and was able to rest knowing I didn't have to kill her. It was pure coincidence that she knew him, now I can focus on this giant Barney acting bitch boy.

"Take her the fuck home after y'all leave here, and you keep it moving." I was serious and my expression along with my growing chest showed him that.

He laughed, looked at her and then at me. "You and the other two niggas think y'all got so much fucking pull. What I do with her ain't none of yo' business, it's her choice what we do when we leave here." He moved closer to me. "You not stupid to make a scene in front of all these people."

I didn't do shit but smile because he didn't know I wouldn't care who was around. I could kill his ass right here, right now. But, I had plans for him. Cyrus told us all about these Philly pussies. They had lives, people they loved and cared about. Oh yes, I was going to have fun with him when the time was right. I turned my attention away from him and back at Symba who was looking at me like she was hoping I wasn't about to do anything crazy.

"D, you ready?" Tish walked on the side of me, holding her bag of shoes she must have bought. I laughed to myself because I forgot she was even here.

Symba looked Tish up and down and then directed her eyes back to me with a look on her face like she wanted to slap the beard off my face. "Who is this?"

Tish was about to say something, but I held my hand up and said, "This is what happens when you play games with me." As far as I was concerned, there was nothing else to say. Symba and *Phillybury* dough boy knew where they stood with me.

"Let's go." I told Tish, and we left Footlocker, leaving them where they stood.

I made sure we didn't leave the mall until I was done, though. I didn't see them anymore and it was a chilled time with Tish. She knew not to question me about shit and she didn't. I grabbed a new blue and yellow diamond Rolex from the jewelry store for my party. I decided I wanted my three-piece suit custom, so I needed to see my tailor. I did find a good pair of Christian Louboutin loafers that was going to go perfect.

Tish got her a few things and I fronted the tab because it wasn't shit but money. A lousy grand wasn't about to put a dent on shit. After the mall, we went to eat and I kept thinking about how fine Symba looked. I bet my lifeline that after the mall, she had that clown drive her home. I know how Symba thinks; she's spoiled and used to shit going her way.

I wasn't kissing her ass and she wanted me to, so believe me, she was bothered. Tish showing up was fuel to the fire and I know I was going to hear about it ASAP. As pissed as she was, she definitely was going to want to go off face to face and I was here for it. This game she was playing had about run its course and I was collecting on the trophy. But today, right now, I was horny thinking about Symba, so you know where me and Tish were headed to.

"You look handsome as hell in that Polo, D." Tish said while drinking the rest of her wine cooler.

We were at my hoe pad and I was sitting on the couch with my arms stretched out on the back of it. I was looking at her standing a few feet in front of me. It was dark outside so I had the living room dim lights on.

"Stop calling me handsome and *handsome* pussy over my way," I said, tilting my head looking at her pussy practically fall out her skirt.

Tish smirked and took the half shirt she had on off. The strapless bra had her titties sitting up real nice. She had a big rose tattoo on her left breast and stars going down her thigh. She was about to take her bra off when someone was banging on my door so hard that it shook a little. I didn't grab my revolver because I was about to bash their head on the pavement. Opening the door, I was shocked to see Symba standing there like she was next up in the fighting ring. Before I could even say something, she pushed the door all the way open, looking at Tish standing there with no shirt on.

"You were about to fuck this nasty ass thot, or you already did?!" She yelled looking at me, but before I could answer, Tish spoke up.

"Ain't shit about me a thot baby, and you shouldn't even be here. He left yo' ass standing looking stupid at the mall."

Symba was about to charge for her, but I blocked her with my arm, laughing. I knew Symba had a crazy side, but damn.

"Get the fuck off me, Dominick! Don't be protecting this bitch!" Her wild ass was trying to hop over me to get to

Tish.

"Calm yo' ass down, woman!" I raised my voice, but I was still cracking up.

"Naw, D, let that hoe go so I can fuck her up!" Tish had her phone out, pushing something on it. I know damn well she ain't stupid enough to call the police. "D fuck this shit. You need to control your groupies better, either she leaves or I'm out. I'll just call me an Uber!"

"Well take that shit and bounce, Tish, because she ain't going nowhere." I had Symba over my shoulder, caveman style, trying to keep her tamed.

"Ha stupid, get the fuck out!" Symba yelled.

Tish was ticked off looking at me with her mouth on the floor. She came charging at Symba and was close to hitting her but I used my other free arm, blocking her. I was able to push Tish all the way out the open door.

"Vegas isn't that big bitch, I'll get at you, again!" Tish yelled.

Symba managed to climb over me and snatched

Tish's wig completely off. I ain't never seen no shit like this before face to face. Tish had these prison braids pointing in all directions. When she realized her wig was in Symba's hands, she tried to run back inside but I slammed the door, locking it. While she banged on it calling Symba every name, I stood in front of the door looking at this crazy girl holding the wig like it was nothing.

"Tish get'cho ass away from this door and get in your ride." My voice was hard enough that I knew she could hear me through the door. No one wanted to see my crazy side, so she stopped banging on it. I still heard her cussing but I saw the headlights from her ride and I heard her get inside. Looking at Symba again, I shook my head at her.

"How the fuck you even know where I was at?" I asked, really curious on how because I never had her here. We only went on dates and I would take her back home.

"I went to the complex first; Quest was there and when I told him what happened he joked about me cock blocking but he told me where your hoe house is. You didn't answer my question. Did you fuck her?" Putting her hands on her hips with a smug expression, she was still holding the wig waiting for me to answer.

I snickered and rubbed the side of my beard. "Yea I fucked her, but not today."

Symba turned her nose up and threw the wig at me, making me laugh. "You so fucking nasty!"

Getting serious I asked her, "Did you fuck ol' boy?" If she said yes, mannnn, I can't even say what I was going to do.

"No." She looked offended. "That was our first time hanging out since I gave him my number. He took me home after we left the mall." Her voice got a little low; she looked down real quick and looked back up at me with kind eyes.

I smiled to myself because she did what I said. "You bothered as fuck about seeing me with her, but you the one that won't stop playing." Symba stood quietly, but that wasn't about to work with me. "Why are you here, Symba?"

Looking down again for a second, she bit the corner

of her lip and looked at me, shrugging her shoulders. "I don't know."

I wasn't about to let her off that easily; she was going to say those words to me sooner or later. But right now, she was turning me on with how gorgeous she was and the fact that she had a crazy side. I pulled her to me and gave her a deep kiss. Her soft, fluffy lips felt amazing on mine. Our wet tongues were wrapping around each other; my hands went down her back and gripped all that peach shape ass hard.

Symba's ass was literally shaped like a perfect peach with the line down the middle of it. Anyway, as soon as I gripped it, I lifted her up by it. Her legs wrapped around my waist and her arms around my neck as I walked her to the bedroom. The time was here for me to show this fucking woman that I was done playing. She had a decision to make after this and she better make the right one.

Y'all know I don't let no female fuck me, so I was about to put the work on her. No mercy, none of her begging me to stop, either. I put her down in the middle of the floor and took my clothes off. I kept my eyes on her the entire time I was stripping. When I dropped my boxers, Symba's eyes popped open wider and she looked at me, fast as hell.

"Take your clothes off," I demanded from her while I stepped back a little.

I stroked my already hard dick slowly while she got undressed. Biting my lip, I watched her intensely strip and fuckkkk, Symba was so sexy. Her weight almost put her at plus size, but her stomach was flat; the way she was juicy and natural was everything. Her thighs touched together that I could hear that soft separating sound before I even had the chance to part them.

Her titties were Double-D's with round caramel circles and sexy, hard nipples. While she took her shoes off, I opened the drawer on the nightstand and grabbed a magnum putting it on. Her pretty feet touched the carpet as she pulled her shorts down. Her thong was black and sexy and when she pulled it down, that perfect pretty pussy had a gold light shining from it.

Her lips were fat, hairless and the same toffee complexion she was. I roughly wrapped one arm around her waist, lifting her naked body up making those chunky legs wrap around me. My strength surprised her and turned her on because as soon as her pussy touched my chest, I felt her juices. We were kissing so wild and nasty, the more we stood in the middle of the floor making out, the harder I got and the wetter she got.

I still had that one arm around her waist and the other one hanging by my side. Her skin and body felt so right against mine this close. Finally, I laid her on the bed and started licking and sucking on her neck. I put hickeys all on it on purpose. Symba was moaning and my eyes would cross her face from time to time. Hers were closed shut like she was just enjoying every single thing I was doing.

I licked from her neck til' I got back to her lips and she opened her mouth for a tongue kiss. Then, I moved down to them big, soft titties. I wanted to lick every inch of her body, so I was. Nothing was better than this; swear God made a black woman like no other. Sensual, perfect skin, and a potent energy vibration that he only chose to give to them. The right black woman was like a gift for the right man and I was showing appreciation to mine.

I licked and kissed all over her stomach and when I got to them thighs, I put hickeys all over them. I had been wanting to do this from the first time I saw her at the club I was performing at. Her pussy made a light sound and her juices spilled out a little more.

"Hold on baby, I'm coming." Grabbing her legs I bent them all the way back to her ears, automatically opening her pussy lips up like a blooming rose. I gripped my hands on her thighs so those legs would stay back.

Symba looked down at me, biting her lip. My eyes were burning looking into hers. We kept eye contact as I went in tongue first on her clit. Her head immediately fell back as I continued to lick her. I had a wide tongue and it was licking every inch of her golden goodness; I folded it and slid it inside her hole and sucked while I fucked her. I was able to wiggle in all inside her walls while pressing in against them. When I slid it out, her juices were all on it and I swallowed it all then went back on her clit.

"Ohhhh Dom...inickkkk. Oh my goodness, daddy, yes eat that pussy." Her moans was making me show the fuck out.

I put two fingers inside her tightness and used my lips as a suction on her clit. I held it in my mouth while swirling my tongue around it and finger fucking her.

Symba was losing her verbal skills. "Dom...Oh my fuck...Ahhh, I'm c-cumming! Fuck, you're the best, ughhh!!"

I was watching her while swallowing all her juices that let go in my mouth. Her head was back so far, I swear any minute now she was about to snap her neck. Her titties were jiggling while her body shook like a fucking earthquake.

My lips made a smacking sound when I released her clit and I held my head up so I could look at that soaking wet kat. It screamed loud when I slowly slid my two fingers out, which were covered in her creamy goodness.

"Mmm." I moaned while licking my fingers clean.

Symba was breathing so hard when I came up, I looked back down at her kat and it was having contractions like a muthafucka. She slowly dropped her legs, but I caught them before they could go all the way down.

"Did I say to fucking move?" I pushed them all the way back to her ears again.

"Baby, wait—" I shut that shit up with pushing my tongue in her mouth.

Symba was about to learn the most important lesson in her life: don't fuck with my feelings. I took my dick and swirled it all around the inside of her pussy lips. We both watched with just the sounds of her moistness barricading the room. Her eyes got wide when my tip pressed against her hole. Seeing how she was nervous, I looked at her.

"I would die first before I hurt you, Symba. Relax." I started sliding in and her hands gripped the sheets. Biting her bottom lip, she didn't stop me at all, her eyes looked up into mine and they were speaking to me… telling me to bring it all on; that pussy wasn't a punk pussy. I knew then that this was going to be my wife. No matter what she thinks or feel like she's not ready for, all her fear of being with me was going to leave.

"Shit. Shit. Shit, Dominick." She moaned out as I was all the way in and now fucking her so good. Her big'ole, juicy legs touching her ears had my dick in heaven. Symba was tight, wet and had a grip like a CEO's handshake.

I was doing what I said I was going to do, fucking the hell out of her. The sounds of her moaning, calling my name back to back and telling me she can't come again was everything. This was my pussy now, I owned it, but I wasn't going to tell her that because I knew she wasn't ready. I knew after we fucked she was going to still be scared. It was going to take me to show my ass just like she did today for her to understand that we *will* be together.

"Ooo, shit, Sym, tight ass pussy you got." I let slip

out, but I couldn't help it, her shit was gripping. I looked at her and she had her mouth open, but no sound coming out. "You 'bout to cum, I can tell. Scream that shit out my Queen, let it out, baby." I put my hand on her neck and squeezed just a little and she came so good.

"Argh...Uhhhh...Ahhh, yes!" Shit, her cries were so sexy.

I got on my knees and slid my dick out slowly because the sight was unbelievable. Once it was all the way out, I grabbed it and slapped it on her clit a few times while her juices poured out. She was breathing even harder from when I ate her out. I let her legs down and looked at her with a big grin. Symba's eyes were low, and she gave me a sexy smirk. I bit my lip looking at her perfect, naked body. We both watched my dick get longer and before she could object, I flipped her thick ass over and put that ass in the air. We were about to be at it for some time, so she might as well fall back and let it happen.

MARLO

I watched Nina pull up at her job in a new Camry. I knew she wasn't driving her old car that I bought her because I would have been tracked her down. That car was parked in my driveway. One day I woke up and it was just there. I knew it was her doing and it pissed me off even more. All her belongings were still at our house. Every day from when Nina was released from jail after our son died, she always kept his pictures with her.

I wish she didn't because I knew that would make her come home. I've been around this damn girl for ten years; I had that pussy first and I was the only nigga to ever touch her. She gave me my first son. Even though he died, it still counts. We had history. An entire life to live together; I was going to get my shit right and spoil her with everything. I don't know why this stupid bitch thought she could stay away from me, like I'm something that can easily be erased.

Nina was mine and always would be. The only way she would get rid of me was by killing herself or me killing her. I had been found her weeks ago going to work. I decided to sleep in my car parked in the alley a few buildings down from her job. Every morning, her boss would make sure he was outside when she pulled up, looking around and making sure I wasn't anywhere in sight. At first, I thought they were fucking.

I always thought they were fucking because he always looked out for Nina. From the moment he hired her, and she didn't have a license, I said he wanted her. Nina of course denied it and I knew I had nothing to worry about when it came to her because she loved the ground I walked on. Cheating wasn't even her character, but that didn't mean that old poot didn't want her. Every time Nina was in a bind, he was right there and even sometimes his wife.

I don't know what kind of freaky shit they were on, but no one was that damn nice to their employees. Anyway, I saw with my own eyes that I was wrong, Nina wasn't fucking that old nigga. She was giving my pussy to Angel, The fucking Law. Y'all knew how the fuck I felt about them as far as how they run shit.

I never had an issue with them or wanted to be in any business with them in any kind of way. I break into houses, snatch purses, rob corner boys and stash houses. I wasn't on no outlaw, Robin Hood shit that The Law was on, so I always figured it was best to stay out of each other's way and I made good of that until I saw Angel take Nina to work.

I was high off some shit so I had to blink my eyes over and over to make sure I was seeing the truth. He pulled up in this G-Class with chrome and opened the passenger door for her. Nina didn't even look like herself; she was smiling widely and had a glow about her. Her style was still the same, but the clothes she wore were on her differently. It was like she wore them with happiness, peace and confidence again like when I met her.

Then, I watched them share a weak ass laugh. Angel

was saying some shit in her ear, making her blush. He had his hands on her waist, back, her round booty and she was all on him, too. Her small hands kept touching his arms and his face. I knew then that this wasn't just a fuck, I could handle that. This was love. Nina was in love with him, but what I was looking at was something I never seen her have with me.

It was like she admired that nigga, like he was mentioned in her punk ass prayers she says every night. When they finally parted ways, he watched until she went inside, and it was like they didn't want to be apart. When Angel pulled off, I had so many homicidal thoughts run through my mind. How could she do this to me and so easily without even giving us another thought?

What about our life, our son and our commitment to each other? Now look at her; she was getting out her car while talking on her phone. Smiling again and probably talking to Angel, I bet she doesn't even know the kind of nigga she has. Nina wasn't a street bitch at all; she wasn't about that life so I knew when she found out she would run for the hills.

But right now, I was breathing so hard, sweating while looking at her through the telescope of my gun. I swear I should pull the trigger and just end her right now. The betrayal, the fact that someone else was touching her, inside of her and making her happy. Why wasn't I good enough? Nina was looking for any excuse to leave me, probably been messing with Angel for years and she used one little fuck up I did as a reason to dip.

"Why you doing this shit to me, Nina?" I said to myself.

I was shaking so badly because my adrenaline was high from my thoughts, the cocaine and molly I was on. I had sweat dripping from my top lip as my fingertip touched the trigger. This shot would kill her and even though I wouldn't have her anymore, neither would Angel. As she walked to the entrance, my heart raced rapidly. My chance was slipping away as she got closer to the door. Finally, she went inside, and I dropped my gun on the seat so I could take a deep breath.

I was so in my feelings that tears were coming down my face, I loved the hell out of Nina. I wasn't about to live without her in my life and I damn sure wasn't about to let her be with anybody else. It was like she was rubbing it in my face; she had to know I was watching her. How could she not think that I would give up and just let her be?

It's like she doesn't even care about my feelings, like I'm some lame ass nigga who will bow out easily. Looking at her job and car one more time, I pulled off. I'm glad I didn't kill her just then, even though she called herself moving on with Angel. I still wasn't giving up, she was hearing me out and we were fixing this or the outcome would be her in a body bag.

**

"Oh, fuck!" I yelled out when I shot a load of my cum all in his warm hole. I needed this stress relief and the molly had me on a hundred in energy. My entire body was sweating from the hard fucking I just did.

"Yo', did you send them fools you run with to Nina's mama's house?" I asked Tino while I put my boxers and basketball shorts back on. I came to his crib for some more coke and to chill before I went home. I had been meaning to catch up to him when I heard about Nina's mama. Wasn't nobody about to fuck with her and leave Nina's fine ass untouched. It had Tino's name written all over it.

"Yea, I did, because I told you to handle that bitch and you didn't." He said looking at me with his nostrils flared like a wild boar.

"What the fuck you mean handle Nina? Wasn't shit to handle because she ain't said nothing. I told you she wasn't, so what you did was a waste of time and messy as hell."

Tino snapped, picked up his machine gun and came at me. "Naw, what the fuck I did was send that uppity bitch a warning! What I did was make sure my street cred was secured because you wouldn't do it!" He held the gun on the side of my forehead.

I moved it down slowly. "You need to chill, Tino,

ain't nobody said shit because that's not her. She'd rather break up with me and act like I don't exist, plus it would make her look like a fool. It's done and over, she ain't even friends with yo' sister anymore. I know Nina, she just wants to put that shit behind her." I was looking at him so he knew I wasn't lying, which I wasn't. Nina wasn't about to be blabbing that shit around. It would have been happened by now.

"As long as she stays quiet then it's all good, but I had to send a message." He walked away, back over to his tray with all the weed on it.

"You got any more hits you know about? I ran through the money we took from Mrs. Newman." I asked him, putting my rolled up blunt behind my left ear.

Tino sat on the edge of his bed so he could put his weed in dime bags. "Fuck that change, I got some more work that you might be into. He only needs two more guys, so you'll have to pick between Mick, Reese and Abe. Just make sure they don't fuck anything up."

"What's the job?" Putting my Adidas on, I leaned on his closed bedroom door, waiting for him to answer me.

"My boy Gunna from Philly need some dirty work done," Tino answered.

"Why won't you do it?"

"Nigga I am. He needs more guys, so I told him about you. Don't embarrass me, Marlo, I'm tryna get put on permanently doing business with him."

"What kind of business does he do?" I asked now, because money always got my attention.

"He into the hoe business; his bitches clean up big every night and they about to be taking over Las Vegas."

I laughed. I wasn't scared of The Law but I wasn't trying to take over anything. All I cared about was having money in my pocket and eating every day. "Shittt, them niggas must don't know. In order to take over anything here, they gotta get through The Law. It's best if they just make their little change low key and stay out the way."

Tino looked up at me from his tray. "Naw, my nig,

Gunna and his people the real deal. I been knowing him for some years."

I turned my nose up, not out of no in-my-feelings shit, but because I didn't know Tino got down like that. "You know him the way you know me?"

He put his tray down, picked up his gun and walked in front of me with a hateful expression on his face. He was already a little wider than me, had a bottom gold grill and tats everywhere.

"Ask me that shit again my G. Come at me again like I'm some fag ass nigga."

I wasn't scared of shit, so I put my hard face on and pulled my gun out. "You think you the only one with heat, Tino? You not about to keep pulling no gun on me—"

"You questioning me like I ain't no full grown man about some homo shit! That's asking to die, is'chu a fag or something?"

I pushed him. "Hell naw you son-of-a-bitch, ain't a bone on me gay!" I gripped the handle of my gun tighter. "I just wanted to know how good you know the nigga. You basically telling me they tryna snatch this city from The Law. I'm not scared of them, but I'm not tryna be down with some shit that's gone fail."

"All I do is win G, so if you down then you gone win, too."

I nodded my head and put my gun back on my waist. "Aight, then I'm in." I told him as I opened his bedroom door and headed out.

On my ride to my crib, I thought about The Law and how it's time for them to get got. I don't even know the plan, but I was down. This would make it so I wouldn't have to kill Nina; killing Angel would for sure guarantee her back to me. If Tino says these niggas are good, then I believed him; besides, I like working with a lot of people. That way I'd flip the switch and have them get killed before me...I would turn sides with whoever was losing and go straight over to the winning team no matter who I had to lie on, set up or kill. I wanted my life back, my woman, I wanted us to get married and have more kids. I missed Nina so damn much, that's why I stayed so high on something so I wouldn't have to think about her all day. Like right now, as soon as I got home, I showered, put boxers on and fixed me a sandwich.

After I ate I went in my bedroom which I kept the same as if Nina was walking through the door any minute. Sitting down, I took my glass tre\ay from under my nightstand and snorted two lines. Nina didn't even know that she was killing me by treating me this way. I never popped this many pills or snorted this much when we were together. It's like she doesn't even care about shit but erasing me. Putting the tray back down, I picked up my phone and went to PornoHub website.

Getting high always made my dick hard and I would fuck Nina for hours. Her pussy was like no other and not because it was mine or untouched. I pulled my dick out and started jacking it off slowly. The video was turning me on; I only liked watching black on black people fucking because it was more realistic.

"Hell yes, fuck that asshole good."

I bit my lip watching this big black nigga give dick to this Tyga looking nigga. You could tell his ass wasn't blown out because it took him a minute to get in. What else I loved was he wasn't wearing a condom; I hated them and loved sex without it. I felt my breathing picking up when all of a sudden, I heard glass shattering. I put my dick up, picked my shorts off the floor and put them on. Grabbing my .9, I hurried to the door as more glass started breaking.

"Yo' what the fuck are you doing!?" I yelled at Talia.

She was standing in front of my house with a garbage bag of bottles and was throwing them at my crib. "Fuck youuuu, Marlo!" Her words slurred out and she was about to throw another bottle, but I ran up and caught her. The liquor was strong as hell coming from her and I knew then she was pissy drunk.

"Talia, have you lost your fucking mind?!"

Snatching away from me she said, "No! But I lost my best friend because of you and my brother wanna be—"

I put my hand over her mouth and snatched her in my house. "Get'cho drunk, sloppy ass in here! I swear I never liked yo' ass when Nina was hanging with you." I spit at her.

"I wouldn't give a damn, I told her to run from yo' black ass but she didn't listen. You're a faggot, you and my brother."

Because she was Tino's sister, it was saving her right now. Her skinny, raggedy ass was sitting on the arm of my couch, all fucked up. Talia always had long hair in her head whether it was braids or that straight shit. Hood rat at its finest.

"I ain't no damn faggot, and if your brother hear you say that, you might be eating them words." I told her drunk ass.

Talia staggered up and flipped her hair. I swear if this hoe throws up, I was going to make her sleep in it. Instead, she unbuttoned her shorts, pulled them down, challenged me and said.

"Prove it."

SYMBA

"I can't believe you are a high school senior; seems like yesterday you and your mom came in to enroll you."

I smiled at Lanail. I was at work and since it was the end of summer, a lot of the students who attended the summer classes were going back to regular school. For some of them, this was their last year because they would be seniors and the program here is from three years old to eighteen. Lanail was one of my favorite students and she's been enrolled in the summer program since her freshman year. Four years came and went so fast; that's how long I've been an aide here.

After high school, I didn't go straight to college. I took three years off school and worked at the mall, paid my rent to Mama and had fun. I assumed she would flip on me for not wanting to go to college right away, but if I worked and paid her $150 a month, she told me to take time a discover myself. When I hit twenty-one, I decided to rent a house with Christian and go to college. Because of my major, I got a job as a teacher aide at a dance school.

It wasn't like the school I wanted to have of my own, but I loved working here. The fall/winter season, professional dancers enrolled here and then in the summer it was open to the public. My school would be just like a general school including the education of dance. You'd be able to get a high school diploma at my school. Anyway, I graduate next fall and I probably would still be working here. It pays good and my boss knew what my goal was, so she educated me on how the school operates.

"I know, I can't wait to go dress shopping for prom and start saving for my senior trip." Lanail grinned at me all excitedly.

"It's going to be so fun; my senior class went to Miami for our trip and girl, I had the best time." I shared with her. Lanail was helping me clean up the dance room until her aunt came and picked her up. As she was sweeping, I noticed she had a very nice white gold bracelet and watch on. The diamonds were shining brightly; I don't know how I missed it.

"That's a really nice bracelet and watch girl." I smiled and said.

"Thank you, my aunt and mama brought it for me for senior year."

"Oh shoot! You deserve it Lanail. You get good grades and have more credits than required to graduate. I'm very proud of you, too."

"Thank you, Symba." She gave me a warm hug. "Can I talk to you about anything and it stays between me and you?"

"Well yes, but if it's something that I think will cause you harm then I can't ignore that." I told her honestly.

"Ok. Um I have a friend. She's older than me, not that much older... she's nineteen. She told me about a new job she got that pays good and helps her pay some of the bills her mama has." Lanail seemed a little jumpy as she was talking. "At first I didn't care, but she started wearing a lot of nice things and always having money—" She stopped talking when her phone rang.

"I gotta go, my ride is here." Lanail scrambled getting her things together.

"Lanail wait, what was the—"

"Nothing, please forget about what I said." She rushed out the room and ran down the hall so fast I couldn't get out the door fast enough.

I went back to the window and watched her go out the doors. The car she got into wasn't her aunt's car, it was a white and red Challenger. I hurried up and went to the camera on my phone and took pictures of it and the driver. He was older, looked to be in his early thirties. When he got out and opened the trunk for Lanail to put her bags inside, I saw the name *Money* tattooed big on his arm. I took pictures of all that shit, what I did notice was they did not embrace.

Lanail was a seventeen-year-old girl. If he were her

nigga she would have blushed, touched him or smiled at him. Instead she got in the car and they did not even speak, what the hell. Lanail's family were from the hood. Her aunt and mama worked some bullshit jobs, they stayed in a three-bedroom house with Lanail two siblings who are under ten.

The only reason she can come here in the summer is because the program is free. I've given her lunch money a few times but that still doesn't mean she needed to be out here doing anything dangerous. I went to Mrs. Lupe, her dance teacher's, laptop and got Lanail's number. I sent her a quick text.

Me: Lanail it's Symba. I just wanted to tell you that you can talk to me about anything. Now that you have my number, call me anytime day or night. I promise I'll come.

I put my phone back in my purse and tried to finish working while trying not to worry about Lanail. I let work distract me all the way up until it was time for me to go home.

"I think she's a stripper, you know there are so many

strip-clubs that hire underage girls to dance," Christian said as she sat in the kitchen with me while I cooked.

After work, I stopped at the grocery store to pick some food up and then I came home. After my shower, I threw on some pajama shorts and a wire bra then I came in here to cook. I was annoyed not only by Lanail, but I had some other shit on my mind too. So of course, I was making some greens with my turkey leg, cornbread, and I decided to throw some macaroni and cheese with it too. Christian was already home from work, so she came in here to talk to me and I told her about Lanail.

"I think so, too." I turned my nose up. "You should have seen the guy; he was cute but he had that 'ain't shit' look about him." I took my phone out, went to the pics and showed her.

"He do look good, but yup, he looks like he fucks old women for their social security checks."

I snatched my phone laughing at her. "Why do you always got to say some stupid shit?!"

"So, I get why that will have you bent but ummm, you not just cooking greens." I looked at her and she was smirking. "What else is wrong with my auntie Sym-Sym?"

Rolling my eyes, I figured I might as well tell her. "Me and Dominick slept together."

"Wheeeeew, chile!" My dumbass niece got up dancing, laughing and acting all wild. "You done shamed all our ancestors and gave the white devil some punanny! Yessss!"

I stood there looking at her, shaking my head and trying not to laugh.

"Oh shit girl, you got my got damn titty falling out my shirt." She finally sat down while fixing her shirt. "Ok. Ok. Tell me everything, and don't leave shit out."

"You sure you ready to hear this, with yo' crazy ass?!" I asked her, chuckling.

"Spill, bih!"

I began telling her about what happened at the mall. Then I told her about me going to the complex and talking to

Quest. When I told her I went to Dominick's spot, Christian was shocked as hell. I told her about that stupid thot he had over there and me snatching her wig off.

"That's exactly what I would have did, threw her ass out the house with her prison braids." Christian joked.

"Girl, that bitch was trying me to the fullest and I was ready to fuck her up. Bad enough when we were at the mall she walked up on Dominick and put her hand on his arm. I swear I wanted to break it off." I was getting upset just thinking about it.

"Christian, having sex with Dominick was something I've never experienced before. I planned to put it on his ass, but babyyyy, that man had me folded like a closed piece of luggage. Then when he ate me out that long hair was hanging and those cat-like eyes were looking at me. It was like watching a wild lion slowly drink some water.

He didn't fuck me like I imagined; he was in control and wouldn't let me forget it. The next morning, he was holding me tight as fuck and his dick was poking me all in my back. Next thing I knew, I was bent over taking every inch he had again. *Every* inch he had!" I snapped out of my recap daze and looked at Christian.

"Damn Symba, you got it bad. I have never seen you like this." She wasn't laughing, but her mouth was open and she was looking at me like I was a project.

"I can't stop thinking about him, Christian. It was like that before, but now that we have reached a new level, I stay with him on my mind. Before I left him the next day, I told him we were still not a couple." I started shredding my cheese for the macaroni.

"Why the hell did you do that if you got it bad for him?" She hit her forehead.

I stopped for a second and stared at the cheese. "I don't know...he scares the fuck out of me, niece. I've never fought over a guy or pulled up on one the way I did with him. I know I wouldn't be able to take it if he plays me." My eyes watered. "I watched what love and relationships—" I stopped talking because I didn't want to hurt her feelings.

"I know auntie; we haven't exactly been a good example for you, but then again, you can't let that get in your way. Life happens to everyone; hearts get broken but it's what you do after. It's what you learn from it, that's all that matters. If you let Dominick slip away, you'll always wonder *what if*. Don't do that to yourself. I think you love him."

I hurried and looked at her, but I couldn't say anything. I couldn't deny or agree with what she just said; I'd never said those words to anyone aside from my family. I didn't even know how it felt to be in love, but I did know it made me sick to my stomach the thought of if Dominick and I failed.

"Auntie." Christian called out to me.

"Huh?"

"You're about to shred your damn fingers off if you don't stop."

I looked down at all the cheese I just shredded and I had a tiny cube left in my hand. "Oh, shit. I don't know if I love him, but I do know I don't like where we are."

Christian laughed and I only did because she was laughing so hard.

"What, slut?"

"How the hell you don't like where you and Dominick are when you're the one who put y'all there?"

I smacked my lips. "Yea, but he was supposed to be all up my ass. I gave him some of this good-good, he should be calling, texting and on me. Instead he acts like he doesn't even care that I friend-zoned him. I thought white boys were supposed to climb ladders for you to declare their love outside of your bedroom window."

I was so serious, and Christian's ass started cracking up. "Naw, white boys do shit like break in your house when you're not home and smell yo' shit. They another type of crazy."

"I don't think that's crazy, I think that's commitment," I said stirring my pot of greens.

Christian looked at me like I had two heads. "You're a weirdo. Anyway, basically you just mad because he's not pressed. Girl, if you don't stop acting childish."

I looked at her throwed, with my hands on my hip, I scoffed. "Since when…when the hell does the mistress of Vegas get all this wisdom? You usually love how I treat these niggas, well in Dominick's case…Naw, fuck that. He acting like a nigga, so he's one too, but what happened to you?" I turned to her after I put my macaroni in the oven.

"You so stupid, and nothing happened to me, I'm just seeing things different."

"Mm." I said, putting the lid over my pot. "Does Quest have anything to do with this? Y'all claim to be done, but ummm, night before last I could have sworn I heard him in the kitchen." I smirked looking at her.

"Oh, my goodness, that nigga is addictive. We said some foul shit to each other last week and I was done. But he blew me up and when I didn't answer, he popped up over here. I planned on cussing his ass out but we know how that worked. You know that fucker told me I'm his, but I'm not his. Ol' funky bitch."

We both laughed as the front door opened and we both knew who it was.

"Nina-Bina!" We said smiling in unison. Seems like we haven't seen her in a minute, but we all worked and I had school so it seemed a little normal.

"Hey my pookies—" She stopped when she saw the food on the stove. "Oh, yes. I love when you're mad and I didn't have lunch today." After she hugged us, she grabbed a chair and set next to Christian.

The macaroni wasn't done yet, so I got started on my cornbread. "What's been up, Nina? I feel like you've been missing?" I asked her while taking out two Jiffy cornbread mix boxes.

"I know, right? I've been working so much, plus furnishing my new place." Nina moved into a nice, one-bedroom apartment last month and we were so happy for her. Marlo was completely out of the picture and it was like sex wrapped in a big dick. "But that's why I'm here; let's have a girl's night tonight."

Me and Christian looked at each other and then at Nina.

"Like watch movies all night or a club?" Christian asked.

I wanted to see what Nina meant too, because she hasn't been clubbin' with us since we were teens. I just knew she wasn't talking about an actual club.

"I mean a club, a nice ass one, too. Let's get dolled up, dance, drinks and just have a good time." When she looked from me to Symba all excited, I think we both were about to lose our shit. Nina was smiling and it immediately made my eyes water, again.

"Nina-Bina you're smiling! Oh, my goodness, who is cutting onions in this kitchen?!" Christian yelled as she hugged Nina.

I hugged her too and she wiped my tears. "You a cry baby, auntie."

"I swear I'm not trying to, but damn niece, it feels so good seeing you smile. Hell yea, we are going out tonight.

Grown and Sexy is the theme and we are living it up!"

I did a spin in my full-length mirror, as I was looking drop dead sexy. I wore some tight jeans that were ripped on the sides, exposing a little side cheek action. My top was a light pink crop that hugged me and fell off my shoulders. I un-did the first three buttons so my pretty breasts could peek out. I put my feet in some blush color pumps and I parted my hair on the side, did my baby hair and ran my fingers through my wand curls. No make-up tonight, just some lip gloss and my eyebrows were done.

"Sexyyyy!" Christian said when she came in my room. My coco niece's skin was flawless, as usual, and her slim-thick frame was in some olive-green jeggings. Her shape was perfect, and she had on a white tight tube top, I loved the Burberry heels she wore.

"Thank you. Your hair is straight tonight, damn you look like trouble for any man." I teased her.

"Y'all ready?" Nina came in our room and once

again, our mouths dropped. She was always beautiful, but we hadn't seen this side of her in years. Her floral black romper fit her body like a glove and her booty looked good sitting up as the romper squeezed right under her cheeks. Her long hair was straight as well, with a side part and her pretty legs were in a pair of black ankle strap heels.

"Nina-Bina!" We geeked her up, making her crack up.

"Hell yes, tonight is about to be hella hot!" I said while I took my phone out and ordered our SUV Lyft ride.

Drop that pussy bitch

What ya twerkin' wit'?

I'm young Papi,

Champagne they know the face, and they know the name

Drop that pussy bitch

What you twerkin' with?

Work, work, work, work, bounce

French Montana-Pop That was playing all through

the club. Me and my two nieces were tearin' it the fuck up on the floor. *Lust* was a new joint that opened about three years ago. Me and Christian have been wanting to come here for a while. We used to talk about dragging Nina out with us; every celebrity that comes to Las Vegas makes their way to this spot. It was sexy, exclusive and the music was a whole mood.

We had been out for about an hour and it felt so good because it was all three of us. We had a little section, enjoyed some drinks, took in the atmosphere for a second and now we were ready to turn-up. The men in here were from the window to the damn wall and they looked good. Of course, they were on the three of us so tough, but we flirted and kept it pushing. I started twerking in front of Christian and Nina was twerking in front of her.

"Ayeeee!"

Get it, bish!"

"Aye! Ayeeeee!!" We were hyping each other up, dancing to the beat. This was the third straight song we had danced to. The women were so bent because their niggas' eyes were on us, but we didn't give a fuck. Hell, I blew a kiss at one girl who was looking bothered.

"Whew! It's hot, let's get a drink and head back to our table," Nina said to us and we agreed.

We locked arms and made our way to the bar. "Can we get three whiskey sours?!" Christian told the bartender over the loud music. While we waited for our drinks, we were dancing where we stood to the music. *Chris Brown-Tempo* was playing so the feel mellowed out. I snapped my fingers while singing along. Some fine ass guy walked past me and Nina but stopped in front of Christian. They laughed and flirted with each other; me and Nina talked about the way some of these bitches were dressing until the bartender gave us our drinks. Christian gave the guy her phone and he put his number in it.

"Bish, he was fine!" I teased her as we walked back with our drinks to our section.

"I know right, I haven't had any new beef since I met

Quest. He still got his bitch so it's time for me to get me something."

I shook my head laughing. When we made it back to our little section, the waitress was cleaning up and she had the small 'Open' sign sitting back on the table.

"Um excuse me, this was our section that we paid for." Christian was the first to say something to the waiter. Hell, we paid a hundred dollars for this section and that's not even VIP.

"Oh I apologize, my boss told me to open it back up. He moved you ladies to VVIP." She pointed up to the club's third floor, which was like a whole other club.

When we looked up, Angel was standing at the top, looking directly at Nina. Me and Christian looked at her and that girl's cheeks were turning red as hell. He was holding a drink in his hand and he tilted it towards the elevator, telling us to come up. We locked arms again and made our way through the crowd.

"You ok over there?" I asked Nina, laughing because

she was looking anxious as hell and she started fixing her hair.

"What? Oh, yeah, I'm fine." She answered, giving us a fake big smile. "I didn't even know he was here or that he manages this place. Fuck, he looks good."

She was surprising me and Christian over and over tonight from the moment she asked us to go out. It was different seeing her actually get butterflies and blush about someone who wasn't Marlo's booty-bandit ass.

"Damn sis, you like him! Y'all should go out or something." Christian's loud ass said, sticking her tongue out.

"We've already gone out." Nina responded.

"What!?" Me and Christian said in unison.

Nina gave us a guilty, nervous grin. "Um yeah, we are sort of together."

"What!?" We repeated ourselves as the elevator door opened, and she practically skipped off.

"Bitch, don't you think that's some tea you should

have spilled all on our lap?" I didn't have to shout so loud up here, because the velvet walls made the music not boom so loud. There were other people up here. The sections were separated by long round booths, a mini bar, two stripper poles and a curtain you could choose to close or not.

"I was going to tell y'all tonight when we got home," she said, holding my hand while I had Christian's.

"You gave him some?" She asked Nina and this damn girl smiled and bit her lip.

If y'all could see me and Christian's faces right now! It was excitement mixed with shock and a little bit of annoyance because Nina knows she should have been told us. "Oh, so he's the working overtime you were talking about. Bitch, you owe us big time when we get home." Christian said, and I agreed laughing.

We finally made it to Angel who was in the VVIP part, broken off from regular VIP. He was still standing in the same spot. When he turned and saw us, his eyes were glued to my niece. They were admiring her from head to toe.

I know Christian was feeling like I was; he loved her. You could tell.

"What's up, Christian, Symba." He looked at us and spoke, then his eyes went right back on Nina. "You had fun out there shaking all my ass for the world to see?" Angel grabbed her hand, pulled her to him and kissed her so deeply I think every woman in here felt the heat. His hand was on her lower back, practically pressing her into him.

"Ladies, would you please excuse us? I need to talk to my woman. Right around that corner is my section. It's food and drinks, help yourself." He told us without taking his eyes off Nina.

Me and Christian were cheesing hard like some creeps and we nodded our heads ok. I grabbed her hand and we walked off to the section.

"That muthafucka is all man, just what she needs." Christian said to me.

"I know right she—" I stopped when we got to the section. Dominick and Quest were sitting down drinking and smoking weed.

"Ouch shit, bitch, damn." Christian snatched her hand from mine because I was squeezing it too hard.

"Sorry." I said low, trying to take my eyes off of Dominick, but it was hard.

He was leaning back with his legs wide and looking like an entire buffet. His hair was in that high man bun I love and that mahogany color beard was freshly lined up. I just wanted to kiss his lips and look in those cat-like eyes. The jeans he had on were black and draped off him perfectly, but what I love the most was how the Fendi shirt he had on was tight on him. I could see that hard chest, those pecs and those big ass, muscular arms. Oh gosh, my pussy just squeaked. That's what he was teasing me about the day after we had sex. He kept saying she was making a squeaky sound every time he went deep.

"Why the fuck y'all standing there looking stupid?! Don't act shy now; you were just face down ass up on the dance floor." Quest cracked as he walked towards us.

"Um, excuse me, but whatever I do with my ass is my business so close your damn mouth." Christian folded her arms and rolled her eyes.

"And the last time I remember, you ain't my daddy." I said back to his smart ass, too. Quest was always saying some loud silly shit. Swear, I hope him and Christian get together because they act just alike.

He looked at Christian and gave her a nasty look. "It is my business when I'm the one eatin' that ass."

I fell out laughing and so did Christian. "Quest, you can eat my ass all day, but at the end of the day, I still don't belong to you. Now move, because I'm hungry." She walked off towards the table of food that was behind the booth. He followed her, cussing her out and she was cussing right back at his ass.

Oh shit, I was left standing alone with nothing to do but go sit down. Maybe I should sit across...hell naw, I wasn't even about to front. I wanted to sit next to him. What I don't like is how nervous I was, especially because we've had sex. He's literally licked and sucked on me inside and out, but yet my nerves and butterflies were through the roof. I flipped my hair and walked over to where he was and sat down.

"Get up and sit on my lap."

"What?" I asked to make sure I heard what he said. Dominick looked at me like he wasn't about to repeat himself. I cleared my throat, got up and sat on his lap. Immediately, I felt that thick dick.

His right hand went up and down my back slowly and then to my waist. Repeating his touch, I looked back at him and he was biting his lip while watching his hand trace me. My skin was on fire and goosebumps started forming. Then his eyes met mine and he pulled me back to him by my arm. He then began kissing me. Oh, fuck, this man had me in every way imagined. My hand laid on his big arm. He kept his legs the same way as if my juicy ass weren't even on them.

"Why the fuck you showing out like that?" He got

wrinkles in his forehead.

"I wasn't showing out, I was dancing and having fun." I told him, still nose to nose with his face.

Dominick smelled so damn good, then he put his nose on my neck and inhaled my scent. I loved when he did that because his lips would graze my neck a little. It gave me shivers and I bet y'all can feel it too.

"Naw, that looked like showing out to me." He pulled my ear to his mouth and whispered. "Do I gotta fuck you up with this dick again?" His voice had a hard grunt to it, then he licked my ear, causing me to release a small moan.

"Why have you been acting funny towards me?" I asked him, trying not to stare in his eyes the way he did mine, but it was hard.

"I would never act funny towards you." He responded eyes dead on me.

"I can't tell, but if you say so. What have you been up to these past few days? Or shall I say who?" My eyebrow curved up, waiting for him to answer.

He gave off a cocky laugh. "I work every day, Symba baby. Not a day goes by that I don't make money.

"And what about girls, you been in they face?" I know I shouldn't ask what I don't want to know, but I don't care.

"I'm never in anyone's face, they be in mine."

I wanted to smack the smirk off his face. I turned my nose up at him. "Well, I'm not about to be one of them." I said, about to get up but he wrapped around my waist tighter.

"You ain't bout to go no damn where; you gone sit that juicy ass right here and stop acting like a child. Now, you made it clear that we weren't together, so." He shrugged and put his blunt out in the gold ashtray next to him.

"Yeah but—"

"Ain't no fuckin' buts. If you not mine, then ain't no in between." He had a grimness to his face underlined with no fucks given. My feelings were kind of hurt and I was ready to go.

"Let me up." I said to him and I swear I wasn't

playing, I wanted him away from me.

When he unlocked his arms from around my waist and looked at me like 'bye,' I got up and tried not to cry. I've never behaved this way before, I hoe men all day, every day. Now I'm in my feelings over this man. Quest and Christian were sitting down across from us; she was eating and he was looking at her like he wanted to kick her ass. Christian looking unbothered made me laugh and I was able to shadow my tears from falling. I went over to the food and three guys were coming from around the corner towards my direction.

"Got damn boo, gimme some of that fat ass." The dark skin guy said then he squeezed my ass cheek.

Before I could go off on him, Dominick hopped over the table and ran towards the guy like lightening. I blinked and he was punching the guy in his face so hard, I didn't even know a punch had an actual sound. When Angel and Quest came over, I thought they were about to break it up but they looked at the guy's friends. Those two scary niggas held their hands up and stepped back while allowing Dominick to beat their friend's ass. I mean he was on top of him just punching over and over.

"Stop him!" I yelled at Quest and Angel. They both blocked me from interfering.

"It's best to let him get it out, baby sister, trust me. He ain't himself when he get like that." Angel said.

"He'll kill that poor man!" Christian said and Quest shook his head no to her.

"He won't kill him, he might make it so the nigga will eat through a straw for a while, but he won't kill him."

Fuck this. I hurried and pushed through their big asses, but it was useless so I ran around them and grabbed Dominick's arm. "That's enough, Dominick stop!" I shouted at him.

"Get the fuck off me!" He snatched away from me and hit the guy again.

Hell no. I stepped back and this time, my tears fell. I wasn't about to stay here and take this shit.

"Symba!" I heard Nina and Christian call out to me as

I hurried away from all of this.

"I'm fine, I wanna be alone!" I yelled behind me as I reached the elevator. As soon as I pressed the down button, it opened and I got on.

Taking my phone out I ordered my Lyft and made my way through the club until I reached outside. I should have just left the first time he hurt my feelings. Now this nigga gone yell at me for trying to stop his crazy ass? No sir, I'm out, and I never want to talk to Dominick again. My phone rang back to back and it was either Nina or Christian. Ignoring them, I sent them a quick text.

Me: I'm in a Lyft on my way home. Have fun but I don't want anything to do with that son-of-a-bitch anymore.

I put my phone back in my purse, sat back and looked out the window of the car. See, this is why I stayed away from feelings, relationships and love. It's all messy and drama, I wanna kick Dominick's ass when he practically admitted that he was around bitches. He said everything as if he didn't care, then dismissed me off his lap. Nobody does that to me; men practically begged at my feet to even get me to return a phone call. Dominick was so cocky and I hated that I liked it so much.

"Thank you," I said to the driver as I got out the car. When I closed the door, I looked on my porch and rolled my eyes because Dominick was on our porch chairs with his feet propped up on the ottoman. See, he just did everything like he was the shit, ugh!

"You know you're right, my mama can be a bitch." He said putting his feet down.

"Huh?"

"In the text, you called me a son-of-a-bitch, you're right." He chuckled and stood up walking towards me.

I folded my arms and grimed him. "Did you kill that man?"

He shook his head no. "He's at our complex getting fixed up then he'll be sent on his way."

I grabbed the bridge of my nose. "You're speaking with no remorse."

"Because I don't have an ounce in me for that clown ass muthafucka. He touched you, Symba, so I reacted. I apologize for doing that in front of you and I deeply apologize for snapping at you. I'm a different person when my temper kicks in, but you need to know I would never hurt you." His eyes were so soft, completely different from what I saw earlier. They were pleading for me to believe him and I did.

"You were unrecognizable and psycho like," I told him honestly.

"I know and I hate you saw that, but then again it's good you did because I don't want to hide shit from you about me." He walked so close to me my back pressed against the front door. "I have three questions for you."

"Ok." I answered while looking at his handsome face. Dominick was so close to me, he smelled so good and it was turning me on. I bit my lip looking at him and my breathing was speeding up.

"Do you forgive me?" He asked me his first question.

357

"Yes, I do." I answered.

He trailed his index finger down the side of my face then he lifted my chin up some, asking me his second question. "Will you be my woman, no games or confusion. All mine and I'll be all yours."

I didn't even need time to think, I knew what I wanted and I was done playing hard to get. "Yes, Dominick, I'll be your woman."

He gave me the biggest, sexiest smile and I returned the gesture. Kissing me hungrily, we both got lost for a second.

"What's your third question?" I asked him, both of us breathing hard.

"Will you ride somewhere with me?"

I was a little surprised he asked me that, but I agreed. "Sure." Taking my hand, we walked to his truck and got in.

**

"Is this your home?" I asked when we pulled up to this gorgeous palace-like home.

"Yes, it is." He answered and turned his truck off. "Before we go inside, I need to tell you something." It was quiet in the truck and in his neighborhood.

I nervously looked at him because I didn't know what he was about to say. "Is it bad?" I asked him, trying not to look panicky but I couldn't help it.

Dominick gave a light chuckle and got out his truck. I watched him come to my side and open the door. He undid my seatbelt and turned me around to face him.

"I've never, ever brought a woman here because this is my peace, my haven. Now you're becoming that, so it feels right that I bring you here. I don't want to play with you, Symba, and I don't want you to play with me. I've fallen in love with you, woman and what you saw me do at the club is only the start of what I'll do to any man who fucks with you. I don't want you scared of me, but you should be scared of how I love you because it's deeper than you could imagine."

I put my hand under his chin and pulled him to my lips so we could kiss. "That was the sweetest and scariest thing anyone has ever told me." I smiled at him. "I love you, too, Dominick. I'm in love with you. I've never said those words to a guy before; just keep your promise and don't hurt me. I'm fragile as hell." I confessed to him.

"On my life." He said and then helped me out his truck.

Dominick's home was breathtaking from top to bottom. It was so him and I knew he put his touch of personality in every room. My favorite was the outside nook room he had, it reminded me of a café that would be in Paris or Italy. The pebble ground, rustic table and chair and because it was night-time, the clear lights lined through the vine was so romantic.

"My goodness Dominick this is…I'm lost for words." I smiled looking at his lit-up pool; the view was magnificent.

He stood behind me and put his arms around my waist. "Treat this place like your second home until you're ready to make it permanent." Speaking in my ear he put his nose in my neck and inhaled like he always did.

"I love when you do that," I told him, closing my eyes while he still smelled me.

"I know; you do this low moan all the damn time. Shit is mad sexy. You did that the first time we were on the phone, too."

I blushed and laughed. "I swear I never thought you could hear it."

He laughed too and took my hand so we could walk inside. We got to his bedroom and once again it was wonderful. His master bedroom had a fireplace that pulled it all together, it made me feel like I was in a luxury cabin suite.

"Take a shower with me." He said and of course, I agreed.

I got to soap his sexy body down. I couldn't believe how fine this white boy was. I mean every inch turned me on but my favorite were his eyes. They burn into mine no matter the mood, if they met mine then they burned with desire, passion and love. Like he'd do anything for me, no matter what. We got out the shower and we were drying off, I picked up my purse and took the Ziploc bag out.

"What is that?" He asked me.

"Oh um, well." I was stumbling over my words because I didn't want to tell him what it was.

Dominick took it out my hand and when he saw what was inside, he squinted his eyes at me, looking pissed. "This a hoe bag. I ain't stupid. Mini deodorant, toothpaste, toothbrush and what is this?"

I snickered because he was really mad. "That's HER by Burberry lotion." I snatched the bag back from him and put the deodorant and lotion on.

"Why the fuck did you have that, you planned on fucking tonight? And I dare you say you planned on fucking me because the three of y'all didn't know we were there."

Now I was cracking up.

"It ain't funny, Symba. I swear to God I would have found you and killed him."

"Dominick, I forgot this was even in my purse but I

won't lie, I used to keep it on me when I go out." I pulled some condoms out. "These too, I'm single and believe in safe sex, but no. I didn't plan on fucking tonight. I didn't check my purse before I went out."

"You *were* single, woman. You'll never be single again and you bet not have that shit in your purse again. Get rid of these, too." He threw the condoms in the garbage.

"Whatever, I'm on birth-control," I said, putting lotion on my thigh.

"Not for long." He mumbled and I looked at him like he was crazy.

"I sleep naked." I told him. "Is that a problem?"

"Hell no, I sleep naked too. Come here."

I walked over to him, swaying my wide, thick hips. He was looking at me from head to toe and he bit his bottom lip. When I got to him, we kissed and he was about to push me on the bed, but I stopped him.

"You are always in control Dominick. Sometimes, you have to let me be," I told him.

He furrowed his eyebrows, but he did what I said and laid down at the head of his bed on his back. He put both his hands behind his head and watched me. That man bun made his masculine face show more.

"Can I turn this on?" I asked him, pointing to his in-wall speaker.

"You can do whatever you want." He responded.

When I touched the speaker it lit up like a screen. There were all the music streaming apps on it so I went to Spotify and the artist name in the search. As soon as it did, it played all through the room. I love this song and always wanted to have sex to it; it was perfect and set the mood for what I was about to do to him.

Tender lovin', its one on one
Don't want to rush it, nah
Lets take it nice n slow, honey
Caress my body, and hold me tight
Don't let me go, baby until I get enough

Kut Klose- I like was playing as I crawled between his legs and looked down at his long dick that was sitting on his thigh. I didn't even have to pick it up because it was already bouncing on hard, up and down. I grabbed it with both my hands and stroked it for a second. Then I put the head in my wet mouth and sucked. I knew a good eight of it I could get down my throat. But it was all good because that eight was about to get sucked good and the other three was going to get licked by my tongue.

I like the way you tease me
I like the way you squeeze me
I like the way you touch
I like the way you sex me

I sucked on his dick and massaged his balls while I did it. My mouth was getting so wet my saliva slid down in my hand, becoming a lubricant on his balls. Dominick was loving it but his dominant controlling side wouldn't let him moan. Instead, he grunted and his thigh muscle was tensing up. He is so hard, I just wish he would let loose and enjoy me in control. I knew I was satisfying him, but I wanted to hear it. I definitely made sure he heard me when he was licking my pussy.

Dominick probably let out one moan when he was fucking me but he talked shit and knew when to kiss, lick and massage me. After I sucked his dick for some time, I went to his balls and got sloppy on them. He was going crazy grunting and that damn thigh muscle was about to pop out his thigh. After I was done, I bit my lip looking at how wet his dick was. Never in a million years would I think a white boy's dick would turn me on this much. It didn't look how I thought, and that tip was like a mushroom. I climbed on top of him and rubbed my hands all over his hard chest.

"It's just me and you, Dominick. Open up to me."

I told him then I bent down and kissed him feverishly. While we were making out, I reached between my legs, grabbed his dick and started sliding down on it. Inch by inch he was stretching me out but oh, my goodness, his bare flesh inside of mine was a trip on its own. Once all of it was in me, I froze and sat all the way up and I started grinding slowly. My walls were getting used to his girth and my clit was enjoying the massage I was doing as I got wetter.

Turn down the lights, baby take off what you have on
Lets do it to the music, come bring your lovin' on
My body's yearnin' for you, baby
For a taste of your love
Only you can fill this appetite, come on and satisfy my love

His hands were on the side of my hips and he was lightly squeezing them. I held my head back a little, closed my eyes and started winding my hips some more. I was enjoying the ride, you could hear that squeaky sound my pussy made the last time we fucked. Opening my eyes, I looked back down at Dominick and oh my gosh, I could have come and never stopped. He looked so damn good; his eye color changed to that dark gold with a hint of hazel. He squinted them and started staring in my soul. I knew when he squeezed my waist harder it was because it was feeling good.

"It's ok to enjoy this pussy, Daddy. Get lost in it. Uhhh. Ahhhh." I moaned as my spot was hit. I leaned down and kissed him again. I sucked on his neck and licked his ear, then whispered. "This dick is the best, Dominick. I'm so proud of it." Licking his lips again, I nibbled on the tip of it.

His giant hands squeezed my ass cheeks. "Ugh, fuck Symba."

I smiled against his neck hearing his sexy voice moan out. I sat all the way up again and turned in reverse. I got in squat position and started doing the froggy on him, making sure my walls squeezed him tight each time I came down. The feeling was sensational, and he didn't hold back which made my kat drenched.

"Ugh! Juicy muthafucka, bounce that ass." He held both my cheeks up with his nails gripping in my skin. It was so hot.

I slowed down; he let my ass go and went back to squeezing my hips. I leaned all the way down on my stomach and started bouncing my ass like a basketball.

"Ssssss daddy, oh shit. Oh shit. Oh shit. Oh shit." I cried out over and over.

SLAP! SLAP!

Dominick hit both my ass cheeks while I kept going up and down on him. "Where you want it gorgeous queen, tell daddy where you want this nut."

I don't know what I was thinking but I was lost in the feels and he was sounding so good. "Cum in me, cum inside this pussy, daddy! Ahh shit!" I came and he was right with me.

"Oh fuck! Argh!" He squeezed my cheeks while cumming what felt like forever.

I felt the whole load shoot in me. I was grinding my ass nice and slow, making sure I emptied him all out. Then when I did, I leaned up and let his dick pop out of me. While still bent over, I pushed his nut out, letting it fall all down his dick before I slid back down on it.

"Oooh, shit Symba you so fucking nasty. I love that shit girl and I love you." He said as he sat all the way up, wrapped his arms around my waist, grabbed my jaw and kissed me so damn nasty. I wanted to go to sleep, but I knew by how hard he was that we were about to go again.

CHRISTIAN

"What, Quest!?"

I answered my phone yelling and angry because he kept calling me. I was trying to be done with him for good this time. I know every time I said I was done, I relapsed like a muthafucka. I couldn't help it, Quest was beyond sexy and everything he did made me weak. But he wouldn't leave his bitch alone. I even stopped fucking around, but when I realized Quest was stuck on stupid, I went back to doing me. After me, Nina and Symba went to the club the other night, I went to Mama's house.

I knew Quest wouldn't be quick to pop up over there and I wouldn't be quick to give in. Nina left with Angel and Symba texted us and said she was with Dominick. I was glad for my auntie and sister. They were getting dicked down left and right, plus I liked Angel and Dominick for them. I just wish things were different between me and Quest, but now I'm over it. He can stay with his girlfriend and just leave me be. I was back to my savage ways. Fucking women's husbands and sending them home with my pussy on their lips. I gave no fucks even more than before.

"Yo' why the fuck you been dodging me like I'm some lame ass nigga!? I been trying to talk to you for three days. What the fuck!" He was yelling in my ear with that bass almost busting my speakers.

"Because I have nothing to say to you!" I hung up, put my phone in the back of my Jean pocket and walked out the bathroom.

"Why you doing my bro like that?" Angel asked me when I sat back down at Nina's dining room table.

Her place was fully furnished and really nice. She picked teal, rust and grey as her décor colors. You knew Angel paid for everything because of the quality all the pieces were. I don't even recall seeing any of these in the furniture stores; it all looked custom. The dining room table was my favorite because the cushion on the seats was so soft, it was like a mini pillow top.

Once Nina was set up, she wanted to host a little get together. She made bacon burgers, French fries and wing dings for us. The music was a cool down vibe, we had some board and card games. Right now, we were playing an intense game of Monopoly. I adored seeing Nina happy with Angel and Symba happy with Dominick.

"I'm not doing your bro any way. He won't leave his bitch alone so I want him to leave me alone. Then he has the nerve to get pissed because I'm doing me." I sat down, so aggravated. "I promise, being a woman is so stressful. Imagine someone giving you attitude over your own coochie. That shit is sick!" They all cracked up, but I was for real. Quest had no right to be jealous.

"Man, I wasn't even with this one." Dominick said and pointed to Symba. "And I was still in my feelings about what she was doing with her coochie. That's just how men are, it's your fault he that way."

My mouth dropped while Dominick and Angel laughed. "How is it my fault!?"

"Did you ride his dick any of the times that y'all fucked?" Dominick asked me and the rest of them fools were looking like they were eager for me to answer.

"I mean yeah, why wouldn't I?"

"Aw shit, well there you go. That's why he on yo' head so tough. You saw how I flipped out at *Lust* the other night on ol'dude and that was *before* Symba rode me. Now that I know what that shit is like, I'll be up at her job with footie socks and pajama pants on if she even thought of giving my coochie away."

Why did we all fall out laughing, especially Angel. "My muthafuckin' brother!" He gave Dominick a fist pound. "School these damn women about how serious that shit is; fuck head or any other kinky shit. Nina rode my shit so good I signed over the rights to my entire life to her!"

"Oh my goodnessss!" Nina yelled, laughing and covering his mouth, trying to shut him up.

"I just want to know what's with the footie socks and pajamas?!" Symba asked, giggling and looking at Dominick.

He put his beer down and said, "That's that ain't right in the head type of man. You don't wanna even fuck with that kind."

"Well why the hell you didn't warn me before so I could have the option to flee from you?"

When she asked him that, he looked at her and bit his lip. "Because you were mine when I first saw you, so there were no options."

When they were about to kiss, I threw a french-fry at them. "Uhh, none of that please. I'm having a crisis!" I shouted playfully at them. "I don't get how a man will have a whole girlfriend and still be obsessed with you."

"With a baby on the way!" Nina said, coming out the kitchen with wine coolers for me and Symba.

Symba laughed and added. "And still tryna get you pregnant along with running ya' new nigga off!" We were cracking up and giving each other high-fives.

The guys didn't find what we were saying funny, which made us laugh even more.

"All I know is I treat my relationships like math problems. Once I get confused...I start cheating." I flipped my hair and said.

"I promise, I don't know how we're related." Nina laughed and joked.

"Naw but for real, I'm done with Quest," I said picking up the dice so I could roll. A knock came to Nina's door and she got up to answer it.

"What's up, baby sister?"

A wall was blocking the front door but we all could hear Quest's voice. I rolled my eyes and took a deep breath. Symba was giggling with her fat head butt and Dominick looked at me and said, "I bet that man got his footie socks on."

I smacked my lips at him while they laughed.

"Sup bros! My other baby sister!" Quest came in the dining room greeting the rest of them.

"Sugar tits, you can't speak or all that mouth gone 'cause I'm face to face?"

"Ugh, Nina what the hell you let him in for." I scoffed at her and got up, heading to the kitchen.

"Y'all bet not break shit in my baby's house!" Angel shouted at us.

Quest followed me to the kitchen, which I knew he would. I sat my wine cooler down and turned to face him. How could someone be so damn perfect? That long beard that touched his chest made me get chills because I thought about how it tickles against my body. It was so soft and his light pink lips were full and soft too. I loved his waves, his coco skin and his body was a gorgeous masterpiece. Even now with him looking at me like we had strong beef was turning me on.

"This flip-flop shit you doin' with me needs to stop," he said.

"I know, you're right, that's why I decided to stop and just remove you from my life. Or remove myself from

377

your life, whatever you need to hear so you can sleep at night. I'm tired, Quest. All we do is fuck and stay in our feelings about one another. Just leave me be." I folded my arms and just shook my head at him.

"Aight fuck it, you wanna be done, you got it." He said and I couldn't tell if he was telling the truth or not. Regardless, he heard me loud and clear so there was nothing left to do but walk out the kitchen.

I went to walk past him but he grabbed my arm and pulled me in front of him. "Christian, stop playing with me. You haven't given me the chance to talk to you for a few days—"

"Because I. Don't. Want. To. Hear. It. I already know what you have to say—"

"Shut the fuck up, woman." I looked him up and down like he was crazy. "You talk so damn much instead of sometimes listening…You know what, get'cho shit, we bout' to go to my house."

"Excuse you?" I said with an attitude, making sure I

heard him.

He didn't even repeat himself, he just grabbed my hand and we walked out the kitchen. "Aye y'all, we gone head on out. Baby sister yo' place lit as fuck. Congratulations, I'll holla at you niggas tomorrow."

Symba and Nina were laughing. "This isn't funny, you bitches need to call the police because this is kidnapping." I told them while putting my purse on my shoulder.

"Call it what you want, let's roll." Quest said and I pushed past him and left out the apartment.

I shouldn't have gone with him; I knew it, but he had a magnetic pull on me. This is why I was so hurt because when I called myself cutting dudes off, he still wouldn't dump his girlfriend. So, I went back to my defensive behavior and told him I didn't give a damn.

I went back to doing me and claimed to only use Quest for dick. That didn't last long. When I knew he was with her, I got in my feelings heavy as hell. When he knew I was with someone, he acted out. We'd cuss each other out, claim to be done and my legs would open for him on sight after missing him.

"We not done, so you can get that out ya' head," Quest said when we got inside his house. The whole ride we let music play and didn't say shit to each other.

"Yes we are done...Quest, move out my space." I said, putting my arm out so I could block him. We were standing in the middle of his living room where I loved having sex with him at. I'd been in his bed a few times, but the couch was our main thing.

"I ain't moving shit and you really don't want me to. I'm done with her, Christian. I swear to God, I am. I want you." He kissed on my neck which caused me to bite my lip.

"Yeah right, how many times have you said that? Stop kissing on me, I don't know where your lips been." I knew that would piss him off.

He looked at me with his eyes tight and his nose turned up. "I ain't ate no bitch pussy or ass but yours since I met you." He put his hand around my neck, looking like a deranged person. Through gritted teeth he said, "Stop, Christian, before you see me set shit all the way off." Quest went back to kissing my neck and then unbuttoning my jeans.

"Sex isn't about to fix anything Quest." I said watching him pull my jeans down.

"But it'll shut you the fuck up for about three hours." He sat on the couch and made me straddle his lap.

He was right, our sex had me on hush and I got lost in it. While we kissed, I pulled his shirt over his head and we both started getting naked. Within seconds, my legs were wrapped around his neck in reverse; he was eating my ass so good while sitting up and I was sucking his dick.

"Mmmm! Mm!" I moaned while I slobbed his dick down. Quest's tongue felt so good I didn't even understand it. I mean this nigga really enjoyed eating my ass out like a buffet.

"Get them balls, bitch. Don't you forget them fucking balls." He grunted out and I did what he said. He lifted me up some more and started licking my pussy. The sounds were everything. He slurped, licked and sucked all of me. The more he showed out, the more I showed out until we both came in each other's mouths.

I was gyrating my hips all in his face, basically smearing my juices all over him and he was loving it. I got down and he turned me around. Putting my legs in the crook of his arm, he put my pussy down on his dick. As it slid all in me, I wrapped my arms around his neck and started licking my juices off his face. Me and Quest were so damn nasty with each other, and this is what fucked me up.

"You been giving my pussy away Christian, I already fucking know it." He said while angrily slamming me up and down on his big dick. "You gone make me kill him and his entire fuckin' family, I swear to God."

I should have believed him, I should have stopped his crazy ass right then and there. But I couldn't, even if I wanted to. He was fucking me out of this world, hitting my spot, making it fart and gush loudly. He was slamming me up and down like he wasn't putting work on his arm muscles.

"Whose pussy is this? Whose damn pussy is this, Christian!?"

"Ugh! Shit! It's y-yours—"

"Yours who!? Who am I muthafucka!? Who the fuck am I?!" Oh my goodness, his voice was so deep and demanding, it bounced off the walls and over the entire room.

"Quest! Q-Quest, ssss, ugh this pussy is Quest's!" I screamed out while cumming all on his dick and he wasn't lightening up on the pounding. "I can't take it, bae! I can't take it!" I had never tapped out before, but he was making me shake like an old lady at church.

"You can't take it?" He asked me in the sexiest tone.

"No bae, I can't take it. Ahhhh…Sssss shit."

"Naw, you doing good, be a big girl, make that pussy woman up and take all this dick."

My arms wrapped tighter around his neck and he slowed down a little while making me grind on him. Quest fucked me in that position so good, I don't know how many times I came. Once we were done, we showered, and I rode him good as fuck in his bed that he passed out after his nut.

**

I was sleeping so good that it didn't dawn on me what was happening until I hit the floor hard. I assumed I fell out his high ass bed, but instead a bitch was over my naked body, hitting me. Not just any bitch either, Kamila from work.

"This whole damn time, you been fucking my man!" She yelled, and her fist was about to come down on my face.

But by now, I was wide awake, so I kicked that hoe in her stomach, causing her boney ass to fall back.

"KAMILA, WHAT THE FUCK IS'CHU DOING!?" I heard Quests voice shout.

Only thing on my mind was my target, Kamila. "Bitch you gone sneak me!?" I stood up the same time she did and I was on her neck. I don't slap, I punch like Mama taught me, Nina and Symba. I might slap a hoe once or twice, but Kamila was getting all punches. All she did was grab my hair but I kept hitting, then I felt her being pulled away.

"Get yo' stupid ass the fuck out my house!" Quest had her in the air while he had his boxers on inside out. "Stay here!" He yelled at me while slamming his bedroom door.

Kamila had blood coming from her lip but that wasn't enough for me. My clothes were downstairs, so I went to Quest's closet and grabbed his basketball shorts and a t-shirt. I could hear them yelling and cussing outside. Running down his stairs like Rocky, I saw my gym-shoes by the door so I put them on and ran outside. Immediately, me and Kamila were back fighting. I was fucking her up. I won't lie, she got two hits in, one in my back the other on the side of my neck.

"Christian! Ok bae, you done fucked her up enough!" Quest yelled, pulling me off her.

"Fuck her and fuck you!" I said to him then looked at her. "Dumb ass bitch, I didn't even know this was your man, but it makes it even better that he been giving me raw dick *and* eating my ass!" I spit on her and snatched away from Quest.

"Yo' what the fuck you doing, where you going?!"

He asked me, looking shocked because I was so angry and I started walking down his hill while ordering an Uber.

"STAY THE FUCK AWAY FROM ME, NIGGA!" I shouted and kept walking. I was done with him and all his drama.

QUEST

Ain't this bout a bitch. How the hell did my night go from fantastic, with a fantastic bitch and some fantastic pussy, to a big mess? Kamila and Christian fighting and me basically watching her walk off on me. I don't even know how Kamila got in my house; I been took my key back from her last year when she moved out. Stupid ass must have made a copy. This shit was beyond anything she ever did.

I usually would sit and laugh while she fuck a bitch up. But Christian wasn't just any bitch, she was mine and I swear I feel like blowing Kamila's head off. I wasn't lying to Christian; I really did choose her and I had left Kamila alone. It's only been almost two weeks since I dropped her ass, but I still did. I didn't halfway do it either, I told her face to face, gave her all her stuff back and I closed the chapter.

Of course, Kamila didn't take no for an answer, she

cussed me out. Tried to fight me, she called, texted me all day and left a bunch of voice mails. I usually would have given in but I didn't want her anymore. Christian had me gone. I was addicted to her chocolate ass from head to toe. It wasn't just our perfect sex, I loved her attitude, how she carried herself and how she talked to me.

I couldn't feed Christian bullshit without her calling me out; she made me laugh and her mouth matched mine. Every time I saw her, I just wanted to kiss on her and stick my dick all in that wet pussy. How she got me like this so fast is what throws me; I went in a rage when I knew she was with someone. Like I just wanted to cut a muthafucka up in pieces.

Then when she talked about being done, I flipped out. Like right now, I know she's not fucking around. Christian really wanted me to stay away from her. I should kill Kamila right now. The only thing that's making me not do it is her old ass parents. She's their only child and I didn't want to put them through that.

"Man, get the fuck up so you can leave before I chop you in bits! What the fuck was you thinking showing up at my shit? Give me the fucking key you got." I watched her stand up. Christian had her bleeding form her nose and mouth.

Kamila spit blood on the ground. "How dare you fuck with a bitch at my job! Do you have no respect for me!?"

"Ain't nobody do this to you on purpose, we didn't know y'all worked together. I never told her your name." I snatched the key from her.

"Yeah right Quest, so she's why you want to throw away five-years? Over her black ass, you don't even know the type of woman she is. That slut fucks married men for a living, she'll never be completely yours."

I laughed. "Thank you, Wikipedia, you telling me shit I already know. Look Kamila, go home and put us to rest, love. We are done. We toxic as fuck and before Christian came along we should have been done. It's over, and I swear after this, I won't be this nice." I was about to turn and leave and she ran in front of me.

This woman got on her knees and started begging. "Quest please boo, please don't do this to me. Five years we have, you don't even know that fucking girl." She started balling bad. "Quest pleaseeee, I'll go crazy if you we break up, I-I-I won't think right." Putting her face in her hands, she just cried.

I'm no heartless nigga when it came to shit like this. Women have higher emotions than men and Kamila was hurt. Christian worked at her job and she probably does think I was on some *Baby Boy, Jody* type of shit, but I wasn't. I knew Christian didn't know either; it was all just a coincidence, but it wasn't shit I could do about it.

I wanted who I wanted and needed who I needed. But still, I got history with Kamila. We've had good times and I didn't need her on her damn knees over me. That didn't make me feel good or my pride increase. I felt bad, so I decided to soften up a little.

I bent down and helped her up. "Come on Kamila, get

up and stop crying." I hugged her and we went inside so I could clean up her face. It didn't take me long, about ten-minutes, then we walked out of my downstairs bathroom.

"Don't do this shit no more Kamila. Someone can really get hurt and I don't want that for you. We ain't no good together, and you know I'm right. Fuck blaming one another. Let's just walk away and move on."

"You mean you move on with Christian. Why her, Quest? Out of all people. We hate each other and she's jealous as hell of me. Did you know she's fucking my boss just so she can move up in the company? She's sneaky, slutty and doesn't give a damn about anyone's feelings, Quest. You can do better." Kamila told me with a lot of hate in her eyes; she hated Christian.

I wasn't about to hang on shit she was saying, only a lame man would do that. Kamila was my ex talking about my next; if anything was foul about Christian, I didn't need Kamila's help finding out.

"I'm a grown ass man, I don't need you schooling me

or trying to save me on any decision I make. That's no longer your concern." I opened my door for her to go out and I followed her to her car. The one thing I fucked up on was not changing my gate code key when she moved out. I was changing it as soon as her car pulled off.

Kamila gave me a nasty look, but she got her ass in her car and pulled off. I took my phone out and didn't even waste time calling Christian. I knew she wouldn't answer, but I needed to know she was safe.

"What up bro?" Angel answered.

"Shit, nigga. I'll catch you up later, right now do me a favor. Ask Nina has she talked to Christian today, and if she's good." I answered going back in the house.

"Aw shit, what the fuck did you do?"

I turned my nose up. "I ain't do shit, Kamila's ass trippin'."

"Chicken nugget, you talk to your sister today?" I heard him ask her.

"Yes, is that Quest? Because I'ma kick his ass."

Angel laughed. "Yea man, she's good. Fix whatever you did because Nina won't let me hear the end of it."

I hung up because I had too much on my mind. As long as Christian's good, then I could calm down a little. After I changed the code on my gate and alarm system, I got dressed and headed out so I could go visit my Ma.

"Sup boss man, you good?" I greeted the security guard when I walked inside Ma's treatment facility.

"Yup, feeling blessed. I hope you are too." He said back.

Nodding my head at him I made it to Edith's desk. "Good afternoon." I gave her some flowers. Edith looked out for Ma all the time so I sometimes did little nice shit for her to make her smile.

"Why thank you so much handsome, you just made my day." She smiled and smelled the flowers then she told me Ma was outside on the porch swing.

"Hey, gorgeous." I smiled at her.

When she saw me, her face lit up. "Oh my goodness,

nephew what a surprise." Lately, she's been being her sister for a few weeks. Ma's therapist told me it was because her sister was the opposite of her. It's like in Ma's head, herself was evil and her sister was good.

I hugged her and kissed her forehead. "You doing ok?" I asked her, sitting down next to her on the swing.

"I am now that you're here; I was arguing with your mother a few minutes ago."

"Oh really, what about?" I asked her and I noticed her hair was a little messy. "Hold that thought." I told her, getting up and heading to her room. I grabbed her brush and one of her hair tie things. I didn't know how to do hair, but I used to put her hair in a ponytail all the time when I was younger. Pops taught me how, so I always did if I saw her hair looking wild. I came back outside and stood behind the swing so I could do her hair.

"Ok, I'm listening. Why were y'all arguing?" I asked her.

"Because I was telling her about that pretty dark skin

girl that was at your house. I told Sonequa that she was the one for you, and she hit the roof. Talking about Kamila is the one and you should marry her. I told her stupid ass that she only feels that way because Kamila acts like her."

I chuckled while brushing the back of her hair. Ma had some long, thick hair and if you a nigga like me who don't know what the hell you doing, then it was going to take some time.

"Oh yeah, so you like Christian?"

She turned her head around smiling widely. "Yes, I do nephew. Please don't listen to your stupid Ma. That girl knows Kamila is your downfall; she'll hurt you in ways you can't imagine. I see it when I look at her, that's why I always make sure I go away when you two visit me. Speaking of visiting, when is that dark skin goddess going to come and visit me?"

"I don't know M—Auntie, I messed up with her and she's not speaking to me right now."

She turned her head all the way around just as I was

done brushing. Now I gotta do all that again. "No nephew, please don't go back to Kamila. She's dangerous just like Sonequa. Spoiled rotten and will do the worst if she doesn't get her way. Be with the pretty dark skin girl, fix it."

I walked over to her and got on my knee so I could be face to face with her. "I promise you I will fix things between me and Christian and I will bring her up here to visit you." I smiled at her and she returned it.

"Ok, thank you nephew." I hugged her and went back to doing her hair.

After we were done, I had lunch with her, played two games of Goldfish with her. Then it was time for her medication and a nap, so I headed out.

**

"Man I wish a bitch would pop up at my shit and act crazy like that. You should have killed Kamila." Dominick said, then he stepped on this nigga's face like it was nothing.

It was two days after the shit with Kamila and Christian. We were working, taking care of these wild ass

Mexican cartel. They had money over money and the safe was wide open. But we weren't here for that, and it wasn't shit to us anyway. We were paid to kill these fools and let the rival gang come in and take what they wanted. All we wanted was the bodies.

"I thought about it; trust me I did, but Christian already kicked her ass so I figured that was good enough." I told him and then I put stuck my Bowie machete all the way inside this fat nigga's forehead. His ass shot at me and almost hit, so he was getting his.

"You know you ain't heard the last of Kamila, right?" Angel walked in the room holding a whole arm.

"Bro you got an eyeball hanging from your brass knuckles." Dominick told him.

Angel flicked it off the spike and put the arm in a plastic bag. "Christian probably gon' have to stomp that bitch again."

"Kamila knows not to do no shit like that, again. Anyway, Christian cussed my ass out and now she ain't tryna have nothing to do with me. My fucking feelings hurt." I didn't mean to say that out loud, especially in front of these two dick heads because they started cracking up. I knew they were about to clown me.

"Aww tink-tink feelings hurt!" Angel started first.

"Want me to take my guitar out and play a song for you?" Then Dominick added some jokes.

"Fuck both of y'all with a herpes dick and I hope it skeet corona on you." I was mad as fuck and them laughing harder wasn't helping. "You niggas play all damn day."

I walked out the room, dragging fat ass in the body bag. Once we did our job we contacted the ones who hired us and they pulled up, ready to perform a raid of the mansion. We got in our van ad took the bodies back to the complex for the doctors to do their thing. We switched up our normal way of doing things since them Philly rats came on the scene.

My phone rang and I saw it was Edith. Ma probably had another nightmare or some shit. "Everything good, Edith?" I answered and she didn't say anything, she was just crying.

"Mr. Foster it's your mother she…uh…she passed away in her sleep."

I stopped doing what I was doing and stood in place. I just know damn well she didn't say that, no fucking way. "Wait a minute, what the fuck are you talking about? I just left from seeing my mama day before yesterday and I talked to her this morning."

Angel and Dominick came outside to where I was and when they saw my face, they walked up to me.

"I'm on my way." I said and hung up.

"You good, bro?" Dominick asked me.

"Yeah it's just a mix-up at Ma's facility, I gotta roll."

"Of course go handle it, kiss Ma for us." Angel said and I nodded, taking off towards my ride.

I just knew damn well Edith was wrong, not my damn mama. I just seen her and she was in a good mood; I did her hair and we had a good time. Naw, these muthafuckas were wrong. My whole drive was in a panic. I had one-way vision and my hands were sweating. I don't know how I got here so fast, but here I was. Storming through the doors, the security guards were giving me sympathetic looks and the nurses were crying.

I made it to Edith, and she was still crying. The emergency responders were inside Ma's room. I walked through the doors and straight to her bed. When I looked at her, I was about to cuss everybody out because she looked like she was sleep. Her skin was glowing and looking flawless; her hair was in a ponytail, she was lying on her side with her pretty hands folded together on her pillow.

I walked over to her and I couldn't even touch her; I felt like I was going to break down. I took a deep breath and touched her, and she felt lifeless. Her face looked peaceful, but her body held no life. I picked her hand up, squeezed it and kissed it while getting on my knees and getting closer to her. I forgot about the other people in here with me. I pressed my forehead lightly against hers and closed my eyes.

"I'm so sorry Ma, I couldn't save you and get you

well. You were supposed to see my kids and start your life. I fucked up, I failed you and I apologize." Kissing her hand and then her forehead again, I got up. I wasn't crying because I'm a man and we don't do shit like that. I walked out the room and Edith was standing by the door.

"I am so sorry Mr. Foster, I was doing my rounds and went to—" I held my hand up, cutting her off.

"I don't need the details." I said to her and looked at the police officer who was talking to her. "If you need me, get my contact information from her." I told him and he said yes sir.

I left out the facility numb as hell and I knew I was going to the liquor store once I made it to my car. Angel and Dominick texted me and asked me was everything ok. I told them it was cool and I was headed home. I wasn't ready to say the words or have people around me right now. If I tell them what happened then they would come my way. I didn't need that right now, I needed a few days to sit on this. I needed to get drunk and suppress my feelings.

**

It had been a whole twenty-four hours since you know what happened. I still hadn't told anyone, I got drunk all day and night. I wasn't in the mood for anything or anybody, I kept lying to my brothers that shit was fine because I wasn't ready yet. I didn't even call my aunt and tell her; hell she's in Cancun with her boyfriend so I wasn't about to fuck her vacation up. I had no siblings to lean on. I know I got my bros, but I'm talking about blood.

I was swallowing my feelings and making sure I didn't fucking cry. Right now, I was drunk as hell holding my big almost empty bottle of Bacardi in my hand. Taking another swig of it, I burped and made my way up the porch. I knew she was home because I saw her car in the driveway, and I didn't see Symba's, so I knew she was home alone. I pray to God she's home alone because if she wasn't, I was slicing up somebody tonight. I knocked on the door a few times until the porch light came on.

"Who is it?!" Her voice asked loudly.

I had the hiccups, but I slurred my name out. "Quest."

I heard her sigh. "Quest what do you want? We are over, I told you to stay away from me."

I chuckled and drank some more Bacardi. "I al...*Hiccup*...I already told you I can't leave you alone. It's been a...*Hiccup*...week Christian. I miss you bae, please just let me talk to you." Damn I sounded like a first-class drunk; my speech was broken up by my hiccups and my words were stretched out.

"Are you drunk?" She asked me, still behind the closed door.

I held up my hand in the shape of a C as if she could see me. "I might be, just a little." I downed the last sip and I sat the bottle down in her porch chair. "There. No more liquor, it's all gone. Now please open the door bae, come on please...*Hiccup*...I love you, Christian, I can't live without you. I need you bad as fuck right now—"

"Quest, you're drunk, and you don't know what you're saying. Leave!"

I got mad when she said that and I kicked her door. My stupid ass almost fell doing that. "I know what the hell I'm saying, mannn. We both know I can come in if I want to, so just open the door!" I didn't mean to yell, but I was wasted and she was rejecting me. When she turned the porch light out, I don't know why that hurt me so badly.

"I'm sorry Christian, I apologize for yelling...*Hiccup*. I'm sorry." I said in a medium tone. I knew she was still at the door because I could feel her.

Then in a the same tone she said, "Go home, Quest."

Those words cut me deep as hell. I remember when I first took her to my house and she called it a home. I had to correct her because I never felt like that.

"That ain't my damn home, it's not, and I told you that." I put my hand flat on the door. "You're my home, Christian. Your voice, smile, laugh, that sexy chocolate skin, that warm spot between your legs. That's my home, bae." All of a sudden, my eyes watered. "Ma died yesterday, I'm alone, man. My bros have family left; they got they woman to hold them, I'm alone. I need you." I said, and tears fell. I ain't cried since I was a child, but here I was, crying.

Christian opened her door and when she saw me, her face turned sad as well. "I am so sorry, Quest." She took my hand and pulled me inside.

I was so drunk that I tripped and fell over the little step. I heard her close the door and lock it then she bent down to help me up. I pulled her down to me because I needed some love at that moment. As soon as she wrapped her arms around my neck for a hug, I broke down. I cried my eyes out like a bitch all on her. I couldn't get how Ma looked out my head and the fact that I just saw her.

"I failed her Christian, I couldn't fix her." I confessed out loud.

"Shhh, stop saying that Quest, you didn't fail her at all." She put her hands on the side of my wet face and made me look at her. When I did ,I saw she was crying too. "You were the best son to your mother; I don't know the whole story, but I just know you were. Sometimes people have problems that are bigger than us. All we can do is love them, pray for them and be there when they need us. As long as you did those things, then you didn't fail her, ok?"

I nodded my head and she hugged me so tightly again. It was the sincerest hug I ever had.

"Come on," she said helping me up.

I followed her to her room where she took her robe off and had on a short silk gown that barely covered her pussy. I wasn't even thinking about sex; after she took her robe off she undressed me and left my boxers on. We got inside her bed and she just held me tight as fuck. I couldn't believe a woman could feel so good without us fucking.

Her warm skin with mine was life. My head was laying on top of her soft titties and I could hear her heartbeat. We were on our sides and she had her arms around my neck, rubbing my head. Every now and then she'd kiss the top of my head and forehead. I never had no shit like this before; this was a lot if intimacy that I didn't even know I needed.

"Tell me about her, your mom." Her soft voice said to

me.

I began telling her all about Ma from the earliest memories to yesterday. I told her about the good times, my Pops, I told her about my birthdays when I used to cry for my mama when I was a child. I got into her mental illness and how it got worse when Pops died, then I got into details about what made us do the line of work we did. Christian listened, laughed when some stuff was funny and she made sure to hold me tight when I spoke on things that were hurtful. I was opening up, telling her everything and I dug the hell out of it. We stayed up talking until seven in the morning.

Five o'clock in the evening.

"I tried not to wake you, you were knocked the hell out." Christian finally opened her eyes.

"What time is it?" She asked me while stretching.

"Five o'clock." I looked at my watch.

"Damn, we slept that long, I'm glad I'm off work today," she said, getting out of bed.

"You let me talk yo' ear off till the sun came up. I appreciate that Christian, more than you know."

I told her before she walked out the room. I let her handle her business in the bathroom while I checked my phone. Of course, Kamila called me and texted me a lot. It was time to block her for real. I put my phone back on Christian's nightstand as she walked back in her room. I put my jeans on and realized I had my Kukri knife on me just in case Christian had company last night. I put my socks and my NIKE slides on. I then grabbed my shirt on the bed so I could put it on later.

"How long you been up? I see your toothbrush is wet." She asked me, and I watched her take her gown off and cover up her titties before putting a sports bra on. Then she put some shorts on but made sure she covered up her pussy.

"I only been up about fifteen minutes before you. Yo' why are you covering your body up like I ain't never seen it?" I was a little bothered by that.

"Because I don't want anything read into what

happened last night."

I felt wrinkles form in my forehead. "I know I was drunk, but I remember all that I said to you and I swear I meant every word, Christian." I was dead ass.

"I know you did, I felt it." She said, looking at me with a soft face.

I was pleased that she believed me. "Then what's the problem?" I asked her.

She took that shower cap thing she sleeps with off and her pretty ass hair was back in those big twisted braids. "That's my problem." Pointing to my phone, Kamila's name was on the screen meaning she was calling, again.

"I don't fuck with that girl on any level bae, phone, texts or anything."

"Yet her number is still saved. She's not blocked." She chuckled. "Quest we just need to—"

I stood up, mad. "No! Fuck that; you my woman, Christian, so get wit' it. I fucking love you, I don't want her. I ain't confused or need time for shit, all I need is you."

I looked her in her eyes because I wanted her to feel this shit just like she did last night.

"What day is it?" She asked randomly as hell.

"Wednesday. Did you hear me? We together," I repeated myself.

But she looked confused as hell, "You said Wednesday?"

Now I was looking confused, "Christian what—" My words were cut off when she fell backwards hitting the floor hard as hell. Her body was straight as an arrow and she started shaking hard as hell. Her eyes were rolled in the back of her head.

"What the fuck!? Bae!" I ran to her and didn't know what the hell was going on except she was shaking so damn bad. I grabbed my cell phone and called 911, it was instincts; she wasn't no damn criminal so she didn't need our complex. I told the lady I needed an ambulance, gave her the address and told her what was happening.

"Ok sir, it sounds like a seizure. You need to put her

on her side so she doesn't swallow her tongue and choke to death."

I did what the lady said and when I put Christian on her side, the shaking calmed down a little. Then I saw blood pour from her mouth.

"Why she got blood coming out her mouth!" I was trying not to panic, but I couldn't help it, I didn't know what was going on with my woman or how this was about to play out.

"She might have bitten her tongue, just keep her on her side until the EMS comes."

I did and all of a sudden, Christian started shaking like crazy again. "The shaking started up again! Yo', her eyes don't look right!" I yelled and dropped my phone, I laid down next to her and wrapped my arms around her tight ,keeping her on her side.

"Calm down bae, the ambulance is almost here, just hold on." I closed my eyes and prayed while Christian was shaking. Love them, pray for them and be there for them, I repeated what she just told me last night. "Don't die on me bae, please don't. Not when I just found you, we got to much shit to do. I got a whole world I wanna show you, don't leave me alone." My tears came again and suddenly, she stopped shaking. I looked at her face and her eyes were wide open, looking vacant. She didn't blink or anything.

Then I heard a hard knock on the door, I kept her on her side then ran and opened the door. The responders came in and went to the room I told them. The way Christian was lying reminded me of my mama. My heart started breaking all over again. I swear to God if they say she was dead, I was going to die my damn self. My phone rang and I saw it said Las Vegas Police Department. I answered it while keeping my eyes on the responders handling Christian.

"Hello."

"Hi Mr. Foster, this is officer Albright, I'm in charge of your mother's death."

"Get to the point!" I wasn't trying to yell because I know it's about Ma, but I saw Christian black out again and the responders' faces was stressing me.

"Yes, I apologize. An autopsy was performed on your mother and there was a trace of Ricin in her blood."

I scrunched my face up, "What the hell is Ricin?"

"It's a poison sir, we believe your mother was poisoned."

You have gots to be shittin' me!

NINA

Rewind to the night before...

"Is everything ok with Quest?" I asked Angel when I walked out his bathroom. He told me Quest had an emergency with his mom and he was worried.

"Yup, it's cool. He just text me and Dominick back."

I took a nice long bath and then a shower so I could wash my hair. I stood in the doorway with my robe on, drying my hair with the towel. I was enjoying the view in front of me, Angel was laying on his back, watching TV. His chest was bare and he had one leg up while his arm rested on his knee. He was so beautiful, even though he hates when I tell him that. It was so fast how Angel became so important to me, I was hopelessly in love with him.

The type of relationship we have it feels like he is my

first. We have deep conversations about life, goals, dreams, fantasies and dream destinations. Angel sooths my mind, body and spirit; he handles me with care and treats me like a rare treasure. I know what love his from my family, but to know someone is not blood and can love you all the same amazes me. Angel thinks about me and it shows, like he knows I love *The Walking Dead* so he got me a fleece blanket with my boo *Rick Grimes* on it.

He has his cook get my favorite snacks, he sends me funny memes to my phone just to make me laugh. It took me a minute to convince myself that he was real. What I loved the most about Angel was, he prayed with me. I was done not talking to God thinking he was angry with me, so one night I was praying and Angel walked in the room. I was about to get up but he grabbed my hand and we prayed together. I knew what Angel did for a living, but God loves all of us and it's not for me to judge.

I moved into my new apartment and I was obsessed with it, Angel took me to his furniture lady who makes custom pieces for celebrities. The way he spent money so freely was new to me; I was still working and taking care of myself, but he made sure that money went into my savings and he handled the rest. It was something I had to get used to, but it didn't take me long, however I didn't spend like he always reminded me I could. I never felt this good before and things would be almost perfect except for a few things.

One of them is Marlo. I haven't seen or heard from him but I always had this weird feeling that he was watching me. It would happen throughout the day; I'd get a wave of fear and a little panic when I'm outside. Like he was around the corner waiting on me. Part of me felt it was just me being skeptical, but then the other part of me knows Marlo. He doesn't like not getting what he wanted and he can act out if he felt disrespected. But hell, in our situation I wasn't the one doing the disrespecting.

Marlo was the undercover fruit cake, he was the liar and deceiver. Because of him, I have to get tested again in three months to make sure I absolutely have nothing. I had the day marked on my calendar in my kitchen and on my phone. The other problem I had was myself. I may have been in love with Angel, but I haven't fallen in love with myself yet. I still had many moments when I would hurt. I'd think the devil was laughing at me because I actually felt this new life would last.

After what I did, why would things work out in my favor? I looked at my son pictures so much in my car. I kept them in my closet but one I kept in my glove compartment. Angel doesn't know about him or Marlo; I wanted to tell him so bad because I didn't want secrets between us. However, I didn't want Angel to judge me and leave so I didn't say anything. I still cried for my baby boy and sometimes, Angel would talk about kids.

I get so uncomfortable and I have to put on my best performance in order for him not to think something is wrong. I'd love to give Angel kids, but I don't know if I can. I don't know if I'll be a good mother, make the right decisions or even if I'll be blessed to have that opportunity again. That alone would break Angel's heart because he had plans on being a father. I tried not to think about it a lot, but it sneaks up on me from time to time.

Right now, I was pushing any doubt, fear or sadness out my head and I was going to enjoy my guy. After I dried my hair off, I put lotion all over my body then I took my robe off. I went over to his drawer and grabbed a long cami that stopped right over my booty and I put it on. I went and got a sew-in the other day, so I braided the twenty-six inches of wavy hair in a big braid to the side. After that, I but some oil droppings on my pretty edges and watched them wave up, looking like the weave. Grabbing my silk scarf, I tied it around my head, put some Dove deodorant on and walked over to the bed.

"Sup chicken nugget, how was your day?" He asked me when I got in bed and laid on his chest.

"It was good. Burt and Mary were arguing over who made the best chili. It was so funny because she slashes him with her words. They had me do a taste test and she was right, she makes the best chili." I laughed and so did he.

"Oh that's without a doubt, Mary can cook her ass off. Burt can cook his African dishes good as hell, but that's about it." He trailed his fingers down my arms.

"How was your day?" I asked him, doing the same thing to his arm he was doing to mine.

"My day was colorful and eventful."

I chuckled because I know that meant the other side of Angel, The Law. "As long as you return to me, then I don't mind a little color in your day." I joked and kissed his chest. I was so affectionate with him because that's how he was with me.

"I'll always return to you baby, that's a promise."

"You can't make that kind of promise, Angel." I was serious. Nothing was promised, and I didn't want to hold him to that.

"Aye." He pulled my chin up, forcing me to look at his fine face. Those puppy doe eyes bore into mine, that five' o clock beard shaped his face and brought out his brown lips.

"What I just say Nina?"

"That you'll always return to me, but—"

"No buts, that's what it is. You love me?" That deep voice asked me.

"Very much." I smiled up at him.

"On God Nina, that smile is everything to me. I love you too, come give me a kiss."

I did what he said and kissed those tender soft lips. "So, I've been thinking about the nickname I want to give you." I climbed on top of him while I talked. Angel always joked about how he called me chicken nugget and I need to come up with something to call him. "I heard this song while I was driving over here today, and I felt it was perfect." I told him, reaching over to his Alexa and turned it on.

"Oh really, tell me more baby." He said while rubbing his hands up and down my thighs. The bedroom was dark with the TV off and the light of Las Vegas attractions making a sexy dim light beam through the bay window.

After I put the song on, I pulled my shirt over my

head while on top of him, Then I pulled his boxers down and got right back on top of him.

Ooh, ooh, ooh, ooh, ooh, ooh, ooh, ooh

If I could I'd give you the world

Wrap it all around you

Won't be satisfied with just a piece of this heart

Anita Baker-Angel played and her voice matched the mood and the feel of our surroundings. Angel did this sexy smirk when the song started and I licked his lips then kissed him deeply. I felt his dick rise under me, so I grind my pussy against it while we made out. I had become so sexually open with this man. He awakened a hunger and desire in me that I didn't know existed. I felt sexy all the time when I was in his presence, no matter what I was doing or what I had on. He was indeed my Angel.

My angel, oh, angel

You're my angel, oh, angel

"You're my Angel bae, that's what I'll call you." I moaned in his ear while I was riding his dick nice and slow. I still wasn't used to his size, but it was ok. Once his dick touched my pussy, she welcomed it. I sucked on his neck while I moved my hips in a circle.

"Got damn, Nina baby, work that pussy out on this dick." His hands were squeezing my waist and then grabbed my round little ass.

Since fucking him, I noticed my thighs got a little thicker and my ass a little fuller as well. Happy weight, Mama called it. I put my hands flat on his chest and worked my handful of booty on him. I started coming up slow then coming down on it all at once, making his tip tickle my stomach.

"Oooo, Angel. Oooo, you feel so good. You're my heaven, my Angel, ooooh." I started cumming, but I still kept riding.

"Yea, chicken nugget, I feel all that pussy juice sliding down my balls. Pour out all them juices on me."

When I started slowing down he grabbed my ass with one hand and started bouncing me up and down rapidly. "Naw, you ain't slowing down on me. I want you to cum again, make that kitty cum again." He bit my bottom lip like I loved, then sucked on it.

"B-Baby shit! Oh my goodness!"

"You love me?" He asked me with his husky deep voice in my ear.

"Yesss, oh gosh, yes!"

"That's not gone work. Let me hear it." Angel then wrapped both his arms around my waist so tight and started thrusting his hips in me up and down fast. With me on top, he reversed it and started pounding me so hard.

I was moaning so loudly because the feeling was out of this world. My body got warm all over and that feeling came over me. "I love youuuu! Oh fuck, Angel, I'm cumming! Oh!"

He didn't chill; I don't know how he did it but he made this orgasm feel like forever and I thought I was going to faint.

"Shit I'm 'bout to nut, Nina!"

"I wanna catch it baby, let me catch it." I moaned out.

He let me go and I hurried down between his legs. Grabbing his hard-soaked dick, I started sucking on it and in about a second, he came all down my throat. I could taste my juices along with his. "Mmm!" I moaned out, because Angel always tasted so good to me.

"Argh fuck, fuck, fuck, girl! Fuck!" I loved the sound he makes when he comes.

I swallowed every drop and then stroked him slowly. Once he was done, I got up and cleaned us up. When I was done, I got back in bed and before I could get in the covers, Angel was pulling me to him, kissing me.

"I love yo' sexy ass." He said to me, kissing my nose.

"I love you too, my Angel." One more kiss then we both fell asleep.

**

I woke up to an empty bed. Angel told me he had

some work to do at the complex. I didn't want him to go, but I was so sleepy from last night I didn't have any energy to convince him to stay. After I stretched my body out, I got up and headed to the bathroom so I could shower. I was taking Mama to lunch and I wanted to talk to her about hosting a barbecue at her house. That way her and Grandma could meet our guys and we can have some fun.

It was the middle of October, but we still had summer weather. I was off work today so after lunch with Mama, I was going home to just relax. I know for a fact Angel was going to come over or we would video chat all night until we fell asleep. Today I decided to wear a simple maxi dress and some flip-flops. My dress was strapless, and it was the colors of the Jamaican flag. I took my scarf off and decided to keep the side braid. My edges were perfect.

I put on some gold hoop earrings and I wore my Movado watch Angel bought me. I went downstairs to the kitchen and made me a light breakfast. A piece of toast with a smoothie drink. If I went to lunch with an empty stomach then I would order a lot of food, only to carry it all to go. I had about two-and-a-half hours before lunch with Mama, so I chilled and watched TV in the living room. Angel Facetimed me and we talked for a few minutes. I love seeing his handsome face.

After that, I watched a few old episodes of *The Walking Dead* until it was time to go.

Lunch was nice with Mama. I took her to a nice restaurant, and we enjoyed ourselves. I was trying to make up to all my family for being the drag Nina all those years. I wasn't her, I was bubbly, I laughed and spent time with them. Me and Mama talked about Angel, I told her I loved him and I was happy. We talked about the barbeque and she was down to host it at her house.

Supposedly, Grandma was dating a new man so she wanted all of us to meet him. That was a first because was beautiful she always claimed since Symba's dad that all men were useless to her. I guess the right one came along and changed her mind. Mama said Symba didn't know and she didn't want me to tell her. That wasn't good; Symba is overprotective over her Mama so I knew she would feel away.

But I promised I wouldn't say anything. After lunch, I dropped Mama off at home and headed to my place. I went over in my head if I needed to run some errands for anything in the apartment and it was, so before I went home, I stopped at Walmart and picked up a few things. I had that feeling again, like Marlo was around every corner.

I usually would stop and close my eyes for a second to calm myself down. Once I was done, I put my three bags in the car and finally drove home. Walking inside the nice lobby of my apartment, I was on the first floor down the hall. My phone rang and I saw it was Symba. I answered as soon as I turned the key in my door and opened it.

"Hey auntie Sym-Sym what are you—"

"Nina." Her voice was in a panic and I could tell she was crying. "Christian had a seizure and it's not looking too good. Dominick and I were going to the hospital, but he had to drop me off instead of staying with me."

"Oh my goodness, Symba—"

"Nina, Dominick couldn't stay because while we were driving here, he got a call that the complex was up in flames."

My grocery bags slid out my hand and, on the floor when she said that. My sister and my boyfriend could be dead. My heart dropped and my hands became soaking wet. I turned around to head back out, but instead my door was slammed shut before I could leave.

"You ain't going no fucking where." Marlo had his hand pressed on my door and he was looking at me like I was a target. "What's up, boss bae?"

Ew, he said that name and my stomach turned and did flips. I stepped back slowly and Symba was yelling in my ear.

"Nina, is that Marlo!?"

TO BE CONTINUED

KEEP UP WITH ME:

My Facebook Reading Group: Londyn Lenz Besty Bratz
Readers

Facebook Author Page: Author Londyn Lenz

Please SUBSCRIBE to my YouTube channel: Through
Londyn Lenz Reading Group

Email: **Londyn_Lenz@yahoo.com**

Thank you so much for the love & support.

-Londyn Lenz

Made in the USA
Middletown, DE
23 August 2022

71265577R00255